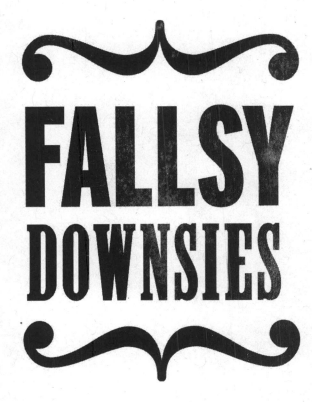

FALLSY
DOWNSIES

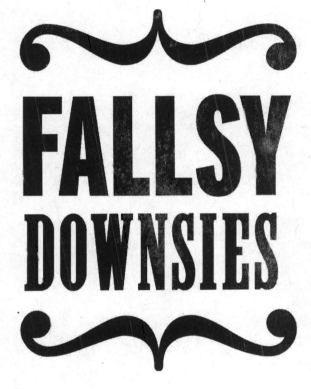

FALLSY
DOWNSIES

STEPHANIE DOMET

Invisible Publishing

Halifax & Toronto

Library and Archives Canada Cataloguing in Publication

Domet, Stephanie, 1970-, author
    Fallsy downsies / Stephanie Domet.

ISBN 978-1-926743-41-7 (pbk.)

I. Title.

PS8607.O49F35 2013   C813'.6   C2013-904322-5

Cover & Interior designed by Megan Fildes

Typeset in Laurentian and Slate by Megan Fildes
With thanks to type designer Rod McDonald

Printed and bound in Canada

Invisible Publishing
Halifax & Toronto
www.invisiblepublishing.com

We acknowledge the support of the Canada Council for the Arts, which last year invested $157 million to bring the arts to Canadians throughout the country.

Invisible Publishing recognizes the support of the Province of Nova Scotia through the Department of Communities, Culture & Heritage. We are pleased to work in partnership with the Culture Division to develop and promote our cultural resources for all Nova Scotians.

NOVA SCOTIA
Communities, Culture and Heritage

Canada Council   Conseil des Arts
for the Arts   du Canada

For Kev, as always.
And for everyone who reaches.

The big-time is a long climb
you can slide back in no time
but if your star should ever fade
I'll be right here actin' half my age
struttin' all around the stage
still havin' fun and gettin' paid
there will always be a small time
if all the lights go to your head
there will always be a good time
when the nine-to-fivers go to bed
there will always be a nighttime
and all of us who knew you when
there will always be a small time
just come and see us now and then

—"There Will Always Be a Small Time"
(Corin Raymond/Jonathan Byrd 2007)

1

There was one thing Lansing Meadows knew he'd miss. When all was said and done, when all the bullshit was behind him, when all the nosy newspaper articles had been written—hell, when they wrote the book on him—when all the bridges were burned and hearts were broken, there was one thing Lansing Meadows would always yearn for.

The spotlight. The warm glow of it on his grizzled hide.

In fact, when all was said and done, Lansing Meadows knew it was the moment just before the spotlight that he'd miss. The moment on the precipice. When the audience was waiting and when even he wasn't sure what, exactly, was next. That beautiful, vertiginous moment, when he'd step out on the high wire, one shaking foot and then the other. There would be that hush, even in a crowded hall. And he'd inhale all his nerves, and breathe out *possibility*. And they'd be with him or against him, but they'd be there in the moment, alive to him and he'd be alive to them.

That, he would miss, when all was said and done.

2

Lansing Meadows hated sleeping rough. He considered it beneath him, or he would have liked to consider it beneath him, but the truth was he more often than not found himself awakening in positions of great discomfort. On a lumpy bed in a Motel 6, with blinds that wouldn't close all the way and a tap that dripped all night. On a single futon with some anonymous someone who'd tried to doll up her room with scarves over every lamp and patchouli incense in a burner beside the bed. Or on some damn pullout, like now, the ridges of its metal skeleton protruding through the thin and worn foam mattress and right into his soft belly.

And that belly was about as soft as it could be, at this point in his life. Too many late nights, too much bad food, fried to within an inch of its life. Too many beers, pints of rum, red wine and colas.

It was unseemly to be sleeping rough. A man his age and in his position. A man soon to receive a lifetime achievement award in front of whatever friends and fans he had left. And in front of the critics and detractors too, of whom there were plenty. Let's not forget about them, he thought. As if he ever could. Spend your whole life trying to prove something and never know for sure if you did. And then it all came down to—this, wherever this was. Petite Riviere, Nova Scotia, if he remembered correctly.

He lay on the pullout and smelled bacon cooking. Heard it popping in the pan, and wondered what the occasion was. That was one way to take stock of your life. Bacon as a metric of special occasions. He shook his head on the thin pillow and sighed. He looked to the left and saw his trusty hat, its brim a little worse for wear, its crown dimpled as though some tiny fist had punched it in a fury. He looked to the right and saw his own ugly mug. *Lansing Meadows: Greatest Hits*. The album cover was well-worn. It leaned, with a bunch of others, against a cabinet topped with an old turntable. He sized himself up. A pugilist's face, even back then. Asymmetrical and warty, his nose a fleshy tuber, his eyes sunken and glistening in his head.

"What the fuck," he said to the picture, by way of greeting. It had been a while since he'd glimpsed the cover of that particular album, longer still since he'd had a hit, greatest or otherwise. He hoisted himself up to sitting, the bed and his bones creaking equally. He wiped a hand over his face as if he could undo the marks the years had left behind. "Chrissakes." A pack-and-a-half of cigarettes a day obstructed his voice, made the phlegm roll in his throat like thunder. The pullout squawked beneath him in a threatening way, an old man's groan. "I hear ya, brother," Lansing Meadows said, "I hear ya."

Evan Cornfield couldn't cope. It wasn't enough that his head was pounding like a battle of the speed metal bands. Or that he'd had to forcibly peel his tongue from the roof of his mouth this morning. Or that he'd swear he heard it make a sound when it came away, like tearing paper. He could deal with the hangover in his own way; put his sneakers on and run along the river till the endorphins replaced the fog. Get back into bed with Colleen and let her coo over him—though in no way was she his girlfriend, so long as they were clear about that—until he fell back to sleep. Even the making and eating of bacon and eggs was a pretty good hangover-curing strategy. But Jesus Christ, he'd brought Lansing Meadows home last night.

How exactly had that happen? He stood now in front of Colleen's stove, in front of a pan spitting fat he was too slow and stunned to dodge. Tiny oil spots speckled his T-shirt and misted his face. He turned his head toward the coffee maker and thought about putting a pot on. The simple act of twisting his neck had him seeing tracers and everything seemed to be ten or fifteen seconds out of synch. But it was important that he feed Lansing Meadows a good breakfast. It was bad enough he'd made the godfather of Canadian folk music sleep on a pullout. And so he accepted the volley of hot oil and he squinted while he scooped coffee into the filter and poured cold water into the machine. The squinting seemed to help.

The night before—Thursday night at the Alley Oop—there'd been hardly a square inch of space in which to stand. The usual fug of perfume and pheromones and the ghost of a thousand cigarettes hung over the room, accelerated by the heat of a hundred bodies or more. The black light, so popular for the bowling that happened there most other nights of the week, illuminated every speck of dandruff, every errant cat hair, every bit of lint, along with the neon faux graffiti sprayed across every wall and up onto the ceiling.

Evan Cornfield had pushed his way through the regulars,

recognizing the same old faces in the blue glow from the Labatt Beer sign behind the bar. Sindy St. John was on stage, as she was every Thursday around that time. She was done up to the teeth. Bleached blonde hair piled up on her head. Evan thought it might be a wig, but then he wondered, why bother to have a wig that looks like shit? Her lips were outlined in bright pink liner and coloured in with garish red lipstick. She wore a clingy polyester dress splashed with green and yellow roses. It glowed under the black light and her white waist-high underpants glowed through it. Evan shuddered and looked away. Sindy showed up every Thursday to sing "Unchained Melody," and every Thursday she punted the words. She needed glasses, Sindy did, but she was too vain to wear them out to Karaoke Thursdays. Still, you'd see her weekday mornings down at the Tim Horton's with her glasses on and her teeth out.

Thursdays were the worst.

Colleen McKinley swung her ponytail and grabbed Evan's hand, pulling him behind the bar. "I'm dying back here," she said. "I could use a guy like you." Evan felt his cheeks go hot.

"Who's the hat?" he asked, nodding toward the end of the bar. The man sat alone in a swirl of bodies, his hat shielding his face from the lights. He looked vaguely familiar, an uglier, older version of someone Evan thought he knew.

"Some old bastard," Colleen said, and tossed her ponytail again. "Tried to cop a feel," she sniffed.

And right then, Evan knew exactly who it was.

Lansing Meadows pushed away from the table, chair legs scraping floor, grease glinting on his upper lip. He swiped a hand across his mouth, smearing the grease into his stubble.

"Mind if I use the phone," he said. It wasn't a question. He was on his feet, dialing, before Evan's brain could form assent.

"It's long distance," Meadows explained as he tucked the receiver between ear and shoulder, the better to draw a cigarette from the package in his shirt pocket.

Evan Cornfield looked at Colleen, who'd emerged from the bedroom they shared bright-eyed and eager for the day and who had become less so, by degrees, as breakfast unfolded. Now she shook her head doubtfully, her ponytail swinging with less vitality than it had the night before behind the bar. She began to clear the plates, clatteringly. Evan could hear her muttering steadily beneath her breath, a sonic gathering storm that reminded him of his eldest sister Elaine, who could do put-upon like no one else Evan knew.

He leapt to his feet, only slightly mindful of his hangover's echo, the parts that were so deeply embedded they were immune to the persuasive charms of buttered toast, strong coffee, crisp bacon, and perfect yolks. He machinated his lips into a rictus of friendly approachability, took the stack of plates from Colleen's hands, and laid them gently in the sink.

"More coffee?" he asked her, nudging her away from the sink and back toward her chair.

She peered into her cup, then up at him. "Is there more?" she asked.

He checked the pot. "No."

She let out an Elaine-class sigh and pursed her lips unhappily. "But I'll make some," he said, and reached for the grinder.

The sound of it made Lansing Meadows scowl and turn away, phone still balanced between ear and shoulder as he used his free hand to tap the cigarette hard against the wall. Evan was listening for the change in pitch that would indicate beans ground to the right fineness when the drone was overcome entirely by Lansing shouting, "Fine, fuck *you*," and slamming the phone down.

"Son of a *bitch*," Lansing said pointedly to the now-silent phone. He jammed the cigarette in his mouth.

"Son," he said, looking just over Evan's head, "I'ma need a ride to Antigonish tomorrow and a light for this goddamn cigarette."

3

Evan jammed his hands into the pockets of his hoodie and strode along the riverside. The March wind was biting, and though it froze his hands, it barely touched the cotton in his head. He'd left Lansing at Colleen's, playing guitar and chewing on the end of a cigarette. Colleen seemed none too happy about it, but she was off soon for a shift at the Alley Oop, so what did she care, really, Evan thought. He was hangover-stupid, anxious about saying the wrong thing to Lansing Meadows. And so he'd called Saxton Crouse to meet up.

Saxton was Evan's oldest friend. They'd known each other since before they were born. Their thrifty mothers had met at a clothing swap between pregnancies and the friendship outlasted the garments each took home that day. That Evan and Saxton would be friends was pre-ordained; the boys were each other's first and most frequent playmate. That they liked each other, quite independent of the friendship their mothers shared, was incidental and lucky.

Saxton was tall and handsome, the kind of boy who could talk to anyone with ease. Evan was just the opposite. Small and blond and tongue-tied. The two took guitar lessons together when they were twelve. Saxton liked it alright, he said. But Evan—Evan needed it. He had a sense, even then, that the guitar could be his entrée to any situation, both the ones he wanted access to quite badly and the ones he didn't really care about. With a guitar in his hands, he could communicate every thought in his head, every feeling he had or could imagine. He'd hoped to grow into being able to communicate without a guitar in his hands, but so far, it hadn't happened. But it was okay. Guitar was a language in which he was becoming fluent.

His three older sisters had left home by the time he turned thirteen and in a house suddenly quiet, Evan tentatively unfurled the sound of his guitar playing and the first nervous words of songs. He bounced his voice off the walls and the ceilings, and it came back to him as a not-entirely-unpleasant sound. He dug records out of his parents' collection, album covers showing tragic-looking men in newspaper-boy caps, women with long hair and no bras. He spirited these records up to his room, removed the discs reverently from their wrappings and put them on the turntable his sister Annabeth had left behind. When the needle dropped, he lay back and closed his eyes, his fingers moving nimbly over invisible strings.

He and Saxton would haunt the aisles of Tilt-A-Whirl, the local record-shop-slash-post-office. Larry Shingles sold mostly CDs and the odd used cassette, but there was a good selection of vinyl albums to be had as well. There was a room where you could audition records, and Evan did, whole stacks of them. At day's end, when Larry Shingles cleared his throat and looked meaningfully through the door of that little back room, Evan had made his selection. He held it carefully, using both hands. At the cash register he pushed twenty dollars across the counter, money he'd earned working alongside Saxton cleaning up the orchard for old Mrs. Dempsey, who lived just down the road from Saxton's place.

He walked home, hugging his purchase to his chest and barely listening to Saxton chattering on about what girls he liked at school, and which ones he thought Evan could get to give him the time of day. When they reached the end of Evan's driveway, he said simply, "See you tomorrow, Crouse," and turned to go up the walk, single-minded in his desire to be alone with the new record.

He'd been drawn at first to the craggy, desperate face on the album's cover. But once he had it on the turntable in that back room, once the opening chords were ringing out, he knew he had to take it home. Lansing Meadows's voice was urgent and weary and it made Evan ache in surprising and mysterious ways. The songs were about sadness and confusion and loss. And about politics and love and working men, and other things Evan didn't understand. But he wanted to understand, oh, he wanted to. One thing he knew for sure, he understood the language Lansing's guitar was speaking.

When he got home he put it on his own turntable. He had two little old speakers, each cased in its own worn wood cabinet. He turned one of them out into the room so he could get up close to the sound. He took off his T-shirt and pressed his thirteen-year-old chest right up against the speaker. He reached over and dropped the needle and let the music get up inside him.

Evan knew he didn't understand much of anything at all. But Lansing Meadows had given him a key, and he intended to use it.

Faced with the man himself though, Evan was at sea. Saxton Crouse would know what to do. As Evan rounded the bend toward his parents' place, he saw Saxton waiting for him, leaning on the Toyota Corolla Evan's mother had recently given Evan the keys to. Evan held a hand up in greeting. Saxton nodded and pushed himself off the car.

"What do you mean Lansing Meadows slept at your house?" Saxton asked by way of greeting.

"Well, Colleen's house," Evan said.

"Uh-huh," Saxton said. "Colleen's house where you keep all your stuff and spend every night."

Evan scowled; frowning made his hangover pulse. "He was in town, he played at the café last night."

"He did?" Saxton said. "Did you go?"

"No," Evan said. "Karaoke at the Alley Oop. You know what that's like. All hands on deck."

"So how the hell—"

"He came to the Alley Oop after. Said he wanted to see what was so *all-fire great* about it that it kept everyone in town from his show."

"Yikes," said Saxton.

"He had a bunch of drinks, and we were closing, so then I had a bunch of drinks with him—"

"With Lansing Meadows," Saxton said. "You had a bunch of drinks with him. Did you tell him you play too?"

Evan's hands were sweating. He wiped them on his jeans. "Jesus, Crouse. No. I did not."

"Why not, man? It could be your big break."

Evan shuddered. "What would I say, my name is Evan Cornfield, I'm a songwriter too?"

"Why not?"

"Just because, okay? And it doesn't matter. Colleen was

bragging to him about me."

"That girl is in love with you," Saxton said. He gave Evan's shoulder a little push.

"Please, Crouse, you gotta stop saying that," Evan said. "One thing led to another and he didn't want to go back to where he was staying because someone told him the place is haunted."

"Ah, the Beach. That place *is* haunted."

"So we had all these drinks, and I was going to stay at Colleen's—"

"Why don't you just admit that you live there too?"

"Seriously, Crouse, shut the fuck up about that. So I just said, we have a pullout couch, you can stay with us."

"And?"

"And—Lansing Meadows slept over. And he's staying again tonight. And tomorrow, I'm driving him to Antigonish."

"What's he like?" Saxton asked.

"He's Lansing Meadows."

4

Dacey Brown knew that spring was coming. She didn't need to check a calendar. She could feel it rushing like the cascade that gave Grand Falls its name. The winter had been long, but then they almost always were in New Brunswick. And she'd been tired, so tired. But spring was coming, and she could feel herself returning.

Two nights earlier, Dacey had dreamt a sere winter landscape. She was driving two cars, one then the other, treacherous roads, lonely streets. Inching forward in one car, then hopping out to move the other ahead. Two lives, she thought. This workaday one, and the other, the one she barely let herself think about, the one she couldn't let go.

She paged through an envelope of photographs, a season of monotony, rendered frame by frame unthinkingly. She had shot the scenes of ennui—a muddy riverbank, the main street in town after a snowfall, the parking lot at the SipNSlurp—without purpose. She pulled the photos from the envelope and arranged them in colour-blocked stacks. White, grey, brown, black. It was time for a new palate.

She was looking for clues. She'd hauled out all her boxes of photographs—the earliest ones were quite well-organized, with dates written on the boxes and little dividers that separated snapshots of camping trips with her high-school friends from subjects she'd shot for the Grand Falls *Examiner*. She'd started working for the paper when she was fifteen. Phil Cotton, who'd been her grade ten English teacher and the staff advisor for the school yearbook, was also the editor of the *Examiner*, and he paid her a little bit each month to take photos for the paper.

She'd seen the world, it felt, from behind her camera, though she'd rarely left Grand Falls. Whatever happened in her little town, she documented. It was how she made sense of what she was seeing. While her peers drank, got pregnant, dropped out, went to work for their fathers, or considered careers in science, business or health care, Dacey Brown framed their world and shot it, held it fast with light reflected or emitted.

Somehow in that holding fast she had herself become jammed. Alone in her house in Grand Falls, the house in which she'd grown up, she dug for answers. Through the organized boxes of photos, and on to the haphazardly stored ones taken in recent years. There were photos of her time away at Mount Allison University in Sackville, four hundred kilometres and a world away from Grand Falls, and photos that showed her return and the time since. The departure of first her younger brother, then her older sister, and finally her parents, all bound for Alberta: Sam to go to school, Lily to be with her fiancé, her parents to take one last shot at making money before they retired. Dacey hadn't even considered going with them. She couldn't see what there might be for her there. But from where she was sitting now—on the polished hardwood floor of the living room of her childhood home—she couldn't see what there was for her in Grand Falls either.

She had failed to make a plan. She had bobbed along, thinking something would happen to her. But here she was, gone thirty, and nothing yet had.

If she listened hard, she'd swear she could hear sap running. There was no mistaking it. The time of year was upon her. Tamp it down, she wondered, try to dull its roar? Or stoke it and see where it took her? She'd been tamping it down for years and look where it had got her. Nowhere, that's where.

5

Evan Cornfield had planned to play a few songs at the Boite even before Lansing Meadows turned up. He'd been practicing and talking himself into it for several weeks. He had performed in public before, once at a high-school talent show, where he'd been easily beaten by a group of grade ten girls lip-synching to "Leader of the Pack," and dressed in circle skirts and bobby socks. Since then he hadn't taken a stage. He'd played at parties where people were drunk and heedless, and that suited him fine. But he knew it wasn't going to take him anywhere he hadn't already been.

Evan had made the decision not to go to university. It was unusual in his family—all three of his sisters had gone to university and were successfully launched into grown-up life—but not in his community, where most kids went into the family business, whatever it happened to be, got married young, and looked hollowed-out by the time they were thirty. Evan wanted no part of that. His father was a carpenter, but Evan was ill-suited to the work. He was clumsy and dreamy and so afraid of cutting that he'd measure all day rather than sink a saw into wood and risk getting it wrong.

In fact, Evan was unsuited to just about everything.

Everything but music. Music wasn't just a substitute for talking. But music required something of you. If you were going to give yourself to it, you had to go all the way. If you wanted to say something with music, you couldn't just say it to yourself. You had to say it in a larger context. In front of other people. And so unless his plan was to work at the Alley Oop forever, serving dried-out hot dogs and nagging the kids to spray their bowling shoes with Lysol before they returned them, he was going to have to make a move.

And that had been the plan, though it made him feel sick to contemplate standing on a stage again, in front of people who would be paying attention. And now Lansing Meadows was here, and Evan felt paralyzed. Saxton Crouse had determined it was Evan's chance to make an impression. He invited Lansing Meadows to drop by the café—and told him why. Evan narrowed his eyes at his friend and vowed to someday have his revenge.

Evan had a drink, and then he had another one, and then he decided what the hell? What was the worst that could happen? His mind immediately offered him several scenarios, all of them devastating. He pushed them away, and held tight to his guitar. Lansing Meadows was at the bar, all hat and swagger. He'd been holding court, telling road tales to a bevy of locals who hung on his every word.

"Where were you last night, my love?" he asked Lucie D'Entrement, who taught kindergarten at the town school and had rosy red cheeks that bloomed above her smile.

Lucie giggled. "Alley Oop, of course," she said. "Thursday is karaoke!"

"Of course," Lansing turned away. "Karaoke. The whole town go to that?"

"Pretty much," she said.

"That would have been nice to know before I booked a gig here on a Thursday night," Lansing said to Lucie, but also to Brendel, who worked behind the bar. Brendel shrugged.

"I'll give you a drink on the house, make it up to you."

"Amazing grasp of economics," Lansing said. "Perfect."

Brendel shrugged.

"Gimme," Lansing said. "Red wine and cola."

Brendel shook her head at the order, but poured it regardless. Lansing took it and slurped, then turned toward the tiny stage, where Evan was plugging in.

"Play us a song or two, boy!" Lansing shouted.

A wave of nausea washed over Evan, but he swallowed it down and tuned his guitar.

"Here goes nothing," he said into the microphone.

"That's the spirit," Lansing called.

The set passed in a blur. Evan played three songs and never quite settled into it. Perhaps it would have been the same had Lansing not been in the room. In front of a crowd—even such a tiny crowd as the one gathered at the Boite—Evan felt flayed.

On stage he lifted one foot, then the other, shuffling side to side but staying on the spot, like a second grader who has to pee but doesn't want to miss anything. He kept his eyes closed tight, so tight he was almost dizzy by the time his set was over and he opened them again.

"Son, when are you planning to learn to play that goddamn thing," Lansing said to him afterward. "I don't know where you picked up your...I hesitate to call it technique." He closed one eye as he sipped at his wine and cola. He regarded Evan from beneath his hat. "And it wouldn't kill you to resolve the fucking thing at the end, you know. You can't just leave it hanging."

The truth was—and Lansing must have known it as well as Evan did—Evan had learned just about everything he knew about playing guitar from Lansing's records. All that time with his chest pressed up against the speaker.

The truncation of the songs—the way they ended as if Evan had forgotten he was playing, or as if someone had entered the room with a gun pointed at him—that was his alone. He lacked follow-through. Ask his teachers. Ask his parents. Ask his sisters. Ask Colleen.

"Okay," Evan said.

"Okay," Lansing said. "Okay? That's it?"

Evan shrugged. "Okay, thanks."

Lansing shook his head. "Alright," he said. "You want a drink?"

"No thanks," Evan said.

"Mind if I finish mine?"

Evan shook his head, mute with mortification. Saxton Crouse was a dead man.

6

Lansing Meadows sat in the back. He pressed the little tab
that made the window go up and down. He pressed it up,
he pressed it down, he pressed it up again. Evan, steering
the car over the rutted road, around roadkill and potholes
and the various other detritus of an old highway in rural
Nova Scotia, bit back the urge to bark at Meadows to stop
it. He was a nervous driver with little experience, and Lansing Meadows himself was unnerving enough. The added
distraction of the business with the window wasn't helping. They'd been doing just fine, making their way along
the Trans-Canada when suddenly they'd been confronted
by a line of brake lights and orange signs indicating construction ahead. Lansing, complaining they were short of
time, had coached Evan toward this alternate route. Here
there was hardly any traffic, but the road had little else to
recommend it. Still, Evan was happy to be driving Lansing
to Antigonish for his next gig, he was. Meadows couldn't
drive himself, after all. Said he'd had his license suspended
some years earlier, for transgressions Evan Cornfield
could only imagine.

They didn't speak of Evan's performance at the café, and

for that, Evan was grateful. It allowed him to enter a kind of reverie in which he and Lansing were peers, two singer-songwriters on the road together. Just the open highway to egg them on. A road that would become embroidered with story as they travelled it, their guitar cases snugged up against each other in the back seat, the two of them sharing a smoke in the front seat, talking about songs they'd written, gigs they'd played, girls they'd screwed. In Evan's imagination it had the potential to be the start of a new era, a moment the historians of folk music would look back on, a moment when, they'd say, the passing of the mantle had begun.

Evan looked in the rear-view mirror. Lansing Meadows was asleep, his head lolling to the side, his mouth open, a pool of spit gathering at the corner and threatening to spill over the banks of his old-man lips. The trademark hat was crushed between head and shoulder. Evan sighed and clicked on the radio. He twirled the tuner, in the mood for old music. Torch songs from the forties, or the kind of music he imagined farmers played on their porches when their day was done. He let his eyes drift from the road to the radio dial, and he'd just about found something listenable when he felt the *hump...hump* of first the front wheel on his side, then the back wheel, rolling over something that wasn't asphalt.

"Fuck was that?" Lansing Meadows said, suddenly awake. He sat up straight, pulled his black brimmed hat back up onto his head and wiped a rough hand across his mouth.

"Not sure," Evan said, pulling over to the side of the road.

"Gotta get to the gig," Lansing said, starting up with the window again.

"I know," Evan said, "but I think we hit something."

"Christ," Lansing said. He tugged the hat down over his

eyes and leaned back in his seat.

Evan eased out of the car. The road was littered, as it had been since they'd left the main highway, with various things. Small furred bodies were everywhere, the luckless creatures who'd met their end beneath the wheels of cars, or, more likely, the wheels of the pickup trucks that had roared past him at every opportunity.

Evan felt cold. He closed his eyes tightly and breathed. "Please don't be someone's pet," he muttered. "Please not a dog. Not a cat."

The raccoon lay just behind the car. It was a big one, its bottom fat. Its heart was beating, Evan could tell, the chest heaved up and down. It was not lying in a pool of blood, and Evan felt relief wash over him. The eye he could see looked pissed off, perhaps, but not on death's doorstep. Not that Evan had had a ton of experience with wild animals. But in books, their eyes always glassed over when they were about to die, and this raccoon looked pretty spry.

"Be okay," Evan muttered, "please, please be okay." The car door swung open behind him, and Lansing Meadows spilled out onto the road. He fixed a gimlet eye on the situation and said coolly, "Should I brain it with my axe?"

Evan spun around. "You're travelling with an axe?" He could feel a thin wave of hysteria rising in him. The raccoon's breath seemed to rattle behind him. Lansing Meadows laughed a little choking laugh, full of cigarettes and dissolution.

"Fuck, no," Lansing said. "Get a hold of yourself." He reached back into the car. "My guitar, you asshole. Hard case, should do the trick."

Evan turned back to the raccoon, which seemed to be rallying. "I don't think so," he said softly. Then to the creature that was picking itself up, delicately shaking off the stun of having been rolled over by a ten-year-old Toyota Corolla, "Go on, guy. You can do it." And the raccoon slunk off the road into the scrub and away. Lansing Meadows watched it go, waited a beat.

"Okay then," he said. "Sound check's in an hour. And fuck, I'm hungry. Let's get at 'er."

Evan watched a moment longer, stood by the rear wheel of his mother's old car and peered into the low scrub, thinking he could see the bushes moving, thinking he could see the grasses swaying where the raccoon made its way. He gazed down at the dirt and gravel of the shoulder, where little paw prints were barely visible.

The slam of the car door brought him back, the honking of the horn made him turn. Lansing was in the front seat, leaned over to the driver's side, beating a staccato rhythm on the horn.

Two singer-songwriters on the road, Evan thought. The open highway ahead of them. The raccoon would become a myth. He'd write it or Lansing would. It didn't matter. "Alright," he said, reaching for the door handle. "Sound check's in an hour, let's get moving."

The gig in Antigonish was in an old church. The building had the smell old churches do, of mildew and incense and perfume. It had the acoustics too; a perfect place for live music. Lansing stood in front of the altar and strummed his guitar. The warm tone rang out in the almost-empty church, Evan Cornfield and the man checking sound the only audience. Lansing's face was less guarded, his body more relaxed as he stood with the guitar strapped across his torso. Evan tried to be cool, but the sound of the voice he'd grown up with soaring in the empty room and ringing off the rafters, and at such proximity, was dizzying. He wished Saxton were here, if only to have someone to talk with excitedly about what was to come.

He'd seen Lansing Meadows play only once before. His parents had taken him to Halifax to see him at the university theatre. His sister Helen was at school there, and she met them for the show, though Lansing Meadows wasn't really her bag. Evan, however, sat transfixed as Lansing held the audience with just his voice, just his guitar. No tricks, no band to hide behind. Afterward, Lansing stood in the lobby, signing CDs and shaking hands, posing for photos. Helen pushed Evan to say hello, but the very thought made him sick. Lansing was larger than life and Evan was in awe. While Evan cowered with his parents, Helen pushed through the crowd to get a CD signed, and Evan clutched it all the way home to Petite Riviere, not letting go even when the thrum of the tires on the highway pavement sent him to sleep. The next day, he clipped the review out of the Halifax *Chronicle-Herald* and pinned it to the bulletin board above his desk. It was still there, yellowed and brittle, Lansing's face under the hat much the same as it was now.

As satisfying as the sound check had been for Evan, the show itself was a revelation. The room was full, every pew loaded with people sitting shoulder to shoulder, their coats laid across their laps or on the floor to make more room. Fans, Evan thought, but not-fans too. Antigonish was a small town, and Lansing Meadows had come to it. Going to the show was what there was to do. And perhaps karaoke had not taken hold in Antigonish the way it had in Petite.

Evan sat at the very back of the church on a hard wooden

pew, the car keys bunched in his pocket, and he breathed in every moment of the show. Lansing pulled everyone's focus his way. His craggy face came alive, came almost beautiful, Evan thought. Lansing built a rhythm the audience was powerless against. He told stories and made them laugh, then played a song that made them cry. And those songs—Evan remembered the sound, the feeling of the music of Lansing Meadows entering him, pushing in through his thirteen-year-old chest, finding a home, holding fast in his ribcage. That long-ago music heard this music and rose to meet it. Everything else fell away. All he cared about were these songs, this singer. He slid down in the pew, closed his eyes and breathed it in.

"Here's the thing," Lansing Meadows said. His hat was low on his head and Evan couldn't see his eyes, but he imagined them bloodshot. "Here's the thing. My manager and I are coming to a parting of the ways, shall we say." Lansing stabbed his fork into a mound of scrambled eggs on his plate, dragged them through a puddle of ketchup, lifted the fork to his mouth.

"A parting of the ways," Evan said.

Lansing pushed the forkful into his mouth and nodded, chewing. "Can't stand the bastard," he said. "Hateful son-ovabitch." He swallowed, swilled coffee, wiped a calloused hand across his mouth.

They were in the motel's diner, and Evan was barely awake. The previous night's bed had been lumpy, and Lansing's snoring was even worse when he was lying down than when he was slumped in the back seat of a car. Evan poked at his over-mediums with a corner of his toast. He was picky about breakfast, though he rarely complained.

Here, for instance, the kitchen had waited too long to butter his toast, and so the butter—or butter-flavoured topping, more likely—stood apart from the surface, a pale and greasy smear, rather than soaking into the nooks and crevices. The eggs were alright though. He poked harder, broke the yolk. He couldn't figure where this conversation was going. What he wanted to say was, What does this have to do with the price of bacon? It's what his father said any time something seemed irrelevant or puzzling. Instead, he said, "Oh yeah?"

"Yeah," Meadows said, picking up Evan's coffee cup and slurping from it. "I'd kill my own grandmother for another cup of coffee," he said loudly. Then, in a confidential tone, "course, she was a hateful sonovabitch herself."

The yolk pooled on Evan's plate and he mopped at it with his cold toast.

"Any event," Lansing went on, holding Evan's cup out for the server, who'd materialized table-side, "no more road trips." He took a long swallow of fresh, hot coffee.

"You're not going to tour anymore?" Evan's heart sank.

"Oh, *I'm* still gonna tour," Lansing said, sitting back. The hat obscured the top two-thirds of his face. "*He's* not. That's where you come in." He pulled a pack of cigarettes from his shirt, shook one loose, tapped it twice on the table.

"I do?" said Evan.

"Got a light?" Lansing asked.

"Yeah," Evan said, "but you can't smoke in here."

"Son," said Lansing. "I'm Lansing Meadows. I can smoke wherever I want. Just 'cause you're my new road manager doesn't mean you can tell me what to do." He reached in his pocket and pulled out a BlackBerry. He slid it across the table to Evan. "First order of business, take care of this. I have no idea how to use the fucking thing and the vibration is driving me bonkers. Next order of business," he pushed the cigarette between his teeth and leaned forward. "Spark it up, boy."

They had reached a compromise. Evan would load the car with their belongings and Lansing would wait in the motel's diner till he was done—and then Lansing could smoke in the car all he wanted. It was raining as Evan fit Lansing's guitar and his own in the back seat of the Corolla, and then tucked in Lansing's knapsack, which smelled of cigarettes, bacon, and damp. He breathed through his mouth and stowed his own knapsack in the trunk.

The rain was cold and pointy, it sliced through his hair and under his collar, carving a path between his shoulder blades and down his back. Miserable to be out in, and hell to drive through, he imagined. But having tacitly accepted his new position, or having, at least, not turned it down, he had no choice but to be both out in it and to drive through it.

Evan had always been afraid of cars. His earliest nightmare, and the only recurring one he'd ever had, involved the family car, his father at the wheel, his sisters in the various passenger seats, and Evan himself buckled in securely. One minute they were whipping along a highway, all chattering happily, the next his father and sisters had disappeared. The car flew along, little Evan still firmly buckled in, disaster the only possible outcome. He always awoke before that outcome, sweaty, dry-mouthed, with a heart that wouldn't stop pounding for many long moments. As a child he would freeze in parking lots, sure that any car in motion would hit him. His parents tugged him along, their voices as they urged him on edged with frustration. But he couldn't make himself not-afraid. He'd put off learning to drive as long as he could, till finally Crouse shamed him into it. He was a rarity in his community, where the other rural kids learned to drive as soon as they were tall enough to see over the steering wheel and reach the pedals—and some learned before that.

But here he had a chance to travel with Lansing Meadows. To see the hero of his childhood and youth perform six nights out of seven. To sit at his knee, practically, and soak up all that he had to offer. Every scrap of history and experience. Here was an opportunity to ask every question he had ever had about the songs and the stories behind them. Here was an opportunity to be, if not friends, perhaps comrades. Soldiers of song, brothers-in-arms.

Evan closed the door on the jumble of gear and belongings, then folded himself into the front seat to wait for Lansing. The windows fogged over, the smells of bacon and cigarettes making a fog of their own. The rain on the car's roof was relentless.

He pulled out the BlackBerry and dialed Crouse.

"How was it?" Crouse asked.

"Amazing," Evan said. "Better than when I saw him in Halifax. There's something—I don't know. *Holy* about him now. I can't explain it exactly."

"Maybe it's because he was playing in a church," Crouse said. Evan could hear the sound of bullets whizzing in the background.

"Are you playing a video game right now?" he asked.

"No, Evan, I'm paying rapt attention to you and this conversation."

"It's not because of the church," Evan said. "It's something about him. A kind of calm, maybe? He has a presence.

And he seems—sad, or something."

"Articulate as always," Crouse said. "Chopper!" he added. Evan could hear what sounded like helicopter blades slicing through air.

"Listen, Crouse," Evan said. "Lansing wants me to go on tour with him."

"What? Why?"

"What do you mean, why?"

"Why does he want to take some little pipsqueak like you on the road?"

"I'm not a—Jesus, Crouse. You were the one who said this could be my chance. You know, that I could make an impression." Three blasts of gunfire sounded down the phone line.

"Ah, fuck, I'm hit. Evan, I didn't think you actually *would*, is all."

"Very nice, Crouse, very nice."

"Kidding! That's great news. So, you're gonna go?"

"I don't know," Evan said. "I haven't decided yet."

"Why wouldn't you?" Crouse said. "What do you have to keep you in Petite Riviere? Besides me, that is."

"Uh-huh," Evan said. "Well, you've been very helpful, Crouse. In your usual way."

"I'm always at your service. When do you leave?"

"I don't know. Soon as Lansing gets out here. I don't know what's keeping him." He scanned the parking lot and squinted through the rain toward the motel's restaurant. He could barely make out Lansing's figure—the hat, mostly—peering back at him.

"I gotta go," Evan said. "I'll talk to you later, Crouse."

He tapped the horn and gestured *come on*.

The hat shook no. Evan gestured again, half-heartedly.

The rain pelted him as he dashed the short distance, and he gasped at how cold it was. He was drenched by the time he made the diner. Lansing stood by the door.

"What's the holdup?" Evan asked, icy rivulets down his neck for the second time that morning.

"I could ask you the same thing," Lansing said, an unlit cigarette clamped between his teeth. "Whadidya, fall asleep out there?"

"I was waiting for you," Evan said.

"Waiting for me to what?" Lansing said. "I need a light."

"To get in the car," Evan said. "You can't smoke that in here."

Lansing pulled his hat down further till he was all brim and cigarette. "And I was waiting for *you*," he said. "Waiting for you to come get me and light this goddamn cigarette."

Evan fished in his pocket for a lighter or a pack of matches. "Outside," he ordered.

"It's raining," Lansing pointed out.

Water dripped down Evan's collar from his hair. No shit, Sherlock, he thought. "Let's go," he said. "Did you pay?"

Lansing adjusted his hat further still.

Evan sighed and peeled damp bills from his pocket. "Get in the car," he said. "I'll be right there."

Evan settled into the rhythm of a rainy drive. The windshield wipers kept time with the melody that was unfolding between his ears, and Lansing's sandpaper snoring provided the counter-rhythm to the wipers. With the heat up high and the radio down low, it was almost cozy. A little universe unto itself, shuttling through time and space. Lansing at one end, with all he'd seen and done, and Evan at the other, with all he'd yet to see and do. Evan felt he should keep a lid on such romantic thoughts. He sensed Lansing would mock him mercilessly, eviscerate him, were he to say such a thing out loud. But Lansing was fast asleep, his breath creating a patch of fog on the window that ebbed and flowed as it moved in and out of him.

Evan considered Crouse's questions.

He couldn't guess why Lansing wanted him along. Perhaps he'd heard something in Evan's performance that night at the Boite—something that reminded Lansing of himself when he was young? But there Evan was, letting himself entertain romantic notions again.

As for the other question, that one Evan could answer. His choices were clear and he could see them in an instant. On the one hand was Petite Riviere, where he could do what was expected of him. He could work at the Alley Oop, serving dried-out hot dogs and spraying bowling shoes with Lysol and dodging the affections of the local cougars. He could settle down with Colleen, who was lovely and safe, but who inspired in him no romantic notions whatsoever. He could play music at parties and once a week at the Boite, until he and Colleen had kids, at which point he'd have to put those childish dreams away. On the other hand was the chance, as Crouse had put it, to make an impression, the chance at his *big break*. He glanced at Lansing, old, grizzled, seemingly alone in this world. But you couldn't say he hadn't made something of himself. He was famous. He'd written a handful of songs that were part of the fabric of Canadian identity and one bona fide hit that everyone knew the words to. Lansing Meadows played music every night for money, and in between times, it seemed to Evan, he pleased only himself.

Evan glanced in the rear-view mirror at their guitars nestled together in the back seat. He glanced at his passenger in the front seat, slumped against the car window. He pictured Colleen and knew instantly that he'd be doing her a favour.

"Fuck it," he said aloud, as the rain continued to fall. "Fuck it. I'm in."

"Well of course you're *in*, son," Lansing rasped from beneath his hat. "Was there ever any doubt?"

Dacey Brown waited for the kettle to boil. This was something she did at work to make the minutes go. She stood by the kettle, warming her hands on its steam and listening for the muffled bubbling. It was change. It was cold water becoming something else. And with the simple alchemy of a tea bag, it would become something else again.

The door banged open and her boss bolted in, chased by a gust of damp, frigid air. Dacey's heart sank. It was much harder to boil the day away with Phil in the office. She could do it, but it required real effort, which kind of defeated the purpose.

"Cup of tea?" she asked.

"Sure," Phil said. "It's miserable out there. Supposed to get worse, too." He rubbed his hands together. "Rainiest March on record, so far."

"Maybe we should go home," Dacey said hopefully.

"Don't be ridiculous," Phil said. "You'll need to take your camera down to the river and get some photos. And talk to some of the residents there. See what they're doing to prepare."

"The same thing they always do, I imagine," said Dacey. "It's not news to anyone. And they'll all go look at the swollen river themselves. Why bother shooting it for the paper? It'll be old news by the time we come out."

Phil shook his head. "For posterity, Dacey. The first

draft of history. For my grandkids and yours." He blew on his red, chapped hands. "And to think you were one of my best students."

"That was a long time ago, Mr. Cotton." Dacey turned back to the kettle. "Won't it be dangerous by the river?" A last-ditch attempt to squirm off the hook.

"Just stay well back," Phil said. "You'll be able to get the shot without even getting your feet wet."

"Unlikely, if it's raining hard enough to be newsworthy."

"Dacey, Jesus! Don't make me order you to take this assignment! I am your boss. It's not so difficult, what I'm asking you to do, so stop arguing with me and just do it! Christ. What is wrong with you?"

Great question, Dacey thought. She grabbed her camera bag and her notebook.

"I'm sorry I yelled, Dacey," Phil said.

Dacey shook her head. "It's fine. You are my boss, as you so rightly pointed out. I'll go do the assignment. For posterity. For your grandkids."

"I said I'm sorry," Phil sighed.

"Don't worry about it," she said, banging out the door.

The kettle boiled.

"I'll just throw my things in a bag," Evan said as he steered slowly around the curving roads into Petite. "It won't take long."

"Take all the time you need, son." Lansing had tipped the seat back some kilometres earlier and he was reclined like a raja on a fast-moving litter.

Evan felt a moment of terror at what might be waiting for him. Would Colleen be home or at work? Would there be a scene? Could he change his mind at this point—and what would it mean if he did? Surely Lansing had once been at similar crossroads. Evan wondered what advice the older man might have for him and whether he could even presume to ask for it. He squinted at Lansing.

Lansing pushed his hat aside and looked up. "What?"

Evan shook his head. "Nothing."

"Then keep your eyes on the road, son." He patted his own chest. "Precious cargo."

Evan hunched his shoulders and drove.

At Colleen's empty house, he packed hastily. A stack of white T-shirts, another of black ones. An armful of soft plaid shirts. His one good cowboy shirt, the kind Gordon Lightfoot wore in photographs. Brown corduroys, black jeans. Socks, long johns. He stuffed them in his duffel bag. Patted his back pocket for his notebook; it was there. Extra guitar strings and picks. His tuque, a scarf, a deep breath. A note for when Colleen came home. Loaded up with his duffel bag, a water bottle, his wallet, his pockets bulging with strings, he barely looked around and he was gone, clattering down the steps to the car where Lansing waited.

"One more stop," he said, pulling the car door shut. The blood thrummed in him, his heart high in his chest, a kick-drum flutter of impatience and anticipation. Lansing Meadows was still reclined in the front seat, prehistoric tortoise on a sunny rock. All stillness to Evan's flurry. Evan closed his eyes and turned the key. If he could make it through the next ten minutes the rest would be easy.

And in fact, it had proven surprisingly easy to leave that Petite life behind, Evan thought later as the Corolla moved west toward the provincial border. Lou Conners had been nonplussed as Evan tendered his resignation. Lou simply shrugged and turned away, and bellowed to Colleen that she could have all the shifts she wanted. Colleen raised her eyebrows so high they disappeared into her thick bangs and then she turned away from him too, that caramel ponytail a wagging finger of disappointment.

He hadn't stayed to plead his case.

Now, the car was a universe unto itself, Lansing its centre, Evan its willing moon. They flashed down the highway, and Petite and all the memories Evan held of it streamed off behind them. Evan's mind raced with songs and questions. He glanced to the right.

"What?" Lansing said.

"Can I ask you a question?" Evan said.

"Don't ask my permission for that, boy. Jesus, what made you so timid?"

"Sorry," Evan apologized. Then: "My sisters."

"That was a rhetorical question," Lansing replied. "That means it doesn't require an answer. I don't need your life story, boy."

Evan grabbed at the first question that bubbled to the surface of the boiling stew of them. "What did you have in mind when you wrote 'On My Honour'?"

Lansing's jowls seemed to droop. "Whadidya wanna talk about that for? What do you think I had in mind? Jesus, boy, if you have to ask that, I guess I didn't do a very good job of it, did I?"

Evan felt panic. He hadn't meant to be insulting. "It's just," he said, "it was such a huge hit. Everyone covers it. Everyone knows all the words. Like it's some good-times-in-the-Maritimes bar-band sing-along song. But it's not, right?" He was feeling his way toward it, sick with fear he'd plummet over the edge of what was acceptable. "I mean, it's really a sad song."

Lansing pushed his lips together and out, the pressure reddening them slightly, the only colour-counterpoint to his drab clothes and pallid skin. "It's whatever you want it to be," he said sourly. And the rest was silence.

7

Dacey Brown wore rubber boots her mother had left behind, black with a brick-red stripe around the top. The camera was slung around her neck, beneath her raincoat, but she worried the sideways rain was getting through and soaking the lens. The din of rushing water was all Dacey could hear.

She was ten metres from the river, and its rise was unmistakable. It had already begun to colonize the yards of the nearest houses. The water was both fast and insidious—absorbing all it came across and making the land disappear in increments. How do you shoot a thing so violently in motion, she wondered. How do you frame a thing so large and still it on a page? It was beyond her. How could a newspaper that came out once a week possibly tell a story that was as kinetic as this one? First draft of history, sure, but by the time it was in people's hands, the second or third draft was already underway.

She swore she could feel the mud beneath her boots, feel it pulling at her feet, a steady tugging in the wrong direction. She had to focus if she wanted to get her feet back on dry land any time soon. She swiveled her head inside her raincoat's hood. Water coursed down each street that crossed the main one, forming little rivers, going nowhere. Look for specifics, she told herself. That's how you contain a rush of water and mill it into a story.

Each house by the river had a deepening pond where its yard had been. In one such pond an old woman stood surveying. A bright yellow slicker covered her housedress. Thick homemade-looking socks were visible above the tops of her rain boots. Grim determination on her face. Dacey sloshed closer, her hand steadying the camera beneath her jacket. She introduced herself.

"What will you do?" she hollered over the rushing water.

"What I've always done," the woman said. "Wait and watch and hope. Harder now without my husband, but still, what else is there to do?"

"How many of these have you been through?"

The woman turned to face Dacey now, each line on her face a tributary. "A few," she said. "Ten, a dozen. This is the worst since the year we married. That was a biblical year," she said. "Everything but locusts. This year, we got even those."

The water fell in sheets and rose in swells. It poured freely into the woman's yard, overwhelming a little wooden gate in a low fence that stood between the riverfront and her tidy house. The gate swung crazily and the woman turned away from Dacey and splashed to her property's edge and tried to fix the gate back into place.

Dacey drew out her camera and began to shoot. The woman turned and called over her shoulder for help, but Dacey, with the camera to her face and the clamour of rain in her ears, could only work to capture the moment, to fix in time and place a raging river, a woman trying to hold onto that which she had yet to lose.

8

Evan stopped once, for coffee and to pee. Lansing barely moved. Evan thought about checking him for a pulse, but he was scared to get that close and he figured Lansing was probably too mean to die. He put the Corolla in park and said quietly, "Just be a minute." He closed the door as gently as he could.

In the gas station he rolled his shoulders back and stretched his neck out while he waited for the coffee. The country radio station was playing "On My Honour," a version recorded by some new country band Evan had seen on television. They had complicated haircuts and fancy shirts. The woman who took his money and stood waiting for the coffee to complete its brew cycle sang along with every word. She even made a stab at the harmony parts. Evan was glad Lansing had stayed in the car. No doubt his presence would cause a commotion of some kind. No doubt the woman would want an autograph of the man who'd written the song she was singing along to. It was a dreadful version of the song, but the woman seemed to be enjoying it. Which was, perhaps, the hallmark of a truly great song—that it could withstand any indignity.

"Great tune, huh?" he said as she handed him his coffee and took his money.

"Oh yeah," she said. "I love this band."

Two hours later, Evan and Lansing were in Sackville, New Brunswick. A tiny university town with a couple of art galleries, a live music venue, and a vegetarian restaurant on the main street. It was almost as far west as Evan had been and he loved it instantly, its little downtown, the old-fashioned lunch counter, the big church on the corner where Lansing would play that night. He piloted the car along the streets of the town, marveling at its wholeness. You could walk from your tidy home on a nearby street to do an errand at the hardware store, and buy a bestseller at the bookstore, and stop for lunch in between.

He loved it mostly, however, as a harbinger of the larger places he was going to see. Petite Riviere was far behind him now, and ahead were the metropolises he'd only seen on television or read about in the newspaper. He was itching for those further arrivals.

"Where we to, boy?" Lansing asked.

"Sackville," Evan said.

"Am I an idiot, son?" said Lansing, turning his hat toward Evan.

"No sir," Evan said quickly.

Lansing sighed. "You have got to learn to recognize a rhetorical question when it comes along. Jesus Christ. Where are we staying tonight?"

This was a good question, Evan thought. Where were they staying? How could he find that out? Most importantly, how could he find that out without letting Lansing know that he didn't know?

"Hello?" Lansing said. "Anyone home? That last question was not rhetorical, boy, in case you're looking to compare and contrast."

Evan stared through the windshield and tried to think of who he knew in Sackville who could give them a bed.

"God sake," Lansing said at last. "Check the tour bible, son. It should all be there. My good-for-nothing road manager was actually good for some things."

Evan felt a moment of reprieve. He guided the Corolla into a parking spot on the main drag and said, "Right, the tour bible. Of course. Now where'd that get to?" His teeth chattered.

"You cold, son?" Lansing said.

"No sir," Evan chattered. They sat.

"The tour bible," Lansing said. "Jesus, boy, you even know what that is?"

Evan looked at him miserably.

Lansing sighed. "Tour bible's in my pack. Get it out and keep it on you. Know where it is at all times. Hell, commit it to memory if you can. We live and die by that thing."

Evan stared. Five sentences in a row. And helpful ones. Perhaps this was the beginning of their true friendship for the ages, the kind of folk-tradition torch-passing Evan had begun imagining as soon as he learned to pick out a tune on his guitar. Perhaps—

"Son, Chrissake, when I say go get it out, you know I mean now. I been sitting in this goddamn car so long I can barely feel my own legs and I'm about ready to die. So quit mooning around, and find out what's next. 'Fore I bite you."

There was an interview that afternoon at the campus radio station. The station's offices were busy with students who barely looked up when Evan and Lansing arrived. Evan felt self-conscious in his corduroys and plaid shirt, amid the fashion-forward but era-backward clothing the students sported. Those who wore glasses wore plastic frames like the ones Evan remembered in photos of his parents from the 1980s. Outsized and candy-coloured. There were T-shirts printed with wide neon stripes, skinny jeans and long cardigans. The conversation focused on seminal Canadian punk and new wave bands. Evan knew he had nothing to add.

But he did have Lansing Meadows, who was attired in his usual hat and a long canvas coat, the kind a cowboy might wear, weather-proof and with an absurdly dramatic drape. He'd had it, he assured Evan earlier, since before Evan was born. And since long before any of the skinny-jeaned students were born, too, Evan thought. Would that make it vintage to them, he wondered, or just old? The bands they were discussing pre-dated any of them by fifteen years or more, and were about as far removed from Lansing Meadows's music as they could be. Evan began to wonder if they were in the right place.

They stood among the shelves of records and CDs in the little waiting room, surrounded by furniture that looked too beat-up to hold them. A bumper sticker emblazoned in red, white, and blue shouted *Gun, God, and Guts: The Three That Set Us Free*. It was layered-over on the filing cabinet by stickers for bands like The Right Angles, The Alimentary Canals, and Typhoid Mary, and for causes from saving the whales to marriage equality.

Lansing Meadows pushed his shoulders down and back, and brought a half-smile to his face. He lifted his chin and looked down the bridge of his nose at a young woman who sat at what seemed to be a reception desk. She wore tattered jeans, leg warmers, and a floral baby-doll dress. She peered back at him through glasses with neon-green frames. "Lansing Meadows," he said.

"I'm sorry," she said, "I don't know what that means."

"It's my name, darlin'," he said.

"It means folk legend," Evan put in, but Lansing held up a hand.

"I'm here for my interview," he said. The student checked the clock.

"The vegetarian lesbian punk show is on right now," she said doubtfully.

Lansing turned to face Evan, eyebrows raised, a thing like a smile rippling his face. "Uh-huh," he said encouragingly, turning back to the student. She sized him up, squinting again at the schedule.

"Have a seat," she said, gesturing to the sprung sofa in the waiting area. "I'll try to sort it out."

Evan and Lansing stood perusing the posters on the wall over the sofa while the woman padded down the carpeted hallway to an office. Evan heard their voices as they tried to place Lansing or find his name in their logs.

"Some old guy," Evan heard, and he looked quickly at Lansing, feeling protective. But Lansing was grinning and flexing his arms like a circus strongman. His coat flapped ridiculously while he did.

"It's alright, son," Lansing stage-whispered. "I know what I am. And after all," he spoke a little louder now, "even a young 'un like yourself is *some old guy* to the likes of these. They're as green as my father's face after a day on heavy seas, after a night of heavy lifting down at the bar." Lansing laughed a crusty, dusty chuckle.

This was a Lansing Evan hadn't seen. Social and funny,

though still abrasive and utterly unpredictable. Evan laughed a little too, unsure whether Lansing was putting on a show or perhaps having a mild stroke. He was racking his brain for the signs of stroke when the young woman returned.

"You're early," she said, in an almost accusatory tone. "Have a seat."

"So it's not the vegetarian lesbian punks who are interested, then," Lansing said, looking at Evan with broad surprise.

The young woman finally cracked a smile. "Have a seat," she repeated. "*Folk You* is on in twenty minutes. Les should be here shortly."

Lansing arranged his features in a semblance of seriousness and nodded. "Very well," he said, sweeping his great coat around him. "We'll sit."

An hour and a half later, it was all over. Lansing had been charming and loquacious with the radio host, Les, who'd arrived just a few minutes to airtime, red-faced with both embarrassment and exertion. His bike had blown a tire and so he'd run to the studio. Lansing answered his questions generously and told stories and Evan looked on in admiring awe. This showmanship was a revelation. He thought back on his own performance—if you could even call it that—at the Boite, the way he'd felt so hemmed in by his own personality between the songs, his inability to connect to the audience, except *through* the songs, and even then just barely. He could see, watching Lansing, that there was a way to woo a crowd, to woo an interviewer. A way to let them in and to leave them wanting more. Evan couldn't see exactly *how* to do it, but he could see that it could be done. It was one more entry on the list of qualities Evan hoped to someday possess.

Later, in the motel room, Evan itched to draw his guitar from its case, but Lansing was snoring in the other bed, deep in an afternoon nap. So Evan wrapped his scarf around his neck and shrugged into his fleece jacket. He dug his fingerless gloves out of his pockets and felt to make sure his little notebook and pen were still there. He plucked the tour bible out from the pile of belongings on the other bed and eased his way out of the room.

Though the calendar said spring had arrived a week earlier, the Tantramar Marsh hadn't got the memo. The wind whistling off the marsh brought the cold damp of winter with it and Evan shivered in his jacket. The little lunch counter on the town's main street was closing up for the day, so Evan found a table at the café across the street. It was a busy place, with music barely audible above the hiss of the espresso machine and the noisy tide of student voices discussing final exams and assignments. Evan studied the chalkboard menu carefully and ordered a hummus wrap and a cappuccino, and felt very cosmopolitan as he did so. At a table near the front window, he opened the tour bible.

Despite its grand name, it was just a spiral-bound booklet with photocopied pages, lists of phone numbers and a map of the country on which each gig was marked by a number. Evan stared down at the two-page spread, traced a finger from Petite Riviere where he'd been born and raised, to Sackville where he now sat drinking a cappuccino, and westward to big cities he'd only heard of. He paged through the booklet. Each page represented a day on tour. Information about each show, who was presenting it, where it was happening, how much pay Lansing should expect. Evan looked hard at those figures. The pay was good, but not great. Surely a guy who'd been around as long as Lansing, a guy who'd won every kind of award there was, who had more honourary degrees than he had walls upon which to display them, who was due to receive a lifetime achievement award in a few weeks' time, surely a guy who'd written "On My Honour" was worth more than these contracts said he was.

Evan thought about the Alley Oop, the way they jammed in there for karaoke every Thursday. And he thought about the Boite and how often performers sang there for practically no one. People wanted, it seemed, the sound of their own voices, singing the songs they already knew. They'd rather get hammered and egg each other on to sing "On My Honour" with a karaoke backing track, than go down the street to hear the guy who wrote that song, and hundreds more, sing it himself. That was fucked up, Evan thought.

It wasn't the way a big break was supposed to work. Surely writing a hit song, a song that spent time on the charts and got played on the radio and that everyone agreed was a seminal folk song, surely all that counted for something. Surely it was a ticket, at least, to something larger, to the kind of fame that would mean your days of touring the country in someone else's Toyota Corolla, playing for hundreds of dollars, rather than thousands, would be behind you.

He leafed through the contracts, the reckoning sheets, the notes on attractions to check out on days off, and he knew that he would do whatever he could to make sure Lansing Meadows was received the way he should be on this tour. Even if Lansing Meadows was a cranky old bastard. Looking at the tour bible, imagining all the bibles for all the tours that had come before it, Evan knew Lansing had every right to be cranky.

The sun was beginning its descent when Evan turned the key in the motel room door.

"There you are," Lansing growled as the door swung open. "Hell you been, son?"

"You were sleeping," Evan said, tossing the tour bible on the bed. "I wanted to give you some peace."

Lansing eyed him from beneath his hat. "Take more than that," he said. "We're late, gotta get to sound check."

Evan looked out the window. "I can see the venue from here. Why didn't you just walk?"

"I don't just walk anywhere, boy. 'Specially not to sound check, and 'specially not without my road manager or my contract." He looked at the tour bible where Evan had tossed it. "Now get your shit together and let's go, boy. Jesus, do I have to tell you everything?"

Evan wrapped his scarf tighter and picked up the bible. The good-humoured Lansing had disappeared, as if Evan had been the one asleep and dreaming all afternoon. He sighed and held open the motel room door.

"After you," he said.

"Always," said Lansing.

9

Dacey Brown had travelled through her twenties like clear sweet water through a country creek bed. She'd been open-faced and open-hearted. But it hadn't helped her much. It hadn't brought her love or happiness. She had asked for nothing, and that's just what she had received. She had, as they say, failed to launch. So she was determined her thirties would be different. She was sure she knew the score. She was sure she knew what it would take to connect with the life she really wanted. But then, she'd been sure of that before, too. Change, she began to realize, was something in which you had to actively participate, or you'd be left behind.

If people asked—which they rarely did, in this small town no one asked you anything, they just figured they knew your deal—Dacey would say she didn't quite know where things had gone wrong.

But that wasn't entirely true.

Dacey tried not to pay too much attention to her dreams, but the truth was these days that's where all the action was. That sere landscape. Driving one car then running back for the other. The life she was living and the one she wanted to live.

She longed to see something she'd never seen before framed in her camera's lens. She was tired of the streets and people and spring floods of Grand Falls. She lay flat on her back on the picnic table in her backyard, its grooves running along the backs of her legs, like the highway going west, the planks and gaps palpable even through her jeans. She clutched a tumbler of rum and cola in one hand. The ashtray rested just below her breasts and in it burned a cigarette she'd dug out of the freezer. She shivered in the cool night. The stars were crisply spread out across the darkening sky. She put the glass down beside her and lifted her camera to her face. She looked through the lens at the stars. Cold and distant, she thought. The stars are cold and distant.

The world felt big and open, but Dacey had lived her life in small closeness. Her family, its storybook composition of two parents and three kids. The small saltbox they'd lived in. The way the nosiness of her small town was at once liberating and confining. Fredericton felt like a metropolis in comparison. She travelled there with Sam and Lily and their parents to visit her grandfather, diminished by age and circumstance to be just as small as everything else in her life. Even the house he lived in seemed to close around him after Gran died, the already small rooms grew smaller and dimmer, held her grandfather in their crumbling plaster arms. And New Brunswick was small, its ridges of hills and trees pressing in welcomingly, its inlets and islands crowded up against each other in a sweet, companionable way, and also against her, wherever she went.

But now that smallness was pressing her too closely. Dacey thought of her family thousands of kilometres away in a place expansive and free. The night yawned around her and she sensed the bigness of the world beyond, the ever-expanding realm of the possible. The expansion, she saw at once, had been going on without her. Despite her, even, for years. What would happen, she wondered, if she stretched out one foot into it. One and then the other. What would happen if she said yes to it.

She smoked the cigarette and drank the rum and cola and wriggled her toes in the cold night.

10

Evan sat in a pew at the back of the church and watched. Lansing had been impatient during sound check and imperious throughout the supper they'd eaten together before the show. He'd shaken the presenter's hand with a mixture of forced jollity and a detached quality that didn't bode well. Evan had despaired. If only he hadn't been late and made Lansing late. He'd clearly thrown the artist off his game. The night was shaping up to be a disaster.

But then eight thirty came and the rows of the candlelit church were filled with people. A hush came over the room and Lansing Meadows strode out and took his place in front of the altar and it seemed as good a place as any for him to receive the worship that came his way. Evan saw again the good-humoured Lansing. He joked with the crowd, even smiled when someone shouted a request.

"Don't get ahead of me, now," he chided, and the crowd laughed as if it were the funniest thing they'd ever heard. Lansing played all the songs he was known for and he played some new ones too, and the audience listened with rapt attention. He played the request and then as always, he finished with "On My Honour." This crowd sang along with every word, not just the choruses. They sang it so beautifully Lansing stepped back from the microphone and smiled at them, beamed, Evan thought. He beamed at them and let them sing the whole second verse, only joining them again near the end of the second chorus. And there was a feeling in that church, a feeling of what churches are for and what music is for and Evan breathed that feeling in, inhaled it into his lungs and held it there. He tried to get the shape of it and its flavour, he tried to hold it whole inside him so that it'd be there for him when he needed it again. And he knew, given the company he was keeping, he'd need it again before too long.

11

Lansing Meadows lay in the dark of the motel room and listened to Evan Cornfield breathe. If he could get up quietly and get away, he could steal a few minutes to himself. The tour was barely begun—still in the Maritimes, Chrissakes—and already he felt a bone-deep weariness. He didn't need to look at the map in the tour bible to know how big the country ahead of him was. He'd worn out enough pairs of boots crossing it over his lifetime. Some shows were easier than others and some you'd just as soon forget. Last night's had been not as bad as forgettable, but not as good as easy. It didn't bode well for the rest of the tour.

He needed this tour. He needed these shows, these crowds. He knew it wouldn't be long before it all began to slip away from him, and he could not imagine what he'd have left once that happened. Marie—she was a dream to him now. And Caroline he despaired of ever seeing again. It had been, perhaps, a mistake to burn so many bridges. The music had been all to him. And for many years, he'd felt that it had been enough. He was a certified legend. Ask the newspapers. Ask the frigging CBC. But he was fifty-nine years old now and he could hear the clock ticking.

He swung his legs out of the bed, put his feet flat on the floor and waited to feel ready for the next step. He glanced at Evan, but the kid was still sleeping, just a tuft of hair visible above the blankets of the other bed. He'd fired that useless bastard Jake and taken Evan Cornfield on the road because it was expedient. Because he was there, but also because he wouldn't ask too many questions. Kid had stars in his eyes and Lansing was up for being adored. But the volume of adoration, Christ. Kid had a fire hose, and Lansing needed a break.

Quietly he drew a fresh shirt from his suitcase and laid it on the bed. Then he reached for the previous day's shirt and drew from its pocket a packet of letters. In silence he observed his daily ritual: placing Marie's letters gently into the pocket of the fresh shirt and then slipping it on. He kept the letters close to his heart, but he rarely read them. He liked to feel their slight weight pressed against him. He didn't need to unfold the thin pages to know what he had. What he'd had. Words of love and longing, disappointment and despair. Sometimes they were a square of armour over his heart. Sometimes he swore they pulled power away from him. He could feel himself drawn, drained out into those pages. So many years later, she still had such a hold on him. He wondered if she knew.

He pulled on his pants and his boots, and put his coat over his arm. With a last glance at Evan, he let himself out of the motel room and into the brisk morning air.

It was a short walk from the motel to the town's main street and the lunch counter Lansing visited whenever he was in Sackville. His mother had taken him there for grilled cheese and fries the odd time they'd travelled from Windsor Junction to Moncton to visit her sister. They would dunk their sandwiches in pools of ketchup and eat their fries with vinegar and extra salt. Lansing remembered licking the salt off his fingers and how his mother would look away while he did in a way she didn't when they were at their own kitchen table. He thought now about the little smile that would tug at her lips as she turned her head away. That kitchen table, that childhood home, all gone. Windsor Junction a sprawling suburb now. His mother long dead and buried. He shook his head. He was not helping himself rally at all.

Mel's was as he remembered. A pair of bells over the door signaled his entrance. The smell of crisp-cooked bacon and frying potatoes hung in the air. Mel had been an old man when Lansing was a child, and now he was decrepit, older-than-old, tiny, hunched. But his white hat sat jaunty on his head and the towel folded and hung on his apron was as neat and crisp as it could be, given the fug of grease that permeated everything. Mel barely looked up when the bell jingled—a half-turn and the merest tilt of his head passed for a greeting.

Lansing settled himself at the Formica counter that ran the length of the diner, and behind which Mel cooked. Three or four of the booths were occupied—a table of university students looking bleary in the early morning. A young guy in coveralls. An older woman alone at a two-seater booth, her coffee cup's rim slathered in bright lipstick and still plenty more on her mouth. Her cup shook in her hand and jangled in the saucer as she replaced it. Lansing thought of his mother, the way she dabbed her mouth with her own handkerchief, barely touching the thin paper napkin the diner table offered. He nodded at the woman, went to tip his hat to her and realized he'd left it in the room. Oh well. There was a time it had made him less recognizable. Now, the opposite was true. Still he burrowed into his coat collar, not used to exposure.

The sections of a newspaper were loosely piled on the counter nearby, the pages had plainly been read already; the newsprint was soft, the typically neat collation now messy. Lansing drew it toward himself.

"Coffee?" Mel asked, his voice craggy with age and cigarettes, his Greek accent hanging on despite a lifetime in Canada. He had it poured and in front of Lansing before he could answer. "What you want?" Mel asked, as he laid the cup and saucer on the paper placemat in front of Lansing, pushed a bowl of creamers toward him.

"Eggs," Lansing said, "over medium. White toast, extra butter. You have back bacon?"

"Back bacon, yeah," Mel said. "Over medium, white toast, extra butter." He turned away, grasped an egg in his thick fingers, broke it with grace onto the griddle, then another. He turned back to Lansing. "Home fry?" he asked.

Lansing nodded, and Mel added potatoes to the grill. Lansing slurped his coffee and unfolded the newspaper.

More of the same, he thought. Crime, backstabbing, double-dealing, and that was just the news from Parliament Hill. Birds were falling out of the sky dead in Arizona and North Carolina. There was a mysterious fish kill in New Jersey, river banks thick with Piscean bodies, but scientists weren't concerned, the newspaper reported. These kinds of things are happening all the time, the scientists said. It's just that with the environment on everyone's radar, people are paying more attention.

Lansing sipped his coffee and thought about that. He could probably get a song out of it. Then again, if you couldn't get a song out of flocks of birds dropping out of the sky, you probably weren't much of a songwriter.

He read on. Recent storms had caused flooding in New Brunswick and people wanted compensation for damage to their homes. Some politician had said perhaps people shouldn't have built so close to the shore. The houses in question were more than a hundred years old. Lansing took another sip and wished you could still smoke indoors. He could probably get a song out of the plight of those home-owners, too. He patted his pockets for a pen, felt the packet of letters and let his fingers linger a moment. It was going to be a long road, and these moments of peace in an old diner in Sackville were fortifying, just like the letters.

His breakfast arrived, the eggs perfectly turned, the back bacon caramelized at the edges and pink in the centre. The toast was heavy with butter and the home fries were a crispy orange on the crust, meltingly pliable within. Mel refilled Lansing's coffee without a word and Lansing dug in.

He put the main section of the newspaper aside and picked up the entertainment section, only to come eye-to-eye—well, eye-to-hat-brim—with his own ugly mug. A shot from the show the night before, candlelit and as Canadian as—what was the old phrase? As Canadian as possible, under the circumstances. Hat brim, lip curl, bur-nished acoustic guitar.

Lansing smoothed the already flat newsprint. He both saw and did not see the point of reading his own notices. On the one hand, and despite appearances to the contrary, one was never too old to learn, never too set in one's ways to improve. Ideally. On the other, one would be lucky to get anything instructive or insightful out of most of what passed for music criticism these days in this country. This review would no doubt have been written by some recent college graduate, if he was lucky. Someone who hadn't even been conceived when Lansing Meadows was truly riding high, when "On My Honour" had been a hit the first time—a hit for him. This review would have been written by some kid who might have found an old Lansing Meadows record in her parents' collection. Who might have the vaguest—and only the vaguest—notion of who he was, what he'd done. Moreover, this review would have been written by someone who'd never read the great music critics. Someone who had no idea the relationship that could and should evolve between artist and critic. Someone who had no idea there was an art to criticism itself.

Lansing thought back to some of his early reviews, especially the ones written by critics who seemed to get what he was up to. Whether they thought he'd nailed it, that was another matter. But at least he had the sense they'd listened, considered. Put the work in some kind of context and understood what Lansing was aiming at. Those reviews had been worth reading over again. Lansing felt a flush of pleasure remembered. The feeling that artist and critic were working together to create a culture, to open a national conversation not just for their own edification but for the edification of audiences too. They were working together to bring new ideas and new ways of looking to the fore. Heady stuff.

This review, Lansing knew without looking, would start with the word "I" and then would be hard sledding from there. He knew he shouldn't bother. He also knew he wouldn't be able to help it. He picked up a triangle of butter-sodden toast and wondered which was worse for him: its animal-fat-laden charms, or reading a review of a show about which he already felt tender, written by someone young enough to be his third wife. He sighed and poked the triangle of toast into the mound of one of his eggs. It resisted exactly the right amount and then spilled a pool of thick golden yolk. Lansing dug into the review.

"I didn't know what to expect from last night's Lansing Meadows show at St. Agnes Church," the review began. Check and check, Lansing thought. A self-centred start and no background knowledge. He mopped up yolk and read on.

> Meadows, after all, is a folk legend in this country. In just two weeks he'll be honoured with a lifetime achievement award. In fact, some may be surprised to discover that he's not resting on his laurels, but is still active, touring and making music. He took the stage—or altar, in this case—as full of piss and vinegar as the old stories about him promise. He delivered a solid program of hits and a few near misses. His new material finds him in a deeply contemplative mood. "Rubber Chicken" muses on aging and the feeling there's nothing new under the sun, and "Sad Old Bastard" is an elderly bachelor's lament of loneliness. And indeed, Meadows seemed to peter out as the evening wore on. Piss and vinegar aplenty, vim and vigour not so much.

Jesus, Lansing thought, turning the paper over quickly lest the lines of type burn themselves irrevocably into his brain. Jesus Christ. Had it come across as bad as all that, then? His shoulders sagged. Yolk congealed on his plate and the glossy promise of the back bacon dulled while the potatoes went cold. He was fooling no one. He pushed his plate away, drained the last of the coffee in his cup, tasting its bitterness. Mel appeared with the pot, but Lansing waved him off.

"You no like?" Mel asked, gesturing to the plate.

"It was very good," Lansing said. "I just—eyes bigger than my stomach this morning, I guess." He pulled a five-dollar bill from his wallet. "This cover it?" he asked. Mel nodded, and Lansing pushed the bill beneath the plate's rim and scooped up the offending section of newspaper. How many in this diner alone had already read it? He looked around, not wanting to catch anyone's eye. Were they ignoring him on purpose, out of pity? He longed for a hat to hide beneath. He pressed the entertainment section into his coat and it lay against his chest, across from the packet of letters. Twin bundles of words that pushed him out the door, bells ringing behind him.

The air was crisp with Maritime spring, and Lansing hurried along with his head down. He wished he'd woken Evan up. He wished he hadn't read the review after all. He wished he'd finished his breakfast. The coffee jittered in his veins and his stomach growled. He dug for a cigarette, lit it, breathed it in. He hustled back to the motel.

12

Dacey Brown spent the morning at the newspaper, but she didn't do much work. She received and declined to respond to half a dozen emails from her boss. He sat three empty desks away—cutbacks and all—but Dacey kept her head down and her headphones on, faking transcription. Once, she accidentally made eye contact with him and he started to say something to her, but she pointed at the headphones helplessly and clacked her keyboard till he stopped.

She was plugging various destinations into an online map site and daydreaming of following the directions, on foot. Just to see. She was in the midst of figuring out how long it would take her to walk to Edmundston when the phone rang. It was Phil. Calling from his desk.

"I need you to go out and do this interview," he said. Her fingers itched to just disconnect the phone, gently, while she herself was mid-word. It was a surefire way to get out of phone calls you didn't want to be in. But Phil was sitting there, staring at her across the line of empty desks. She put the phone down.

"Okay, you got me," she said, standing in front of Phil's desk. "What's up?"

"Folk legend," he said. "Name of Lansing Meadows. Bring me seven hundred and fifty words and a photo." He held out a thin white hand and in it was a scrap of paper. Dacey Brown took the scrap, saw a phone number scrawled on it. "His cell number," Phil said, "but it's already set up. They're at the SipNSlurp and they're expecting you."

Dacey knew who Meadows was. Her high-school boyfriend had introduced her to the album *Naked as a Jaybird* one memorable afternoon. Nicholas had handed her one of his earphones and shown her how to nestle it in her ear, while he nestled the other in his. As the school bus jounced them home, Lansing Meadows scratched his songs into one of her ears, and Nicholas poured his passion for the album into the other. It had been a formative experience for Dacey. Sex and music and the road. Three things her life in Grand Falls lacked utterly.

"He's not playing here," Dacey said, "is he?"

"Just passing through," Phil said. "But he's getting a lifetime achievement award next month. And you're a fan, aren't you? First draft of history can't be all floods and disaster." Phil smiled.

Dacey folded the scrap and pushed it into her pocket. Her heart began to beat as if she were a rabbit in a snare. She wiped her palms on her pants. "Seven-fifty," she said. "A photo." But in her mind, she was halfway to Edmundston already.

She'd dug out her parents' copies of Lansing Meadows's albums after that fateful bus ride. She found them in a cardboard box in the basement rec room, collecting dust, perhaps on the verge of being tidied out of existence, given away in some spring-cleaning purge. The family's old turntable, too, was covered in dust. Dacey wiped it clean with the hem of her T-shirt and drew the vinyl disc from its sleeve. She blew on it, the way she'd seen her parents do. A few false starts and she had it spinning on the turntable. She plugged in the headphones, greedy to have the sound to herself. She lay down on the braided rug on the floor and closed her eyes. She was listening to the things Nicholas had pointed out. The lyrics, the chord progressions. There was an urgency, a vitality to this music, and Dacey heard it loud and clear. She heard what Lansing Meadows was saying and she knew he was saying it to her. She was young, but she understood what he was saying about love and disappointment—hadn't she had her share of those too, despite her tender age? The latter perhaps more fully than the former.

When the record ended, she flipped it and started again. She turned up the volume and listened as deeply as she could till all there was inside and outside her head was music. She didn't notice when the basement lights flicked on and off. She didn't feel her brother's toe nudge her. It was only when Lansing Meadows stopped singing mid-phrase that she came to and opened her eyes. Sam was standing over her, grinning. "Suppertime, freak," he said. "And if you're going to sing along, at least learn the words." He smirked and was gone.

Dacey sat up and brushed herself off. The turntable still spun and the needle hovered just above.

"Dacey!" She heard the impatience in her mother's voice. "Now!"

She clicked off the power to the stereo but left *Naked as a Jaybird* on the turntable.

At supper Sam talked about the school play he was hoping to land a role in and Lily fretted about the history test she'd written that day and whether she'd got enough of the answers right to pass her least favourite subject. Dacey's parents talked about work and whether the downturn in the economy would likely have an effect on the frozen-food plant where they were both employed. Dacey pushed the peas and potatoes around on her plate, her head still full of Lansing Meadows's songs. Sam was chattering about whether he should sign up for soccer or baseball once summer vacation started and while he was in the midst of listing the pros and cons of each, Dacey Brown couldn't help herself.

"Hey, Dad," she blurted. "Hey, Dad, I don't know if you know but there's this guy, this songwriter Lansing Meadows? And he has this album called *Naked as a Jaybird*? And Dad, I don't know if you've listened to it, but there's this one song called 'Cantina Heart' and it's probably the most amazing song I've ever heard."

By now the other Browns were staring at Dacey. Not only had she interrupted her brother (which none of them ever did), she'd also spoken an enthusiastic paragraph, something she hadn't done among her closest relatives since childhood. A silence fell over the dinner table then, punctuated with the sounds of cutlery on plates and Sam muttering, "I was *talking*."

"As usual," Lily said and stuck out her tongue, as if Dacey's aberration had ushered in a kind of anarchy.

"Lily," their father said. "Manners. Dacey, you shouldn't interrupt your brother." He took a long swallow of water and added, "And how do you think that record got into this house?" He forked a piece of meat into his mouth with finality and Dacey's heart fell. He chewed for a while. Then, "and if you think 'Cantina Heart' is good, wait'll you hear 'Nowhere Bridge' and 'Marching On.' You'll lose your mind."

Dacey could feel her cheeks flushed with pleasure, a rare

moment of connection.

"Sorry for interrupting, Sam," she said. "Mom, that was great, may I be excused?" Her mother nodded and Dacey pushed her chair back, scraped her plate and put it beside the sink, then made for the basement once more.

Her father was right, she thought now, as she packed extra batteries for her tape recorder and got her camera together. Lansing Meadows had many more fine songs than what she'd heard that night. You could spend a lifetime getting to know them, she thought. They retained their hold on her long after Nicholas had released his.

She had so many questions for Lansing Meadows and so much trepidation about asking them. She'd read enough about him to know he didn't suffer fools gladly, or at all. She'd seen him on national television once, drunk first thing in the morning, being asked stupid questions about traditional Maritime music and not even pretending, for the camera's sake, that they weren't stupid questions. This both thrilled and terrified Dacey Brown. She made her way to the SipNSlurp with fear in her heart.

At the coffee shop she spotted his trademark hat right off, before she was even in the door. She wanted to turn around, to go back the way she came. No good could come of meeting one's idols. She knew this. Everyone did. She took a deep breath, then another. She pushed the door open.

The weight of the camera around her neck was comforting. An outsized talisman. She could make sense of a world framed by a lens. If all else failed, she would get a good photo and call it a day.

The SipNSlurp was busy with the lunchtime crowd. Dacey smelled the coffee and wished the place had a liquor license.

She gathered herself, then began to weave through the tables to where Lansing Meadows sat. There was a young guy with him, his dirty-blond hair fell straight into his eyes. He brushed it away and it fell straight back in. He brushed it once more and stood when Dacey arrived table-side.

"You're from the paper?" he asked. He stuck out his hand and Dacey took it in her gloved one. "I'm Evan Cornfield," he said, "Lansing's ..." he paused. "Tour manager, I guess."

"Nice to meet you," she said. She could feel her hands sweating inside her gloves. She touched her camera again to steady herself.

"And this, of course, is Lansing Meadows," Evan said.

Dacey stuck her hand out, but Lansing just nodded toward the empty chair at their table.

"Lansing," Evan said, admonishment in his voice.

"What?" Lansing said, and Dacey could see in his face what she'd seen that time on television, and her fear bubbled again.

"I'm going to get Dacey a coffee," Evan said, looking hard at Lansing. "Would you like anything else?"

Lansing shook his head. Dacey clasped her hands and said to Evan, "I'll help you."

They stood in the lineup at the counter and Evan said, "Sorry about that. He read a lukewarm review of last night's show in the paper and now he's really down on journalists. Once you get him talking, I'm sure he'll be fine."

Dacey swallowed a wave of panic. "Yeah," she said, "sure." She wished for a moment she was still covering the flood, or perhaps at a school board meeting. She touched her camera again.

"What do you take in your coffee?" Evan asked.

"Just coffee," she said. She dug in her coat pocket for change.

"I've got it," he said. He paid for the coffee and handed it to her. "Alright, good luck," he said, "I'm off."

"Off," said Dacey. "Oh no. Where are you going?"

"To see what there is to see here," Evan said. He laughed and shook his head to knock the hair out of his eyes.

"You're seeing it," Dacey said. She felt her face burning. "Please stay. I might have questions for you, too." This was a lie, but Dacey was desperate.

"Okay," he said. She thought maybe he was blushing a little too.

Lansing Meadows seemed at first immune to Dacey Brown's charms. She tried to flatter him, but he resisted her efforts. Eventually he warmed up or took pity on her, she couldn't tell which.

"Bunch of nonsense," he said when she asked about the lifetime achievement award, dismissing the very idea with his hand. "It's pretty cold comfort after a lifetime as an outsider."

"Is that how you feel?" she asked. "Like an outsider?"

He narrowed his eyes at her. "You trying to psychoanalyze me?"

"I'm just trying to get my seven hundred and fifty words and make my deadline, honestly," she said.

Lansing leaned back in his chair. "I do feel like an outsider," he said. "I think it's a necessary condition for an artist. What else are you going to make art out of? If you're inside, what is there to chafe against? What insider ever questions anything? Outside is where it's all happening."

Dacey nodded. "Then do you feel that by accepting this award, you'll compromise your outsider status? What was it W.C. Fields said about not belonging to any club—"

Lansing looked at Evan and grinned. "She's quick, isn't

she?" He tapped Dacey's arm. "That was Groucho Marx, lovey. But nice try."

Dacey leaned across the table. "You make me nervous, Lansing Meadows," she said.

"Proper thing," Lansing said. "If I didn't, I'd have to wonder at your cheek and my own decline." He patted his pockets. "Son," he said, turning to Evan. "Go buy me some cigarettes, would you?"

"You can't smoke in here," Evan said.

"That's certainly true while I don't have any cigarettes," Lansing replied. "Now get."

Evan went, casting a backward glance as he did.

Lansing crooked his finger toward Dacey and she leaned in again. "This'll be my last tour," he said to her, his voice low and craggy. "It's about time they got their shit together to recognize me, and not a moment too soon. But don't go thinking it means something, because it don't. They've just already given one of these things to everyone else." He held up a hand. "And don't write some bullshit about how they're saving the best for last, either." He grinned at her, his mouth a flash of yellowing teeth. "And you know who else was full of it? Goddamn Groucho Marx."

Dacey laughed then, the percolating bubbles of her nerves finding their way out. She couldn't tell if it was truly funny—if Lansing was trying to make her laugh—or if it was horribly sincere, but laugh was all she could do.

As for Lansing, he nodded at her, his sunken eyes seemed to sparkle. "Yes, might as well laugh," he said. There was a note of mirth in his voice too. "It all goes fallsy downsies in the end."

"What do you mean?" she said, coasting now on his unexpected warmth.

"Up one side," he said. He raised one arm up, index finger pointed gracefully into the air, his eyes following its progress. "And down the other." He brought the arm down with force. Dacey could feel the slice of air it displaced. "Happens to us all before too long," he said. And where mirth had been a moment before was a heaviness Dacey couldn't identify. "Happens to some of us sooner than you'd think."

She watched as the shutters closed over his face. What had an instant earlier been a moment of closeness became what it really was, two strangers at a table in a café in Grand Falls, working at cross purposes. One leaning in and the other leaning back.

"Let me come with you," she said impulsively, though she could see clearly the moment had passed. "Let me come along and document what happens. Regardless of what you say, they *have* saved the best for last. It matters, this award. It matters to your fans. It matters to me. Let me take photos of the shows and scenes backstage. It'll give you something to look back on—"

But she didn't get to finish. Lansing stood, shaking his head vehemently. He pushed the chair away behind him and it tipped to the floor. "Fuck that," he said quietly, evenly. "I don't need any vultures picking over my corpse." He pulled his hat down over his face. "Print that in your goddamn newspaper." And he stalked out.

Evan met him at the door. "Going for a smoke?" he asked, and he held out the cigarette package. Lansing swiped it out of his hand.

"Don't make me wait, boy," he growled.

"I...okay," Evan said. He looked around and spied Dacey, who gestured weakly, shrugging her shoulders.

"What happened?" Evan asked, as Dacey picked up the

chair Lansing had knocked over.

"Safe to say he's still down on journalists," Dacey said. "Ah, damn it. I didn't get my photo."

Evan looked out into the parking lot, where Lansing paced, all angry energy and cigarette smoke. "Maybe ..." Evan said.

Dacey shook her head. "Definitely not," she said.

"I'm really sorry," Evan said. "He had a bad morning."

"And a bad afternoon," Dacey said. "Don't worry about it." She held out a card with the Grand Falls *Examiner*'s logo on it. "My cell number is on here," she said. "If you need anything." She picked up her camera from the table. "Good luck," she said.

"Thanks," Evan said. He looked out again at Lansing, who was leaning against a car in the parking lot and scowling. "I think I probably need it."

Dacey sat at her desk at the newspaper office, her story undone, her blood humming. She imagined Evan Cornfield and Lansing Meadows making their way to the next place, wherever that might be. They'd be creeping along that miserable stretch of road between Edmundston and Saint-Louis-du-Ha! Ha! Ninety kilometres that often took just as many minutes to travel. The semis chugging up the hills, four-ways on no matter what the weather. They'd be creeping, but at least they'd be creeping forward. Dacey Brown meanwhile churned in neutral, alone in Grand Falls.

She clicked open the browser window she'd been fooling with before the interview. Noted it would take about twelve-and-a-half hours to walk from Grand Falls to Edmundston. And then what, she wondered. Then you'd be in Edmundston. Not far enough, she thought.

She opened another tab and typed in her search terms. You could take a bus, she found, all the way to Rivière-du-Loup, and that would only take a little under three hours. And then the next day you could take another one to Montreal, and then you'd be starting to get somewhere.

Dacey Brown began to percolate. She'd been asleep, she thought, and now she was suddenly awake. She typed in a fury, seven hundred and fifty words. She found a photo online and downloaded it. She emailed them both to Phil with the subject heading: *first draft of history*. Then she emailed again to say she wouldn't be in the next day, or any other day. She didn't spare the office a backward glance. There wasn't much time and there was plenty to do.

13

They drove in silence for a time, Lansing's sourness seeming to drip off him. Evan darted glances at him till finally he sighed and said, "What is it, boy? You're making me nervous."

"I'm just wondering if you're okay," Evan said. "I'm wondering what happened back there."

"I don't want to talk about that," Lansing said. "But here's a tip for you, son. Journalists are bloodsuckers, they're all the same. Ride to their own kind of fame on your coattails as soon as look at you." He scowled. "They're a necessary evil in this business. Emphasis on the evil." He looked out the window. "It's not like in the old days, when there was respect. They respected that you had a job to do, and you respected that they did too. You could even have a beer together sometimes, and if you happened to slip up, if you kissed a girl who wasn't your wife, or slagged some other songwriter's abilities when you were in your cups, well, they didn't turn it into an international incident. Your secret was safe with them. Not these days. They smell a little blood in the water, they go in for the kill," he said darkly.

"Okay," Evan said. Dacey Brown hadn't seemed the type

to go in for the kill, but she was the only reporter Evan had ever met, so maybe he just didn't know. He decided that for the time being, he'd keep to himself the numerous interview requests that had come in from various outlets via the BlackBerry that day. "We'll be in Quebec soon," he said, to change the subject.

"*La belle province*," Lansing said bitterly. "It's never been particularly good to me. How many gigs we doing there?"

Evan pictured the tour bible. "A house concert in Quebec City. A club in Montreal," he said. "What's a house concert?"

Lansing coughed out a laugh. "A house concert is the last bastion of sanity," he said. "Some enterprising music fan invites twenty or forty of their closest friends, charges them twenty or thirty bucks at the door—all of which they then give to me. I play two sets of forty minutes each, hobnob with the homeowner and guests, eat their snacks and then sleep soundly in their guest room. In the morning, they make me breakfast and send me on my way. It's the best payday we'll have on this tour. Beats the hell out of that soul-killing gig in your neck of the woods, son." He sighed. "They'll drain the life right outta ya, though. It's always either a bunch of people who've never met an artist before and treat you like an animal in the zoo. Or a bunch of people who've met a bunch of artists before and they just wanna drop names and add you to their collection. Money's worth it, though." He pulled his hat down over his eyes. "I'm tired of talking, boy. Leave me alone for a while."

Evan started to protest but Lansing held up a hand. So he drove without a word and wondered how he could make it easier for Lansing. He was beginning to learn what Lansing liked: smoking, rough talk, getting paid. And what he didn't: journalists, being told what to do, karaoke. Evan was pretty sure that what he himself knew the most about, the area in which he was most qualified, uselessly enough, was karaoke. He was going to have to watch and learn, and fast.

The house concert in Quebec City went very much as Lansing had said it would. The audience was mostly people Evan's parents' age, and a few who were older—closer in age, perhaps, to Lansing himself. The couple who owned the house had arranged in rows their kitchen chairs and couches and footstools and whatever else they had that could be sat on, and the audience crammed in the large living-room-turned-concert-venue. At the break, there was a cheese platter and cookies and vegetables and dips all laid out on the dining room table, and people swarmed around Lansing to get a word with him.

It was Evan's job to stay at a little table near the front door and sell CDs to anyone who showed an interest. Lots of people bought them, and many more just stopped to chat with Evan, reminiscing about the number of times they'd seen Lansing play, and how great it was to see him in such intimate quarters.

"He seems tired, poor dear," one woman said to Evan as he counted out her change.

Evan felt himself bristling. "He's fine," he said. "He's just great."

"It must be difficult for him, at his age, to be on the road still," she pressed.

"Oh, don't you worry about Lansing Meadows," he said firmly. "He's got plenty of life left in him."

"Who does?" Lansing said, suddenly at Evan's side. Evan handed the woman her change, and gave her a warning look.

The woman blithely ignored it. "I was just saying it must

be awfully tiring, to be on tour the way you are, at your age."

Evan braced himself, but Lansing laughed heartily. "Still a little gas in the old tank," he said. "At least enough to get through the second set. Tomorrow though, that's another story." He pulled out a thick black marker. "Sign those for you, darlin'?" he asked, reaching for the CDs the woman held.

She smiled and held them out to him. As Lansing signed he said to Evan, "About ready to start up again, I'd say. Don't want to keep them past their bedtimes." He winked at the woman and handed the CDs back.

14

The thing was, Lansing Meadows *was* tired. His body ached most days, and more often than not he woke with a start and spent the first moments of consciousness in a cold panic about where he was. It didn't help that he rarely woke in the same place twice. The doctor had said he was likely to see an increase in *episodes of forgetfulness*. Lansing thought of these episodes as *losing my fucking wits*. It amounted to the same thing. Moments of terrifying disorientation, and an exhaustion the likes of which he'd never felt in forty years on the road.

It was an effort to stuff that fatigue down every day. An effort to wait out those moments of terror, those *episodes of forgetfulness*. He was determined, though. He'd race the clock and beat it. He'd get out across the country one last time, from sea to shining sea. He'd sift through the ashes of the bridges he'd burned, if necessary, in order to get it done. He was not the type to go gently into that good night.

But here again, he'd made it through another night, only to wake in the morning light in yet another strange bedroom, unable to orient himself for several long moments. At last he fought through the morning fog inside his head—

how to differentiate that from an episode, he wondered—
and located himself in the spare room of a house in Quebec
City, a house that had provided him a thoroughly decent
concert the night before. It was comforting, the degree to
which he still had it. And disturbing, the degree to which he
would someday lose it all.

He swung his feet out of the bed and placed them firmly
on the floor, wanting the certainty of hardwood, the unmis-
takability of his feet on it.

Why live in such a wretched future, he admonished himself. It was important, he thought, in the face of inevitable
misery, to live exactly in the moment while the moment was
good. Or, at least, while the moment wasn't bad.

It was good in many ways, to have the boy along. The
boy who knew nothing, which was as much as he should
know. Lansing had seen a glimmer, the night before, of the
way the boy would rise to his defense. It was, he thought,
both good and bad. Certainly it was good for Lansing
Meadows. He thought perhaps it might be bad for Evan
Cornfield, but then he brushed that thought away. Evan
had nothing but time. And that was one thing Lansing
Meadows couldn't spare.

15

Evan Cornfield was stuck between a rock legend and a hard place. The clouds overhead were low and dark grey, and the forecast on the car radio promised heavy rain and thunder. Evan wanted only to get to Montreal, and it shouldn't have been an impossible goal. It was a drive of only a couple of hours from Quebec City. But Lansing was agitating for a stop at a diner, and Evan could sense if he didn't oblige, Lansing would conjure up a worse storm.

Evan had suggested they grab smoked meat sandwiches they could eat in the car, but Lansing dismissed that idea.

"We're not savages, boy," Lansing said, his lip curling. "We'll stop to eat. Find me a diner with waitresses in old-school uniforms. I want a bottomless cup of coffee."

And so Evan had found one. He'd ordered a grilled cheese and fries, and he had to admit they were top-notch. He felt diner food was an area in which he was gaining some expertise. And though Lansing seemed to be in a playful mood, Evan felt himself getting more uptight by the minute. He glanced worriedly out the big front windows of the diner at the darkening sky and tapped the car keys on the Formica table.

"Fuck is a xenomorph," Lansing said, barely looking up from his newspaper crossword. "And your answer better have five letters."

"Alien," Evan said absently. "I think we'd better get going."

"Alien," Lansing said. "I'm impressed."

"Seriously," Evan said, folding the rest of the newspaper. "Time to go." He fingered a scorch mark on the table, the spiny ridge where the plastic buckled up, the granular feel where it had bubbled.

"Patience, boy, I'm nearly done," Lansing said. "What's your hurry?" He held out his coffee cup to the passing server. "More a this, sweetheart, when you get a sec."

Evan shook his head at the woman, but Lansing caught him and said again, pointedly, "When you get a sec, sweetheart." Then, to Evan, "We have loads of time, boy, and I don't care to be rushed."

Evan twisted a paper napkin into a ribbon of worry. "There's gonna be lightning," he muttered darkly. "Lots of it, and I'm the one who has to drive in it."

"Oh, well then," Lansing said, capping his pen and tilting his hat. "In that case we better get going."

Evan felt relief wash him. "Really?" he said.

"No, not really," Lansing scoffed. "It's lightning, boy. It won't kill you."

"It could, though," Evan said. "It does. It could." He slumped against the vinyl booth's back. He pictured again the continent, gigantic, relentless. They'd barely edged across it and already his dream of songwriterly camaraderie was fading. He didn't want to let Lansing Meadows down. But he had never been so far from home and he'd never driven in an electrical storm. He felt a familiar tightness, a humiliating prickle behind his eyes, and forced it down. He had to at least try to be a man.

"I got hit by lightning once," Lansing was saying. "Thank you, sweetheart," as the server filled his cup. "Seventy-eight," he said, "or maybe seventy-nine. I'd gone back to Yorkville just to see what the developers and that crooked city council had done to the place and there wasn't even a trace of the old scene there. I was standing outside where the old Riverboat Café used to be, and they'd turned it into some upscale lunch place, even then, with ridiculous little potatoes, the kind you make with a melon baller, you know?" He slurped his coffee while Evan shredded the paper napkin. "Anyway, who comes out of there but Murray McLauchlan, that yellow bastard. Oh, we hated each other. And just as we made eye contact, *boom*, sky opens up, thunder and lightning and *zing*, *zow*, next thing I know I'm on the ground and all I can smell is barbecue." Lansing drained his cup.

Evan folded the shreds of napkin and laid them carefully over the scorch mark.

"Really?" he said.

Lansing raised an eyebrow. "No, boy, not really. Jesus, you really are gullible. I'm finished my coffee, let's get out of here."

The rain did indeed come, and thunder and lightning too. Evan told himself a moving target was hardest to hit, and made the car go as fast as it felt safe to go. He gripped the wheel and tried to stay calm amid torrents of rain. Streams of cars, their tail lights steady through the rain, pulsed ahead of him and he followed resolutely.

Meanwhile, Lansing was in a voluble mood. His reminiscence of Yorkville, false though it had been, had awakened the storyteller.

"I didn't really hate Murray McLauchlan," he said now.

"I met him in the mid-sixties there in Yorkville, when every alcove with a stage in it was suddenly a coffee house and folk singers were fixing to be kings. It really did seem like something was going to happen to all of us. Like we were going to change something. Instead, we were the ones who were changed. And not all for the better. Of course, a guy like Murray, yeah, he went on to become king. A guy like Gordon Lightfoot. Joni Mitchell, too, I knew them all back then. That pipsqueak from Newfoundland, Ron Hynes. That guy was always eating my lunch, you know? *I* was on track to be the poet troubadour from the east coast, till Hynes swooped in there and punked me." Lansing sighed. "Jake tells me I gotta let this stuff go, but the older I get, the harder it is. I just want to leave something behind when I go. You know?" He looked at Evan, who was gripping the wheel and staring straight ahead.

"Of course you don't know," Lansing said. "You're so young you don't even know what I'm talking about. You can't even imagine a world before any of them—Murray, Joni, Ron."

"I thought you fired Jake," Evan said.

"Eh?" said Lansing.

"Jake. You fired him, right? Called him a sonovabitch, hung up on him? That's why I'm here?"

"Oh, sure," Lansing said. "Yeah, I forgot, I did fire Jake, didn't I?"

"Are you okay, Lansing?" Evan asked, tearing his eyes away from the road long enough to see Lansing's face, unguarded and old for just a moment. Then the hat came down and Lansing laughed.

"Boy, I haven't been alright since the seventies. Aren't you listening to a word I say?"

Sheet lightning crackled. "Better keep your eyes on the road, boy. Don't want to be responsible for killing the once-and-future king."

16

Hours had felt like days to Dacey, travelling down the spine of Quebec, skimming over the highway running alongside the St. Lawrence River, not to mention the night she spent in a grungy hostel in Rivière-du-Loup, a night best soon forgotten. But Dacey Brown was running hot now, every system humming, every follicle alert to the world. She'd watched out the window as the bus bore her further south and west, to see the progressive shrugging off of winter's coat. From town to town, it seemed, the furze of green spread between the river's banks and the highway's edges. While eastern Quebec still slept under a blanket of early spring snow, the closer she got to Montreal, the more the mantle of white receded from the fields.

She'd eaten a toasted western sandwich and a bowl of beef barley soup. She'd had her coffee weak, strong, burnt, and cold. She'd felt every bump of the road in her bladder, and she'd fended off the attentions of would-be suitors in both official languages. But she'd had not a moment of doubt.

She was moving, but she wasn't sure what she was moving toward. Or whether, in fact, she was simply moving away. She knew Lansing had a show in Montreal, and her only plan was to go. Whatever happened next, happened next. There had been a time in her life when she was ruled by what she called cosmic hints—now she recognized them as coincidences, random occurrences into which she'd read meaning. She'd let the universe tell her what to do back then, in her early twenties, when she'd been a student in Sackville. But it had stopped speaking to her—or she had stopped listening—after a time. The universe had left her high and dry in Grand Falls. Now, she would let her instinct lead the way.

Traffic on the highway had slowed. Dacey looked out the window and saw endless chains of brake lights, the highway lanes close and tight, where the ones in New Brunswick were roomy, expansive. The cars too were packed in close and tight. Dacey watched a number of drivers make what she considered questionable lane changes, with little room to spare and seemingly without a moment's notice or hesitation. It was late afternoon and raining, and the brake lights made everything festive, a path of light leading to the city.

The bus was chugging uphill, the on-ramp to a bridge suspended high above the river. Dacey's heart beat hard, at the height and the unknown. There was a tangle of bridges, and on the other side of the water, Dacey could see, was the city. As if Montreal were playing hard to get. As if it wanted to know for sure you meant it. Dacey did. She felt a kind of sick giddiness at what she'd set in motion.

Somewhere down there, on the little streets below, were people who didn't know her father, and his father too. People who didn't know Dacey Brown from a hole in the ground, who hadn't already made up their minds about her. There were things to eat that would confuse and dismay her neighbours in Grand Falls, and Dacey intended to eat them all. And somewhere down there, Lansing Meadows and

Evan Cornfield were pulling into town too.

The bus lurched to a stop. Passengers lifted their sleepy heads and looked around, blinking in the dim light of the bus. Dacey hadn't slept a wink. She'd been asleep too long, she thought, and all she wanted now was wakeful attention. She lifted her camera to her face and froze the moment. She breathed in what she'd done, the choice she'd made, and she breathed out the word *okay*.

A man sitting in front of her twisted around. "It's alright," he said, "if you made the wrong decision you can just climb back on the bus and go on home. It'll still be waiting for you." He smiled kindly. Dacey smiled back, but she was having none of that. She stood up and brushed the crumbs from her lap, pulled her satchel and knapsack from the overhead bin and made her way down the aisle.

Bag in hand she hailed a cab and directed it to an auberge on St. Denis where she'd made a reservation. In the back seat she closed her eyes and savoured the feeling of moving forward.

17

Evan watched Lansing carefully that night for signs of fatigue, but traces of the tired old man had faded and the dynamic performer was back. It was remarkable the way he could turn it on in front of a crowd. Evan tried to imagine what would be involved in that. He pictured himself on stage in front of Lansing again, confident this time, commanding attention from everyone in the room. But especially Lansing. He did have confidence in his songs, the four or five he'd worked and worked, alone in his room in Petite Riviere or on the lumpy couch in the second bedroom at Colleen's place when she was out. He had a natural way with melody it seemed, and words came easy when they were going to be set to music. Everything else was difficult for Evan Cornfield, but writing songs was like breathing.

To perform them, though. To stand on a stage, alone in a spotlight with all eyes trained on him. To sing those songs and not just sing them well, but sing them with such passion and determination, with such conviction that every pair of ears hearing them was convinced too—that was what he wanted. He couldn't see how to get it, though. So he kept a close eye on Lansing Meadows in the hope it would become clear.

The show that night was at an old workers' hall, the walls painted a deep red, with a little wooden stage and folding chairs all crowded in. The room was at capacity—a hundred and fifty people—and CD sales had been brisk. Evan's work done, he caught the bartender's eye and signaled that he wanted to order a beer. Of the stragglers remaining, one seemed familiar. A short woman in jeans and a hoodie, with shoulder-length, smooth, dark hair that parted in the middle and ran down each side of her face. Her eyes were brown, and her heart-shaped face broke into a smile when their gazes connected.

"Evan!" she said, moving toward him. Her hand was on the camera she had slung around her neck.

"Dacey Brown," he said. "What in the world are you doing here?"

"Just taking some pictures," she said. "How *are* you?"

Evan looked at her, his brow wrinkled. "How am I? I'm confused. You're just taking some pictures...for who? The Grand Falls *Examiner*?"

Dacey laughed then, and her laugh, like a silver bell, rang once. "Uh, no. The paper doesn't have a travel budget. No, I just ... well, I just decided to go on a little trip and take some photos."

Evan tried to make sense of what she was saying. "And what a coincidence," he said slowly, "that you'd make your way here?"

Dacey's heart-shaped face pinkened. "Well," she said.

"Well," he said. His mind and pulse raced in tandem. He understood, in a heartbeat, that Dacey Brown had followed them to Montreal.

"What are your plans?" he asked, as casually as he could.

The pink in Dacey's cheeks turned to red. "I guess that kind of depends on you," she said.

Evan felt entirely in over his head. What was the right thing to do, he wondered, when a girl you'd barely met travelled a time zone to catch up with you? This was the kind of thing Saxton Crouse would instinctively know how to handle. As Evan gazed at Dacey and tried to think of something suave to say, he saw her face change, first a flicker of surprise in her eyes, then her lips narrowed and he watched her steel herself. He heard Lansing's voice from behind him.

"You have got to be kidding me," Lansing drawled. "The lengths some people will go to. You're an awful long way from Grand Falls, there, lovey." The words were friendly, but the tone was definitely not. If Evan had felt in over his head a moment before, now he felt he was being swept downstream, bouncing off rocks and driftwood as he went. Lansing pushed past him and stood, hands on hips, just a few inches from Dacey, who faced him head-on, her own hands on her hips.

"I just happened to be passing through Montreal," she said. "And I saw you were playing. And I never did get my photo that day." She lifted the camera, but not all the way to her eye. Just enough to put it between her own body and his.

"Uh-huh," Lansing said. "Well if you got what you came for, it's late and I think the bartender is trying to close up."

The bartender had approached with Evan's beer. "It's okay with me if you stay for a while," he said. "Can I get you a drink?" he asked Dacey.

"She was just going," Lansing said, his eyes not moving from Dacey's face. "But I'll take a red wine and cola."

"You sure?" the bartender said to Dacey. Dacey stared a moment more at Lansing's face, then broke the connection and said to the bartender, "Yeah, no, he's right, I'm just on my way." The bartender shrugged and went to fill Lansing's order.

Dacey Brown zipped up her hoodie and said to Lansing, "If you change your mind, Evan knows where to find me." She gave Evan a half-smile from beneath her cascade of brown hair, and then she turned neatly and was gone.

The room had cleared out by then, and Lansing stood his ground a moment more, hands on hips. Then he turned and said to Evan, "Fuck this. I'm going for a smoke."

And Evan Cornfield stood in the old workers' hall under bright overhead lights that showed all the nicks in the walls you couldn't see when the lights were dim and the spotlight was on the stage. He stood alone and empty-handed.

18

Lansing Meadows should have listened to his gut. There was no gig in Cornwall, Ontario. There just wasn't, and there never had been. There wasn't even a reliable house concert in Cornwall. In fact, the last time Lansing had been through there, the whole town was cloaked in the smell of fire. Looked like there'd been two, maybe more, fires downtown, one of them recent enough that the wreck was still smoking a little. Maybe one of those places would have been a gig. But no. Lansing knew—hell, every folk singer from Gabriola Island to Torbay knew one thing: there was no gig in Cornwall, Ontario.

"So what, I ask you," Lansing said to Evan as Evan steered the Corolla up to the door of their motel room, "am I doing in Cornwall, Ontario?"

"Same thing I'm doing," Evan said, and wished, not for the first time, that he smoked. "Getting ready for the gig."

"There is no—" Lansing began. Evan held up his hand.

"I hear that," he said. "And yet, right here in this tour bible, as anyone can plainly see, there is."

"I should sue that bastard," Lansing growled. "He did this to me on purpose."

"Probably," Evan said. "Or maybe you're wrong. Maybe there is a gig in Cornwall."

Lansing Meadows tipped his hat up. "There's a lot I am, son, but wrong is not on the list."

Evan quavered for a moment, fixed as he was with that gimlet eye. He gathered himself and said, "Regardless, they await you at Piecemeal, so let's get our act together."

Lansing tipped his hat back down. He prided himself on never missing a gig. He'd play one-armed. With stomach flu, a bullet in his brain. If he could, he would. But he heartily wished he could make an exception for Cornwall.

Evan was already out of the car, lifting bags and working the key in the door of their room. Lansing sighed heavily and followed him.

Still, Lansing should have listened to his gut. Piecemeal was a nice enough place, incongruous perhaps, an upscale tapas bar in a downtown that was otherwise hollowed out by fire and economic misfortune. He couldn't imagine who'd have thought it made sense to book a wordy folksinger such as himself in at an upscale tapas bar—where people would no doubt want to chat and drink and do anything but listen to his narrative songs—on a Saturday night. But the pay was generous, and there'd be a meal and a bottle of wine to boot. He was curious about the *poutine boeuf bourguignon* on the menu, but he had a bad feeling about the gig.

That bad feeling was not improved by the stage, which was really a sunken area at the front of the restaurant out of which they'd cleared the tables. Lansing could see that he'd be playing his two forty-five-minute sets with his back to the street-side picture window, and from about a foot below where the diners would be sitting. He looked for Evan, to whom he wanted to complain bitterly about this latest outrage, but Evan was at the back of the room, showing one of the waiters how to operate the mixing board.

"Well, that's just terrific," Lansing said.

"What's that?" said the manager, who'd shown Lansing to the sunken stage.

"Huh?" Lansing looked up. "Oh. Terrific, terrific room."

The manager beamed with pride. "I'm glad you think so," he said. "We're always busy on Saturday nights. Everyone who's anyone in Cornwall comes to Piecemeal to see and be seen."

Lansing grinned, his teeth clamped tight. He was a man on his way to receiving a lifetime achievement award in some splashy ceremony in two weeks. How could this be one of the stops along the way? This goddamn life.

He nursed a glass of wine—"Not the kind of place you can comfortably order a wine and cola," he complained to Evan—and a flickering resentment as the restaurant began to fill.

Bare-shouldered, perfumed young women and sharply coiffed young men in flat-front trousers and crisp cotton shirts mingled by the bar or laughed over small plates of food. Cartoonishly large wine glasses dotted every table. Lansing despaired of ever being able to get the attention of these people, let alone hold it.

He remembered seeing Stompin' Tom Connors at the legendary Horseshoe Tavern in Seventy-three, or maybe Seventy-four. Lansing had been bumming around Toronto for a few years by then. He'd gone down the road, with just his wits and his hitchhiking thumb, at the age of fifteen, striking out from tiny Windsor Junction to arrive in Yorkville as the folk scene was in full boil. He'd been at Mariposa in Seventy-two, when Dylan showed up, and he remembered clearly what it was like back then. When a performer was on stage, the experience was communal. That gig at the Horse-shoe, the room had been packed, absolutely packed. People sat at little tables, not gabbing and flirting with each other, but sitting and listening to Stompin' Tom as if he were delivering the Word of God and they were the faithful. They all clapped along with enthusiasm to every song. None of this wheedling and cajoling that was so necessary these days to guilt even just a handful of people into singing along with a single chorus. And in the middle of the set, when Tom invited some kid from Waterloo, Ontario, to play a few fiddle tunes while Tom smoked a cigarette—inside the bar, mind you—and drank a beer, the room was so crammed he had nowhere to sit. Till someone at the back lifted a chair. It was passed overhead, from hand to hand through the crowd till at last it arrived at Tom, and he sat down to take his break and enjoy the fiddle tunes along with the rest of the audience.

That was then, Lansing thought, slurping his wine. That was then.

"Might as well get it over with," he said to Evan, and put his empty glass down on the little table they were sitting at.

"That's the spirit," Evan said.

Lansing picked up his guitar and strummed it, and could barely hear its tone above the din. He stepped up to the microphone.

"This song is for that group of beautiful ladies in the back," he said, and hated himself. He sang "Cantina Heart" and held the final lovesick note a beat longer than usual. Polite applause from the women in the back, and then they fell back into conversation, chattering and laughing with energy.

Lansing played songs he liked since, he figured, he was the only one really listening. He played some gypsy guitar, and a couple of Robert Johnson tunes. He played a dirty song he'd written on a week-long bender in St. John's. Or had it been Saint John? It didn't matter, and it didn't matter what he played, either. His presence had no impact at all on the people in the room, except for Evan, who applauded diligently and with enthusiasm after each number.

It was the law of diminishing whatsit, Lansing thought as he tuned his guitar between songs. Diminishing responsibility or something—where a crowd was much less likely to help someone than an individual was. It was fucked, but he'd seen it a million times, a million different ways, and here it was again. Sure, each person might think it was rude to talk while there was a singer on stage. Even if "on stage" in this case meant "in a pit." But there was a general din in the room already, and so they could put their manners on hold for the night, and talk as well.

Lansing sighed mid-song and longed for the old days. Even the comforting packet of letters next to his heart couldn't give him the energy to get through this night. "One more," he said into the microphone, "and then we'll take a break." And I'll get very drunk, he thought, since none of you will notice.

Just then the restaurant's front door, which was immediately to Lansing's left, banged open, admitting a wave of cold air and three staggering figures. They were noisy before they were even in the door, and their noisiness was chaotic and rough rather than flirtatious and joyful. They were as out of place as Lansing was, drunk already, and coarse where the other patrons were smooth.

"Awesome," said the small, rabbity one in a Chicago Blackhawks ball cap and what Lansing's mother used to call a Cape Breton dinner jacket, but what was more properly called a doeskin. A blue one, in this case. "There's live music. Live music," he yelped in Lansing's direction.

Lansing smiled. At least someone was excited about it. "Thank you very much," he said, to a smattering of applause. "We'll take a quick break and be right back."

A haze of booze hung over the new arrivals. Besides Rabbity Doeskin, there was a beautiful young woman with caramel-coloured skin, long brown hair and melting almond eyes. She was lovely, but had taken far less care with her appearance than the other women at Piecemeal. And she seemed disoriented, those almond eyes sadly unfocused. And there was a guy who appeared slightly older than Rabbity, who wore an old navy windbreaker, zipped up to the chin. He was silent.

"Get something to eat," Rabbity said to his crew. "Get warmed up. Sarita," he said to the girl, "you're okay?" Sarita nodded once. "We get some menus?" Rabbity asked loudly, of no one in particular. The wait staff were clustered by the bar, well-groomed, fragrant and aloof, shooting worried looks in the direction of the newcomers.

Finally one of the servers peeled off from the pack to wait on Rabbity and friends.

"We would like three Molson Canadians," Rabbity pronounced carefully.

"We don't have that," the waiter said. "Our beer menu is carefully curated—"

"We would like three Labatt Blues," Rabbity tried again.

"—and features only selections from Belgium and Catalan."

Rabbity nodded at this and then said loudly and distinctly, "Three rum and Cokes, please."

The server sighed. "Alright," he said.

Rabbity examined the menu, while Sarita sat with hers open, her eyes unfocused above it. "Shrimp?" Rabbity said.

"The garlic bread, maybe poutine." Sarita smiled, the quiet guy nodded. "Bacon-wrapped scallops." He closed the menu, handed it to the server. "Please," he said. The server sighed again and moved on.

He paused at Evan and Lansing's table, and Lansing ordered extravagantly. "The poutine," he said, "And the oysters. We'll also have the Benedictine blue soufflé and the eggplant and red pepper *sushi*." He replicated the menu's quotation marks in the air with his fingers. "And another bottle of wine," he said.

"Lansing," Evan murmured, "I have to drive."

"I don't," Lansing said.

The waiter gestured to the new arrivals and said, *sotto voce*, "Sorry about that."

"I'm not," Lansing replied at normal volume. "At least they seemed excited about the music." He grinned wolfishly and the man nodded and retreated.

As they ate and drank the din of conversation became a roar. Wine glasses were never empty, and as the room became louder it heated up as well, a mist of mingled perfume and assorted kitchen aromas hanging over the crowd. Lansing began to feel the glasses of wine he'd had.

Behind them, Rabbity's silent friend rested his forehead on the table and appeared to sleep. Sarita had disappeared in the direction of the restrooms and Rabbity, having finished his own drink, was slurping hers through a straw. "More live music," he bellowed in Lansing's direction.

"Right," Lansing said. He swallowed what was left of his wine and descended toward the stage. Second verse, same as the first, he thought. Perhaps a little worse.

"Play something we know," Rabbity called. "Something with words so we can sing along."

Sarita had returned, and nodded her head emphatically. The other guy was still silent, head on table. Sarita popped a shrimp in her mouth and gamely chewed.

"You're eating the shell," Rabbity said loudly. Sarita chewed, staring at him, her eyes vacant. "The shell," Rabbity said. "You're eating the *shell*."

Understanding flickered across her face and she bent toward the little plate in front of her and opened her mouth. She gave a little cough and expelled bits of shell. Rabbity seemed satisfied. He handed her back her drink. "Have a little sip," he said, solicitously.

"Play some blues," he called to Lansing. "Or play that song, you know that song. The one by that band from Manitoba or wherever. Love Allergy. Play their song. Good one to sing along to."

Lansing smiled a wicked smile. "This one?" he asked, and played the opening chords of "On My Honour."

"That's the one," Rabbity said, and loudly sang along. Lansing put his shoulder into it, played it for all he was worth and before long he'd captured the attention of the place, and half the crowd was singing along. It had been a huge hit for Love Allergy. It probably felt more like their song than his. For this crowd it did. So he sang it. He sang Love Allergy's wishy-washy version, leaving out the verse they'd left out to make it the right length for radio play. And when it was over, and the crowd had applauded with the first real enthusiasm they'd shown, Rabbity cried out, "Play another. Play some blues. You look like you know some blues."

Lansing smiled a crooked smile and moved his capo on the neck of the guitar. Oh, he knew the blues alright.

The waiter approached Rabbity's table with the bill. "Hell is this?" Rabbity cried. "We're not done. We want another drink."

"It's time to go," the waiter said. "Do you want me to call the police?"

"Sure," said Rabbity, leaning back with all the little-man bravado he had, "call the cops, see if I care. What am I doing wrong? Eating expensive appetizers and drinking rum and Cokes, like everyone else in here."

Sarita nodded, her brown hair swinging.

"Your friend appears to have been over-served elsewhere," the waiter said, gesturing to the sleeping man.

"He's just very tired," Rabbity said. "He works hard all week."

But the cops had already been called. Red-and-blue lights bounced through the front window, garishly lighting the stage.

"Oh, that's too bad," Lansing said into the microphone. "I feel like we were just getting started."

"This is fucking bullshit," Rabbity said. He nudged his sleeping friend. "Wake up, fucksakes, the cops are here." He looked at Sarita. "You look beautiful tonight." Then his face hardened as the door swung open. "Total fucking bullshit," he announced to the room.

"That it is," Lansing said. "I promised you some blues." He began a standard blues progression. "No change in the weather," he sang, "no change in me." He sang the borrowed folk song in a blues style as the cops entered and headed straight for Rabbity's table.

"Oh, come on," Rabbity said, "how do you even know it's us? It could be *anybody*." His voice rose. "Wake *up*," he nudged his sleeping friend.

"No chaaaaaange in the weather," Lansing sang, "no change in meeee."

"Christ almighty," Rabbity said to the ceiling. "Baby, I'm so sorry," he said to Sarita. "I'm not paying this," he said to the general direction of the bar, where the servers once again clustered. He threw down the miniature clipboard that held the bill. "Total fucking bullshit."

His sleeping friend finally came to and drew a roll of bills from his pocket. He peeled off three twenties and let them fall from his fingers.

"Fuck, whatever," Rabbity said. "Fine. *Fine*." He held his arm out to the nearest cop. "What*ever*."

The cops escorted the little group out of the bar.

"No change in the *weather*," Lansing sang, "and lord lord *lord* no change in me." The door swung shut and Lansing played the final notes, slowing them down and stretching them out till it seemed they might break.

The room erupted into applause. Whether for Lansing or for the cops, it was unclear. And immaterial, Lansing joked later.

"Just another Saturday night in Cornwall, Ontario," he remarked as he had one final glass of wine at the bar, surrounded by wait staff and a few bare-shouldered women who'd stuck around, intrigued.

"I loved your version of 'On My Honour,'" one of them cooed. "So stripped down."

"You should record that," the manager put in. He'd been buying that particular customer drinks all night and saw now it had been in vain.

"Hmm," Lansing said, throwing the last gulp of wine into his mouth. "I'll talk to my guy about that." He gestured toward Evan. "Meanwhile ..."

"Meanwhile, we should get out of here," Evan said. "Long drive tomorrow."

19

Evan was dead tired. A wine-soaked Lansing had wanted to stay up late, talking and playing his guitar, and at the time, Evan was thrilled. A band of brothers they were now, having survived the crucible of Cornwall. Lansing played a couple of new melodies he was thinking about, and suggested perhaps Evan might help him finish them into songs. In the cold light of day though, with the landscape alongside the 401 a blur of drowsy monotony, Evan wished he had back those hours to sleep.

And something was nagging him. "We should have let her come along," he said.

"Who?" said Lansing. His seat was in the rare upright position. It was a drive of just a couple of hours between Cornwall and Kingston and the late night didn't seem to have affected him at all.

"The girl from the newspaper." He'd got it out of Lansing, the night before, that Dacey had offered her photographic services in Grand Falls.

"Now why the hell would we do that?"

"She really wanted to come," Evan said, knowing it was insufficient. "She came all the way from New Brunswick.

On the bus."

"Which proves she's nuts," Lansing said. His finger hovered over the window button. "Whacked as a bag of hammers."

Evan nodded at this, tapped his fingers on the steering wheel. "Or it means she's committed," he said, regretting his word choice almost instantly.

"Should be committed, more like," Lansing said predictably. He started up with the window.

"Don't do that," Evan said, a reflex by now. "I just think she has a certain interest, a certain passion—"

"Oh my God, you want to bang her," Lansing said. "Jesus, boy, why didn't you say so?"

"I do not want to—bang her," Evan said. He could feel even his hair getting hot. Don't be crude. Jesus."

Lansing reclined his seat and hooted. "Good Lord," he yelped, "you don't have to agree to take them across the country for that! Don't you know anything, boy?"

Evan's eyes darted around the car, as if their conversation could be overheard. "I just—she seems—interesting. Someone who wants things. Like we do." Before Lansing could get a word in, he hurried on, having finally hit on a practical reason. "And it would be nice to have someone to share the driving."

Lansing nodded at that. "If you need a little female companionship, boy, just say so. Jesus. I'm not an ogre."

"Oh, God, never mind," Evan said. "Forget I even brought it up. Doesn't matter anyhow. You said no, she's gone home, end of story."

"Well," Lansing drawled, "next time you see some pretty little filly—"

"Just stop," Evan said. "Forget it. It's over." He spritzed the windshield, which was perfectly clear, and ran the wipers.

"Right, well," Lansing said. "Wake me when we get there." He pulled down his hat brim and lay back in the seat.

Evan waited for the smooth road beneath the Corolla's wheels to lull him back to calm. Lansing could wind him tight.

There was something about Dacey Brown. She was cool and detached, but she was also open and seemed curious. She was interested in Lansing Meadows, but it seemed to Evan in an almost scholarly way. As for himself, well, she'd been so easy with him, so funny and sweet. She had that little heart-shaped face and that smooth brown hair that fell like a river on either side. Her eyes were brown and intelligent and she seemed to want nothing from him. Not love nor attention, like Colleen; not a rise, like his sisters. She was so self-contained, so freewheeling. He loved that she lit out after them the way she did, not knowing whether it would come to anything at all. Evan had ended up on the road by default, there because Lansing had chosen him—and Lansing had chosen him, as far as Evan could tell, because Evan had been convenient to choose. Dacey though, she'd thrown caution to the wind. She'd made a bold decision. Evan could only imagine being brave enough for that.

What would it be like, he wondered, to have her along for the ride? On one hand he felt possessive of Lansing, and the time they had together. But the further he got from Petite Riviere and the life he'd had there, the more he longed for everything the world had to offer. Dacey Brown, with her forthright way and her blushing smile, was suddenly a priority on that list.

Still, he could hardly imagine a better way to spend his days than in the company of Lansing Meadows. Lansing had decided Evan's folk music history was woefully lacking, and he'd taken it upon himself to school his protégé.

By the time Lansing was Evan's age, he was jaded and aloof, with a record contract. All the signs indicated stardom was within his grasp. He'd arrived in Yorkville just a kid, green but paying attention. He'd been there when Murray McLauchlan and Ron Hynes wrote "No Change in the Weather." Practically co-wrote it with them, Lansing had said after the show at Piecemeal. Lansing told Evan he'd played a thousand gigs more soul-destroying than the one in that tapas restaurant. In fact, there were a million stories he hadn't yet told anyone, and Evan was grateful for every tale Lansing chose to share with him.

Not only did he get to listen to the history of folk according to Lansing Meadows all day, he got to watch it in action each night. And even on a bad night, Lansing was very good. He read the crowd and gave them what they wanted, or he gave them something they didn't know they wanted but were totally stoked to get. He played many of his hit songs night after night. And he always finished with "On My Honour."

"Don't you ever get sick of singing that song?" Evan asked one night. It had been a hard show. A tipsy woman in the front row had loudly called for "Cantina Heart" after every single song. Lansing ignored for her for a while. Then he thanked her for her passion and dedication to his music. And finally, when it felt like he was about to lose the rest of the crowd, some of whom were beginning to heckle the heckler, Lansing assured the woman that he had indeed devised a set list and that "Cantina Heart" was most definitely on it, and if she could just sit tight and let the others enjoy the show, before the night was out, she'd get her desire. And when at last he played "Cantina Heart," of course she sang along, loudly and off-key. But Lansing smiled and took it in stride. Even that night he sang "On My Honour" with as much conviction and presence as if it were the first time.

"How could you not get tired of it?" Evan insisted.

Lansing thinned his lips into a straight line. "That song brought me a mighty long way," he said seriously. "Not for that song, I might be working in some bowling-alley-slash-karaoke-joint in Petite Riviere, or living in the decrepit family home, God help me, in Windsor Junction. It's what they come to hear, boy. And as long as they want to hear it, as long as it means something to somebody, I'll sing it and I'll mean it."

"But don't you want to move on, as an artist?" Evan persisted.

Lansing leveled a long look at him. "What does that even mean, boy?"

"Do other things," Evan said. "Grow, change, I don't know. It's just, same song every night. For thirty years or whatever. I'd go crazy."

"Then maybe you're not cut out for this line of work," Lansing said, and that was the end of that conversation.

He did that sometimes. Just shut right down. It was an option Evan didn't have. Not between the driving and everything else: looking ahead in the tour bible and calling the next two or three venues down the road to make sure there hadn't been some screw-up, that the gig was still on, had been advertised, that tickets were selling; organizing media in the next town, if there was any media to speak of—and if he could convince Lansing that talking to a journalist wouldn't kill him. (He thought of the emails in the BlackBerry's inbox requesting interviews to which he still hadn't responded.) And then there was checking the motel reservations; and just generally making sure that Lansing was fed, watered, and relatively happy. It was a lot, and he was still learning.

At the very end of the night, once Lansing had passed out with the television remote clutched in his knobby hand, Evan would pull his own guitar out of its case and play a few of his own tunes, just so he didn't forget how. He only did this when he was certain Lansing was dead to the world. He was mortified still at the thought of Lansing hearing him play.

Evan stretched in his seat. It would be nice to have help with the driving. It would be nice to have someone to talk to when Lansing was asleep. It would be nice to have Dacey Brown along for the ride.

"Less than an hour now till Kingston," he muttered. "We'll be there in time for a late lunch."

Lansing Meadows snored in reply.

20

Having come this far, Dacey didn't think she could turn around and go back. Back to what? The same crooked house? The job she barely tolerated? It didn't even bear considering. Thing was, she hadn't made a solid plan. She hadn't finessed the situation at all and she could see that she had appeared crazy in some way. She could have made a case that would have convinced Lansing. She could share the driving, carry the gear, sell the merch. She had excellent credit and was a problem solver.

But so far, she had not solved this problem. She sat with her feet on her knapsack and waited for a westbound bus. If she'd had the presence of mind to offer even one of those things. But no. She'd simply asked, and when Lansing said no, she simply walked away.

She'd walked most of the night, in fact, from the club back to her auberge, and once there, still feeling restless, she walked up and down the little Montreal streets. Montreal was in restless motion, like her. Early April and there were still little crusts of snow here and there, receding just enough along the boulevards to reveal the odd woolen mitten, sodden from a winter trapped in ice. Decaying dog dirt dotted every corner. But along those dirty streets cruised Montrealers of all ages and ethnicities, dressed in what would be formal wear in Grand Falls: on the women, high-heeled shoes or tall leather boots; stockings or dark denim jeans not cut for the woods; leather jackets or fashionable wool coats that nipped in at the waist and flared out over the hips; bright scarves and hats that sat pertly above perfect hairdos, rather than slumping down over the wearer's eyes. The men were equally well appointed, in slim thigh-length cashmere coats or leather bomber jackets, expensive-looking short boots, their own scarves equally bright. These men would be looked upon with suspicion in Grand Falls. Here though, they strode confidently, the men and women both, making frank eye contact with all who passed. It wasn't friendly, exactly, Dacey thought. It was appraising. And in some cases, it was an invitation. In Grand Falls people looked you in the eye to be sure you knew they saw you, they could see who you were and what you were up to. Here in Montreal, the eye contact seemed to be more about—well, about sex.

Dacey sensed the electricity of connection pinging off lamp posts and zinging off buildings, binding strangers who happened to find themselves on the same street at the same time. She herself could not feel the heat. She wanted to be swept along by that current, but she could not find a way in. And so, as always, she put her camera between herself and that world, and she snapped until she felt at ease. By then she'd circled back to her auberge and without a feeling one way or another about what should be next, she bought a mickey of whiskey and took it back to her room. She fell asleep after two shots and the evening news in French.

And now she sat in the bus station and waited. She was sure of one thing, at least: she would go forward, and she would see.

21

Lansing Meadows lay fully clothed atop the blankets on the single bed furthest from the door. They'd opted for the Howard Johnson over the Motel 6 because the former had a swimming pool. Lansing knew he'd never get in it, but he liked to know the option was there.

The kid had stepped out to run errands and Lansing was glad of a minute to himself. They'd been in short supply. The kid was great, there was no question, he'd taken Lansing on like a pro. But there was a certain puppy-dog neediness the kid seemed to sweat in his direction, and after a while, you just needed a break.

The shows had been alright so far, about what you'd expect. Decent houses by and large, and apart from the disaster in Cornwall, real listening audiences, his people, crowds who knew him and his work and who were so goddamn glad to get a chance to see him perform up close. It was refreshing. He'd done big soft-seater tours in recent years, playing theatres in major cities, rather than small halls in little towns as on this tour—the kinds of gigs where you couldn't see the faces in the crowd, the goddamn stage lights were so bright. And afterward you'd go out to the merch table to press a little flesh; but you'd really had no connection with the audience up to that point, and so it was abrasive the ardour that came his way from those strangers, instead of communal, a true exchange, which is what it should be, Lansing thought.

Which is what he got into it for in the first place. Actually, he got into it for the chicks. But now that that was all behind him—all over but the lying, really—it was this connection that mattered most. It was the exchange of energy, the symbiosis of a live show, that really kept him there.

Thing was, he didn't know how much longer he could ride this particular train. A songwriter at the height of his powers, the *Globe and Mail* had said about his latest record, and the four-night stand at Massey Hall that had accompanied its release. The height of his powers, Lansing thought. So what comes after that, then, if this is as good as I get? The long, slow slide down the other side, that's what. And fuck that. He was too old to burn out now. He'd pretty much be stuck with fading away.

He thought of Mick Jagger singing that it was a drag to get old. For Lansing Meadows, maybe, but Jagger seemed to be doing just fine, thanks. Practically seventy years old and still prancing around in spandex pants, waggling that tongue and pursing those lips, and why not? If they were still buying what you were selling, why not? Mick Jagger and his millions could buy supportive spandex and all the facelifts he'd need to maintain the illusion of rock-and-roll bad boy. Lansing Meadows—despite the success of "On My Honour" (which paid for a couple of divorce settlements)—got by on his wits, such as they were, and for however much longer they'd last.

Lansing sat up on the bed, gripped suddenly by the need for his guitar. It stood in the corner near the door, resting in its case against Evan Cornfield's. Kid was getting better. He heard Evan playing sometimes at night while he pretended to sleep with the TV on. He played songs Lansing hadn't heard before. Originals, he imagined. The kid would be alright.

With a guitar in his hands, Lansing was his best self. With Marie he'd come close to being his best self, but he couldn't maintain it for the long haul. The touring, the nights apart, other available women—he was no Mick Jagger, he knew, but there was a certain kind of woman to whom Lansing Meadows appealed. And they were getting fewer and farther between, Lansing thought, as he let his fingers find their way over the strings.

There was a melody that had been plaguing him for some days now. This happened whenever he was in motion. Physical momentum gave way to melodic flights. It was part of the reason he didn't drive. He found the passenger seat, tipped back, with his hat down, most conducive to writing.

He played the chord progression, still working parts of it out. He was unsure what shape it would ultimately take.

The key turned in the lock as he started the melody a second time.

"That's pretty," Evan said as he entered. "What is it?"

"Not sure yet," Lansing said, a little absently. He hastened to arrange his face in neutral. Though he performed his own songs for a living, he'd never got over the vulnerability of a song before it was written. Like being seen naked in the window by a passerby in the middle of the night.

"Success?" he asked Evan, to cover his discomfort.

"Success," Evan said. He held up a plastic grocery bag. "Fruits and vegetables."

"We'll probably never eat them," Lansing said.

"It comforts me to know they're there," Evan replied. He

unpacked the bag on his bed, transferring the groceries into the little Styrofoam cooler he'd bought. "Apples and oranges," he said. "Baby carrots, snow peas. A container of hummus. Chocolate-covered almonds."

"Neither fruit nor vegetable," Lansing noted, "and as such likely to be consumed first and in their entirety. Toss them over." He held out his hand.

"They're for the car," Evan said.

"Actually, they're for the people in the car," Lansing said, "of whom I am one. Toss them over."

"At the moment, you're a person on a bed," Evan pointed out, though the bag was in his hand already and airborne in Lansing's direction before his sentence was done.

"I think we should dip into the States," Lansing said suddenly.

"Not in the tour bible," Evan said. "Pass me those almonds."

"So what," Lansing said. "We have a couple days off."

"Where the tour bible is concerned," Evan said taking a handful of almonds, "I'm a fundamentalist."

"Two weeks ago you'd never seen a tour bible in your life," Lansing said. "Gimme." He held out his hand for the bag. Evan passed it. "I want to see my old stompin' grounds, check on some old friends." He thought of Marie for just a moment, her light brown curls, her thin face. "It'll be fun."

Evan looked unconvinced.

"Don't make me beg," Lansing said. "It's undignified."

"I'm not making you beg," Evan said, "you're choosing to." But he knew he was giving in. He'd take Lansing to the States, if that's where he wanted to go, of course he would. "If we get lost or arrested, it's on you, got it?"

Lansing threw a handful of almonds in his mouth, talked through them. "We will get neither lost, nor arrested."

Chocolate drool formed in the corners of his mouth.

"Don't be gross," Evan said, "or I'll change my mind. And don't eat all the almonds."

"You're not my mother," Lansing said, "but you sure do nag like her." Still, he tied the bag of almonds and tossed it back toward the cooler on Evan's bed.

Evan drew a postcard from the almost-empty plastic bag and said, "Now leave me alone for ten minutes, Chrissakes."

"You're starting to talk like me, boy. Better watch out." Lansing peered at him. "What's that?"

"A postcard."

"Obviously. Who's it for? That girl, whatshername, Colleen?"

Evan blushed. "No, not her," he said.

Lansing looked at him a moment and saw the truth on Evan's face.

He bent again to his guitar.

There was a show that night in Kingston and a workshop the next day at a big high school near the lake. The students there had lately been taught to care who Lansing was, and one or two of them, Evan thought, maybe actually did. They had learned a few of his hits in their school band. Some clever band teacher had arranged horn parts for most of the tunes, and Evan had to admit they added something to some of the folkiest songs, like "Cold Road" and "End of the Line."

After a week or so of slog, the school workshop was invigorating. The kids were enthusiastic, most of them. This visit from an old-man folksinger was something different at least, it wasn't math class or geography. A new generation was being introduced to Lansing Meadows, even if it wasn't likely his tunes were turning up on many of the playlists these kids dialed up on their phones. Still, some of them seemed to care about song, some of them were able to appreciate the vagaries of the human voice without Auto-Tune and Evan began to feel some of his road-weariness lift. Even Lansing looked a little lighter by day's end, his face less grey.

They sat at a pub together that night, drinking a pint in companionable silence. This moment in this pub with his boyhood hero, this was what Evan had longed for.

"So what's in the States?" Evan asked.

"Americans, primarily. And a lot of big fibreglass shit—giant hot dogs by the side of the road, stuff like that." Lansing gulped his beer, fiddled with his cigarettes.

"You can't smoke in here," Evan said reflexively. "I meant, what's in the States for you, in particular."

"Used to live in upstate New York," Lansing said. "Had a farm there before Levon Helm ever thought to."

The thought of Lansing on a farm, wearing coveralls and mucking out a barn or milking a cow with a cigarette clenched tight in his teeth, was both ridiculous and persistent.

"I didn't figure you for a farmer," Evan said drily.

"Didn't do much farming, actually," Lansing said. He stared at a point somewhere to the right of their table, twirled a cigarette between thumb and forefinger.

"Used to have big parties, barn parties. Bales of hay for seats, a bar set up in one of the stalls. Little lights everywhere. Smelled a little like shit, but once the music started, no one cared about that. Play till dawn almost, and people would dance. Then there'd be pancakes for breakfast and bacon and lots of coffee, and anyone who wanted would sit at this long table and just dig in." He stuck the cigarette in his mouth. "I miss that place."

"Why did you leave?" Evan asked.

Lansing pushed his chair back. "Things change," he said. "Going for a smoke."

When he came back his face was closed, the dreaminess of the life he'd described tucked away again. Fresh pints arrived, ordered by Evan in Lansing's absence.

"This is as far west as I've ever been," Evan said. "Farther."

"Jesus, boy," Lansing bristled. "How the hell old are you?"

"Twenty-four," Evan said. "Almost."

"What were you waiting for, Chrissakes?"

"Don't know," Evan said.

"Lucky for you I came along," Lansing said. "Lucky for you my tour manager turned out to be an asshole."

"Yeah," Evan said. "Lucky." He rolled his eyes. "So where to tomorrow? Want to see the old farm?"

A cloud darkened Lansing's face. "Nah," he said. "It's not there anymore. Couple little towns I have friends in, and then we'll wrap around under the lake and pop up in Toronto. Gas and smokes and booze are all cheaper in the States. There's crazy talk radio to listen to and packaged foods you've never even heard of before."

"They don't have ketchup chips," Evan said.

"You're a grown-up now, son. You're almost twenty-four. Have some dignity." Lansing drained his beer. "I'm tired, let's go."

Evan gestured to his pint, still half-full.

"Jesus, boy, you're drinking like a virgin. Down that thing and let's get gone."

Evan could see by the hunch of Lansing's shoulders and the oblique angle of his hat brim it was pointless to argue. The night was over. He gulped his beer, leaving an inch or two in the bottom. Lansing picked up the pint and drained it, then turned on his heel and made for the door.

As they approached the border crossing, Evan could feel himself getting uptight. He'd never been across an international border and the stories he'd heard all indicated that it was a tricky business. He clutched the steering wheel so hard his knuckles turned white.

"What's up?" Lansing said as Evan slowed the car to a crawl about a kilometre from the border.

"I'm nervous," Evan whispered.

Lansing laughed. "About what?" he said.

"Crossing the border," Evan said.

"Oh, don't be ridiculous, son. And don't get all weird. That's the kind of thing that can get you into trouble." He poked Evan in the ribs. "Drive, son, I mean it."

Evan pressed the gas pedal gently. He felt dread, but he made the car go forward. He gripped the steering wheel ever harder.

"Ease up," said Lansing, "you're not in trouble."

"Not yet," Evan chattered.

"Jesus, boy. You are as green as the grass. We are private citizens taking a pleasure trip to the USA. There is nothing to be afraid of here."

"What about the guitars?" Evan asked.

Lansing looked at him, baffled. "What about them?" he said.

"Maybe they'll think we're trying to sneak in to work."

"Oh, for Chrissakes. You gotta stop thinking that right now, you hear me?"

Evan moved the car closer to the wicket.

"And for the love of God, let me do the talking," Lansing said.

The digital sign blazed red at the wicket ahead. Evan stopped the car and breathed deeply, loosening one finger at a time from the wheel. His heart pounded, he told it to stop. Lansing was right. They weren't breaking any laws. They were just going visiting. Green light. He let the car roll forward, rolled down the window.

"Citizenship," the border guard began. He looked a little younger than Lansing. His uniform was snug, his glasses smudged. Evan stayed silent. Lansing took off his hat.

"Canadian," he said. He gestured to Evan. "Both of us."

"Proof of citizenship," the guard said, unmoved by Lansing's deference with the hat.

Evan dug for his driver's license in his little satchel. Lansing drew his passport out of his hat and passed it to Evan who handed them both to the border guard.

"You're a musician," the guard said to Lansing, reading from the well-worn booklet.

"By times," Lansing said.

"Don't recognize your name," the guard said.

"Not surprised," Lansing said. "Never did have much of a profile here."

"And you," the guard said to Evan, "you're a student?"

"I was," Evan squeaked.

"He works in a bowling alley," Lansing said smoothly.

"Nice work if you can get it," the guard said. He and Lansing shared a laugh.

"Purpose of your visit," the guard said.

"Pleasure," said Lansing. "We're en route to Toronto, going to visit a couple of old friends near Rochester on the way."

"Uh-huh," the guard said. He entered information on his keyboard, then cast an eye over the back seat of the car. The guitars nestled together. "Planning to play any concerts while you're here?"

"No sir," said Lansing agreeably. "Just planning to catch up with a couple old friends."

The guard appeared to think about this. Then, "Sir, I'm going to have to ask you to pull the car over up ahead. Remain in the car and turn off your ignition."

Evan wondered what it would feel like to be strip-searched. Not good, he'd bet. He took his foot off the brake and rolled ahead, pulled over and killed the engine.

The guard approached, accompanied by another. They snapped on latex gloves. The second guard, skinny with badly pockmarked skin, appeared at Evan's window.

"Sir, what's in the cooler?"

Evan opened his mouth, but Lansing spoke first. "Just some snacks for the road," he said, "apples, carrots, hummus, that kind of thing."

"Where are the apples from?"

"Grocery store in Kingston," Lansing said.

"They're Canadian," Evan squeaked.

The border guards conferred about this. Then the skinny one asked, "Any citrus in there?"

"A couple of oranges," Evan said.

The guards looked at each other victoriously. Smudged Glasses snapped his latex glove.

"Sir," he said, "please unlock your car door."

"It's unlocked," Evan said, panic rising in him.

"We're going to have to look in your cooler," Skinny said. He removed it from the car and set it on the hood. Smudged clicked his tongue against his teeth as Skinny lifted the lid. "Sir," Skinny said, "it's illegal to transport citrus fruit across the border."

"Okay," Evan said dumbly, "although I think those oranges were grown in Florida"—Lansing was elbowing him—"so really we're repatriating them."

The guards looked at him sternly. He didn't know why he'd said that. He pressed his lips tightly together as if to disavow the sound of his own voice, which hung still in the air.

"It's in contravention of international law," Smudged said. "Sir, we're going to have to confiscate these oranges."

"Okay," Lansing said agreeably. "You're welcome to them. We didn't know."

"Ignorance of the law is no excuse for breaking it," Skinny said grimly. "Sir, I could fine you up to ten thousand dollars."

"We're very sorry," Lansing said. His smile was Canadian and apologetic.

"We're going to have to throw these oranges out," Smudged said, with a kind of aggrieved sorrow.

"Or you could keep them for your lunch," Lansing said. The border guards exchanged looks. Smudged moved toward the Corolla.

"Sir," he said sternly, "that is strictly not allowed, sir. These are contraband citrus, sir." He gestured to the oranges his colleague held above a garbage can. He gave a nod and Skinny let them fall, one at a time, into the can below.

There passed a moment of silence. Then Skinny drew off his latex gloves and dropped them in the garbage can as well. Smudged pulled his off and jammed them in the pocket of his too-tight jacket.

"Enjoy your stay in upstate New York!" he said, his countenance lightened now that illicit oranges had been stopped at the border. He patted the roof of the car twice. "Drive safe," he said.

Evan looked at Lansing, who nodded deeply, an exaggerated smile on his face.

"Okay, thanks," Lansing said.

"Don't forget your cooler," Smudged said, retrieving it from the hood and handing it back through the window.

"Right," said Lansing cheerfully, "thanks again!"

"Drive," he said under his breath to Evan, who turned the ignition without delay and put the car in gear. Lansing reached over and tooted the horn twice. "Bye now," he called out the window.

He sat back, replacing his hat. "Piece of cake," he said. "Oranges were probably woody anyhow. Nothing worse than a woody orange." He looked out the window, then reached over and tooted the horn twice more. "Welcome to America, boy," he said, "land of the free to be stupid."

"You know you're in a different country down here, even though the landscape is the same," Lansing Meadows said. He was flush with triumph after the successful border negotiation. His mood was expansive—practically American. All optimism and bigness. His time in the States had been short, but seminal. There was much to dislike. The political backbiting, the damaging lie of the American Dream, but there was much to recommend it as well. He'd felt free to succeed in the States in a way he never did in Canada. You were expected to succeed, and if you did, it conferred on you admiration, praise even. At home, suspicion was heaped upon the successful. With that freedom to succeed had come some of his best writing. "Cantina Heart" had been the result of a writing weekend in New Mexico. "On My Honour" had its roots here in the fertile soil of upstate New York. And while he had never found commercial success in this country—or any other, for that matter—and while even his critical success here had been very niche indeed, he had found approval, had found a community that respected and responded to his music in an uncomplicated way, and that had been tremendously gratifying. In America he could just be a songwriter, a good one, without having to think about his songs as part of the cultural fabric of the place. There were hundreds of other songwriters, maybe thousands, and he was one of them, each of them getting up each morning and trying to outdo themselves, and each other. It had let him rise above the sometimes-pettiness of his homeland, the unwillingness to let anyone get too big. He'd used America and his American friends as a kind of pump to fill the well so that he could draw from it anew.

"You'll go into a grocery store, son, and you'll see foods you've never seen before. Foods no one should eat. French fries shaped like letters. It's not natural, boy, and you shouldn't eat them, but here in America, goddamn it, if they want to eat over-processed potato pressed into alphabet shapes and deep-fried, you can't stop them, boy, no you cannot. And should a bag or two of those french fries fall out of your grocer's freezer while an American is loading up his or her cart, let them stay on the floor, son. For it is the God-given right of an American to take what's theirs and damn the rest." Lansing's eyes glittered beneath his hat and he turned to Evan. "As a Canadian, son, you will feel compelled to pick up that bag of fries, even if—especially if—you did not cause it to fall. You can do that," Lansing said, his voice taking on a cautionary tone, "but then everyone will know you for what you are, son. A Canadian. And therefore a socialist, just so you know." He rolled down the window, poked his head out. "Better to be confident and cool, son, stay brash and bold. Be mistaken for an American." He shouted to a herd of cows grazing in the sunshine, "Live a little!"

"Cut it out," Evan muttered. "What's the matter with you?" He surveyed the road, hoped there were no other cars to witness Lansing's behaviour.

"Don't be so Canadian," Lansing said. He reached over to honk the horn twice. "Live a little, son, that's all I'm trying to say."

Evan rolled his head from his left shoulder to his right. With one hand on the wheel, he stretched out the other arm and flexed its fingers, then switched sides.

"Jesus, I wish you drove," he said.

"Well, I don't," said Lansing, "so don't waste your time."

"Where are we going, anyway?"

"Little town called Fulton," Lansing said. "Tiny, but bustling. There's all kinds of places to have lunch there, and we can stop in on some old friends of mine."

"Shouldn't we call ahead?" Evan asked doubtfully.

Lansing shook his head in disgust. "What kind of Maritimer are you, boy? Call ahead. Jesus Christ. The drop-in is perfectly acceptable here, just like at home."

"I hate the drop-in," Evan said.

"Well, good thing you don't live here, then, I guess," Lansing said. "You want to take the I-81 a ways, and I'll tell you where to get off."

"No doubt," said Evan.

"You sassing me, boy?"

"No sir."

"Well, why not, son? You're in America, time to start acting like it."

The drive was a monotony of bad highways with potholes that rattled Evan's teeth and crumbly bits that made him worry they'd give way beneath his tires. The monotony was relieved occasionally by toll booths. Evan wondered what they used the money for, since clearly they weren't putting it into road repair.

Lansing had fallen quiet after his initial cross-border euphoria, and Evan too was lost in thought.

"What made you come out of retirement?" he asked suddenly. "You did that last big tour, like, five years ago, and that was supposed to be it."

Lansing shook his head. "I wasn't retired, son."

"Well, but you kind of were. I mean, you told Peter Mansbridge that you were done with songwriting, and especially with touring. I saw it on television."

"Well, then it must be true," Lansing sneered.

"You'd been at it a long time, I guess. Not to say you're old, but anyone would want a break after a while. Is that it?"

Lansing paused. "First of all," he said, "I didn't retire. A break is not retiring. Second of all, fuck Peter Mansbridge. And third of all, I am old, boy, but don't go thinking I'm done. Don't go thinking you can pick the flesh off these bones."

Evan's heart pounded. "I don't know what you mean," he stammered, hands tight on the wheel.

"It's none of your goddamn business why I took a break and why I'm back now." Lansing said, a low threatening note in his voice. "I see the way you watch when I'm on stage, looking for any sign of weakness. I hear those songs you sing when you think I'm asleep."

Evan burned crimson, withered at the thought.

"I'm not done yet," Lansing said evenly. "You can't have it yet."

"Have what?" Evan said. "Lansing, I don't know what you're talking about."

Lansing was stone-faced.

"Look, I know those songs are no good," Evan said. "Not yet. And yes, I watch you. Of course I do. I'm trying to learn something here." He glanced at Lansing who was watching him steadily, with narrowed eyes.

"And more than that," Evan said, his voice hoarsened with a rising pitch of frustration, "I'm just trying to keep the wheels on the road for you. Jesus."

Lansing's mouth turned down at the corners. He shook his head. "Just don't ever think I'm done, boy."

He pushed the seat back further, swung one skinny leg up, then the other, planted his feet in their cowboy boots on the dashboard.

"See these boots," he said. "I'm gonna die with them on. And not 'cause you killed me." He smiled a ghastly smile. "I'm too mean to die even if you want me to."

The wheels bumped over uneven pavement. "I don't want you to die," Evan said. "Don't talk like that."

"We all go sometime, son," Lansing said, philosophically. "But I ain't fixing to go soon, nor on anyone else's schedule, don't you worry." He looked out the window, a storm cloud passing. "Put the radio on," he said at last, "let's hear someone else's voice besides our own."

Evan turned the dial and tuned past rap and classic rock and Top 40 pop.

"Auto-Tuner'll be the death of this country's culture," Lansing said.

"I kinda like that song," Evan said. "It's catchy." He tuned back to the spacey, Auto-Tuned female vocal laid over inorganic-sounding beats.

"You wanna walk, son?" Lansing asked, outraged.

"You can't kick me out," Evan said. "Car doesn't go without me in it." He sang syllabic nonsense along with the radio. "Besides, what's wrong with a little guilty pleasure?"

"Some skinny little pop starlet I got underwear more mature than, some little girl thin enough to floss your teeth with, cracks up, shaves her head for the cameras, stop the presses, you know?" Lansing said "It's headline news around the world. *Around the world*. Meanwhile, Lansing Meadows, *Lansing Meadows*, mind you, so-called godfather of Canadian folk, can't even get a callback on his goddamn press release in his hometown, you know?" He exhaled loudly. "Jesus Christ, a guilty pleasure? You *should* feel guilty. Hell is this world coming to, anyhow."

"Indeed," Evan said, after a moment. "So, I should look for another station?"

Lansing slumped in his seat. "Whatever. You wanna kill me, this is a good way to go about it."

"To clarify," Evan said, "I don't want to kill you, and yes, absolutely you are too mean to die. Just, you know, isn't there room for both? Can't you have the pop starlets and the godfather of Canadian folk—can't I listen to both?"

"Sure," Lansing said with a broad sweep of his arms. "You can listen to both the pop starlet and the godfather of Canadian folk. So long as the latter is a passenger in this car. Only way you can listen to both me and her"—he pointed a finger toward the radio—"is right now, me talking to you while you hear her on the radio. You twist that dial all day, son, you won't hear a Lansing Meadows tune. Unless it's that dreadful techno version of 'On My Honour.'"

He laughed. "Was a time there was room for everyone, for all of us on that dial. But no one wants to see me shake what my mama gave me, and that's the name of the game now, boy. Don't know if you've heard the news, but sex sells. And enough isn't enough anymore. Hell, more is barely enough these days. You know? It's all singles now, and they don't even exist in the real world. Just zeroes and ones organized out there in the ether. The kids who buy that stuff don't give a shit about some old man, singing about shipwrecks and divorce."

He rubbed a worn hand across his forehead. "Jesus. And the geezers who do get me, maybe they would buy something, but no one's interested in their money. They won't be around much longer, I guess. Better to spend your time marketing thongs to eleven-year-olds whose best shopping years are still ahead of them." He was gathering steam again. "And the merch! Some pop tart's face on that thong, that's cute. Lansing Meadows on a thong, well"—he paused, wiped that hand over his face again—"even I'm kinda grossed out by that." He slumped in his seat. "There's a change coming, boy, or maybe it's already here, and nobody knows what's next or how to best profit from it. But they're pretty sure of one thing. It won't have anything to do with Lansing Meadows."

"But you've sold all those records already," Evan said.

"And my various thieving record companies all made much more off them than I did," Lansing said.

"And you've written all those songs," Evan said. "I mean, even you said it, a techno version of 'On My Honour,' 'Cantina Heart,' the others, those are great songs. Songs for the ages."

"Yes," Lansing said, "but what have I done for them lately?"

"You're playing almost every night," Evan said. "That's gotta count for something with someone."

"You'll pardon me if I'm not exactly heartened by that bold assertion," Lansing said. "Listen kid, you asked if there's room for both, and of course there is—but not in that mainstream, money-making world of fame and fortune and Top 40 radio plays. Sure, I sold records, I wrote songs—hits, even—I had fans. Still do. Even some young ones. But by and large, no one wants what I got, and that's okay. My time on that big stage will never come again. But I can still write songs, there are still a few hundred people in most places across the country who'll come and see me play. It's enough. It's enough. And eventually, someone'll give me the Order of Canada just for hanging in there. So don't get all worked up about it."

But it was Lansing, Evan could see, who was worked up. Lansing whose eyes were flashing, whose hands were trembling. Evan stole glances at him till Lansing said, "Cut it out, boy, you're giving me the willies. Just find NPR on the radio and drive." And he pulled his hat down over his blazing eyes, balled his fists and turned his face away, toward the window once more.

They passed signs for places like Calcium, Watertown, Adams Centre, and Adams. On the radio, a call-in show about canning relishes and chutneys. The only other sound was the rhythmic slap of the tires on pavement. There were questions Evan wanted to ask, but he was wary of riling Lansing up all over again. Their conversation about music represented by far the most he'd heard Lansing say, and the most emotion he'd seen him display. Lansing had had decades to perfect his cool, unflappable demeanour and it made Evan nervous to have seen beneath it to the rattled old man inside. Lansing was, in most respects, vital and alive. His hands were big and rough, fingertip pads like baseball gloves. His arms were sinewy and strong, and the work of his tendons and muscles was visible when he played guitar. Lansing was deeply intelligent and funny and engaged. Evan felt a complicated affection well in him.

He was struck by the magnitude of what he'd taken on, the path from thirteen-year-old in love with the twin sounds of voice and guitar to where he sat now, a foot from his idol. It struck him again how inconceivable it was that someone who'd done what Lansing had done—played at Newport, been on the cover of *Maclean's*, written a couple songs everyone knew all the words to, been featured time and again on the CBC—that someone like that was still touring the country by car. Submitting to indignities like the gig in Cornwall. Getting paid hundreds, not thousands, and still scrabbling for every scrap he could get. It didn't make sense somehow. Shouldn't there be some advantage to all that fame? Shouldn't all those years of artistic service amount to something? He wanted to know, but he'd bide his time.

22

Dacey Brown deferred making a decision on what would be next. She'd waited for a westbound bus at the station and at the moment it arrived, she balked. While a steady stream of other passengers filed on, Dacey lingered in the station unable to decide whether to stay or to go. At last, the bus made the decision for her. With a great release of exhaust, it pulled out of the depot and began to leave the city.

So Dacey put her knapsack on her back and headed in the opposite direction. She wandered the streets of Montreal, her camera always close at hand, trying to learn the rhythm of a city, and how to be in it.

She felt the city romancing her. It was familiar in one way—here again, as in Grand Falls, she was an English minority in a French milieu. It was excitingly unfamiliar in every other way. There was the eye-contact that was flirtatious rather than censorious. There were narrow streets with brightly coloured houses, ornate cast-iron balconies, big trees all crammed in together, and the feeling that everywhere was possibility. The streets of Grand Falls were tidier, more polite. The houses were further apart so you could live without having to be all up in your neighbours' business—though in a small town you generally were anyway. Dacey marveled at the feeling in the city. People lived literally on top of each other—one old house might contain four apartments—and yet there was a sense of privacy, a sense that people minded their own business and didn't care too much about yours. She found the opportunity for anonymity intoxicating.

And then there were the little shops, the cafés, and bakeries that dotted every block. She made herself almost sick, stopping for espresso almost as often as it was offered. She felt she wanted to know the whole city all at once. She couldn't walk past a little café without longing to go in, drink the coffee there, overhear the jokes the baristas were cracking with the regulars, pretend she herself was one of them. And the buttery croissants you could order alongside the coffee, the way the outsides shattered pleasantly and the insides were chewy and damp with butter. She swooned. She took pictures. She did not think about the future.

She made her way back to her little auberge and was able to reserve the same room for another night. The day had turned suddenly hot, the way it did sometimes in spring. Montrealers were shedding their jackets, balling up their gloves, not caring if they fell out of their pockets. In her room's tiny bathroom, Dacey splashed cool water on her face and looked at herself in the mirror. She was still queasy from the espressos but she felt a remarkable calm. It wasn't the lethargy of Grand Falls, the damping down of her spirit that had been necessary to keep her there so long. This was a deeper, true peace. She smiled happily at herself.

With the espresso buzz in her veins she knew she'd never sleep, though she was tired from her morning spent wandering, and with the sun beckoning through the window, she knew she couldn't stay inside. She left her knapsack behind, taking only her camera and her wallet back out into the city.

She could hear a steady drum beat and at first thought it was just the city's own thrum, or perhaps her espresso-quickened pulse. But she followed the sound until it was undeniably real, a big grassy park stuffed with people—hundreds or maybe thousands—drumming and dancing and throwing Frisbees.

Dacey reeled. She'd never seen so many people in one place. The sheer scale was overwhelming. She pulled her camera up to her eye and began trying to understand it that way. But she couldn't capture it all in one frame, so she shot a panorama, taking the scene apart in sections, until she had tamed it. Still, to look closely at its individual parts was also dizzying, and Dacey took a deep breath. With her hand on her camera, she moved into the park shyly and found a patch of grass that wasn't taken. She'd tied her hoodie around her waist, and she removed it now, and made a little cushion for herself.

The drumming was urgent, organic, almost frightening. The drummers were uncountable. They were all motion. Their faces showed they were transported. The dancers too looked blissful and free in a way Dacey Brown knew she had never experienced. There were all kinds of people in the park. There were vendors too, little booths that offered food and drink, or hacky sacks and saris.

Dacey sat and took it all in. The sun on her back was a promise of summer, the din in her ears constant and becoming familiar, the riot of colour before her a visual feast for a photographer's eye. She lifted the camera again, but stopped short of raising it to her face. She wanted to be subsumed. She'd never felt that before, always holding herself back a little. Even in her family, she'd kept herself the odd one out, never feeling she could truly connect. Here though, in this ecstatic crowd, connection seemed inevitable. If she could just stay with it. She let the camera fall.

Nearby was a gaggle of teens, their limbs flashing in the spring sun. Three boys and two girls, testing their limits, it seemed to Dacey. Their voices occasionally rose above the din of the drums, shouts of laughter, egging each other on. The boys were engaged in physical feats, play-fighting each other and darting glances over their shoulders toward the girls. Then their focus shifted to acrobatics, and the boys attempted cartwheels while the girls held each other up, giggling helplessly. The cartwheels were stunted things, the boys could barely get their legs into the air. Still, they kept trying, and they kept checking the response they were getting from the girls.

One of the girls stood, finally, as her friend laughed, and said, "I'll show you how it's done." The boys stood back, hands on hips, as the girl stretched her body, arms over her head, one foot raised and daintily pointed. She flashed her eyes at the boys for a moment, and then flung herself forward, cartwheeling with grace, her legs extended high into the air. She hopped up and flung herself forward again, executing three perfect cartwheels in a row before coming to a stop with her arms out and her hair falling around her face.

Her friends burst into applause, and Dacey Brown laughed, and then covered her mouth with her hand. Such freedom in those limbs, she thought, and watched the girl shake her hair back into place and proudly strut back to the blanket she'd been sitting on with her friend. Dacey wondered what that freedom felt like, and vowed to herself she'd find out.

23

Evan thought of the life he'd recently life behind. Petite Riviere would be awash in mud as it was every April. Its residents would be emerging after a winter with the hatches battened down. The river itself would be pounding, rushing with the cold froth of spring runoff, its graceful banks greening, the tumble of rocks on the beaches around Green Bay a chattering on rough days, a susurration when the wind was gentle.

The cottages around the bay were due for painting, and if he'd stayed behind, that's what he'd be doing, picking up the extra work by day. He and Crouse would be outside all day, pushing their muscles to the max, long strokes with the roller, picky detail-work with the angle brush, plenty of time to talk about their plans for the future, the way they'd chase fame and success, whether Colleen was indeed Evan's girlfriend, a topic of conversation with which Crouse seemed to be obsessed. At the end of the day, they would have the sense they'd done something, and that there was a concrete result of a day's aching labour. Shingles would be freshened in candy-grab-bag colours, trim crisply whitened, everything cheerful and ready for a summer's worth of visitors.

And then there was the road. His body ached, but for lack of activity. He longed to feel the spongy ground along the rivers beneath his sneakers, longed to move his legs and arms instead of folding them day after day into the driver's seat and night after night into some lumpy motel room bed. His only exercise was pumping gas, pushing the car's pedals, and carrying Lansing's gear. And his body was not helped by the endless menu of road food. One day he'd eaten three club sandwiches, for breakfast, lunch, and dinner. Pale lettuce, pulpy tomatoes, and ketchup were the only vegetables.

He thought about Colleen, his not-girlfriend, left behind, ponytail swinging, dark eyes flashing. Dacey Brown was a question mark, a missed connection, a feeling that wanted exploring. And then there was him and his guitar, this troubled and troubling genius, and the open road.

He tried to weigh it all, the known quantity of Petite Riviere, the work that would be there for him, the girl he could commit to if he'd only make the decision to. And the possibilities of this life into which he'd been conscripted, where each day was the same but different. You drove, and that was stultifyingly the same, but you drove to somewhere you'd never been before. You never knew which Lansing you'd encounter; he changed minute to minute some days. But Evan could feel their connection growing. He could see the opportunities this tour was offering him. When he sat down at the end of the day with his own guitar on his knee, the result of the day's labour was much less concrete than with house-painting, but no less satisfying. It was another day he'd kept the wheels on the road. Another day he'd taken Lansing Meadows where he needed to go. Another day he'd moved a little closer to being the man he wanted to be.

He glanced at Lansing, whose head hung, chin-to-chest,

though the hat never budged. A tenderness welled in Evan. He could not help it, but he would keep it to himself.

He guided the car to an interstate off-ramp. Pee, coffee, check the map. He'd let Lansing sleep, or pretend to.

Before long, Evan was nosing the Corolla off the highway toward their destination. The signs for Fulton and the map were in accordance for once. The country roads showed spring had made better progress here, a little further south. Violets and bluebells were visible in the roadside ditches, punctuating a landscape of trees. Tucked back from the road were farmhouses in various states of repair. Sagging porches and left-for-dead barns were next door to well-tended gardens and freshly painted shingles. A few rundown houses were obscured by rusting cars and farm machinery parts, batts of insulation in filthy fraying plastic, the detritus of industry and whatever could be collected and hoarded, mounded up in front yards by who-knew-who. A panoply of decay and obsession.

As they got closer to town, more of the houses were well-kept but boarded up, evidence of a recent exodus. As if bad news had come and the townspeople left all at once. It didn't jibe at all with Lansing's description of a bustling, beautiful town with lots of places for lunch. Evan cruised along the main street and saw almost no one. Vacant storefronts with For Rent signs, stone planters with withered plants beside park benches that sat empty. He shivered and drove through.

On the other side of town, the landscape became more pastoral, with rolling hills and the odd farmhouse. Evan slowed the car as he rounded a bend, and there rose a graceful, shapely house, a classic rural construction with gables and a porch that wrapped all the way around. A sign posted at the road read Part and Parcel Farm. They had arrived. A curving drive led to one of three trim outbuildings, and a field of wildflowers rose beside it. Evan turned onto the drive, its gravel crunching below the Corolla's wheels. "Lansing," he said softly. "We're here."

24

Dacey Brown was enervated. She'd walked all over Montreal, and the espresso buzz, when it lifted, left her feeling as weak as a kitten. Too tired to navigate the Metro, she took a taxi back to her auberge and dragged herself up the two flights of stairs to her little room.

She downloaded the photos she'd taken that day to her laptop and sat cross-legged on the bed with the computer on her knees. She scrolled through them, looking for—well, she didn't know exactly what she was looking for. Clues, perhaps. Information about herself or what she should do next.

The Montreal she saw on screen romanced her all over again. The beautiful streets with many doorways, each an offer of the unknown. That park teeming with people who grabbed the day with both hands. If Dacey were looking for a place to belong, Montreal could be it, she thought. Perhaps you became where you lived, and if you lived in a place as alive as this city, you too became alive. Perhaps connection was something she could learn from watching others.

But then she thought of Lansing Meadows, of the way his music had been a beacon in her teenage years. The connection she'd felt with him, with what his songs said to her about herself. She imagined him moving down the highway, always moving away, and of herself once more stuck in place. Even if she made a choice to stay, it would be choosing to remain stationary while others moved on. Again.

She closed the laptop with a decisive click. Moving forward was the only thing to do.

25

Matthew met them at the door with outstretched arms. He was short and plump where Lansing was tall and lean, but Evan could see he was strong, not soft, muscular despite his plumpness. Matthew pulled Lansing in and embraced him, clapping him on the back and hugging him hard till Lansing finally said, "I thought you'd be glad to see me, Matthew. Why so standoffish?" Matthew let him go then, and turned to Evan.

"And who are you?" he said, holding out a hand for Evan to shake.

"Evan Cornfield," Evan said. "I'm glad to meet you."

"Come in," Matthew said, and he stood back to let them pass. "What a surprise to see you, Lansing. What brings you this way after all this time?"

Lansing stood in the foyer, his hat tipped back on his head. "Just passing through the neighbourhood," he said, "on a run out west. Couldn't pass by without sticking my head in to say hello."

"Touring?" Matthew asked. He seemed surprised.

"That's right," Lansing said. "The place looks great," he added.

"Come in, Evan," Matthew said, ushering him further into the house. "You're back out on the road, then," Matthew said to Lansing.

"Where else would I be?" Lansing said. He'd made his voice large, Evan noted, the way it was on stage. It rang off the wooden staircase in Matthew's front hall.

"Where else indeed," Matthew said. "Come in, come all the way in." He led them down the hall to the kitchen. "I just finished lunch," he said, "are you hungry?"

Lansing pulled out a wooden chair and sat, his legs akimbo. "I could murder a cold beer," he said.

Matthew looked at Evan. "You?"

Evan nodded. He leaned against the kitchen counter.

Lansing took a long swallow from the bottle Matthew handed him. "It's good to be back in Fulton," he said.

"A lot has changed," Matthew said.

"Looks like only for the better," Lansing said. Evan pictured the vacant main street, the boarded-up houses he'd seen, the farms that seemed to produce nothing but rusty car parts and sprung mattresses.

Matthew shook his head. "It's not like it used to be, that's for sure."

"Well," Lansing said expansively, "what is, these days? What about you, Matthew? You look like you're doing well." He reached out and poked Matthew in the belly.

Matthew smiled and shook his head. "Yes, I'm fine. This place has been good to me."

"You playing much?" Lansing asked, and Matthew shook his head again.

"Just by the woodstove, really," Matthew said. "I've mostly left that behind. Leave it to the ones coming up."

"Oh, they'll take it from us soon enough," Lansing said,

inclining his head toward Evan. "No need to hand it over without a fight."

"In any event," Matthew said. "I have everything I need right here."

The two men looked at each other. Evan pushed off from the kitchen counter where he'd been leaning and asked, "Where's the bathroom?" Matthew pointed the way, and when Evan returned, the tension had been broken—Lansing and Matthew were laughing together—and there was a fresh bottle of beer awaiting him on the counter.

Evan tilted the cold bottle up and let the beer slide down his throat. The thought of a night off, and no need to be up early the next day to drive, someone besides Lansing to talk to, not to mention someone besides himself to talk to Lansing, had him feeling drunk already, and he was in no hurry to sober up.

Matthew said to him: "So how exactly did you get roped into this racket?" and pointed toward Lansing.

Evan told him about the night at the Alley Oop, and all the locals singing karaoke. He described Sindy St. John till he had both Lansing and Matthew laughing. He improvised the more drunken parts of the night that remained blank spots in his memory, till he got to the part that mattered. "There we were in my kitchen," he said giddily, "hungover, eating breakfast, and the next thing I know, Lansing's on the phone, firing his tour manager, and boom—I'm driving him to Antigonish." Evan felt as if his very blood were carbonated. This was what he'd been waiting for. This brotherhood, swapping war stories, tales from the folk-music trail. He leaned back against the kitchen counter and closed his eyes. "And it's been non-stop since then."

Lansing said, "Non-stop adventure, you mean."

Evan opened his eyes and grinned, awash on the waves of fellowship. Lansing reached over and clinked his bottle against Evan's.

"Those border guards," Lansing said, "and how you distracted them with those illicit citrus fruits."

"The gig at the tapas bar in Cornwall," Evan returned.

Matthew smiled. "There's no gig in Cornwall," he said.

"That's what Lansing kept saying!" Evan could barely contain himself.

"And yet," Lansing said.

"And yet," Evan agreed.

Matthew smiled again. Then: "You fired Jake, Lansing?"

Lansing drained his bottle, keeping an eye on Matthew the whole time. Evan glanced from Matthew to Lansing and back, trying to figure out what was going on. Finally Lansing placed his empty bottle deliberately on the kitchen table. He wiped the beer out of his stubble with the back of his hand. "Got a better tour manager right here," he said, gesturing to Evan.

"Yeah, but you worked with Jake for years," Matthew said.

"And now I don't work with him anymore," Lansing said. "Leave it."

Matthew opened his mouth to speak, but Lansing put his hand up. "Leave it," he said again.

Evan pushed off uncertainly from the kitchen counter. "Maybe I should get our stuff out of the car?" he said.

Matthew arranged his face in a smile again. "Will you stay the night, then?"

"If you'll have us," Lansing said carefully, like a man testing a truce.

"You're always welcome here, Lansing. You always have been, no matter what." He said it quietly but firmly, looking across the kitchen table at his old friend with intensity.

Lansing nodded.

"Okay then," Evan said.

The afternoon passed in industry. Matthew moved around the kitchen, humming as he prepared their evening meal. Lansing grudgingly took their dirty clothes to the basement laundry room and put them through the washing machine. Evan spent the afternoon outside, splitting logs with an axe and sweating, his jacket abandoned, the glorious feel of sunshine on his back.

Later, he stood beneath the steady stream of the shower, feeling alive in every fibre and tendon. He relished what was to come. A home-cooked meal, a soft bed, clean clothes to put on.

They ate well that night. Creamy potatoes, mashed with lots of butter. A little pot roast braised in the oven the whole afternoon while the washing machine churned and the little pile of split logs grew. A simple salad of early spring greens. Homemade pickles from a Mason jar and grainy rolls with sweet butter. They sat at Matthew's dining-room table, a long slab of board atop two sawhorses, simply adorned by a tray crowded with little jars and pots. A small pot of honey, blackberry jam, coarse salt in a bowl with a little spoon stuck in. The honey gleamed a deep amber, and Evan was transfixed.

"Comes from the neighbour's bees," Matthew said, as Evan picked up the jar and turned it in his hands.

Evan had never had honey not in a bear- or beehive-shaped squeeze bottle. "What does it taste like?" he said.

Lansing's jaw was busy working, chewing through the food Matthew had made. Busy as his jaw was, he couldn't conceal his smirk.

"What do you mean what does it taste like?" Matthew asked. "It tastes like honey, of course."

"Jesus, boy," Lansing said, the bolus of pot roast dispatched. "What you don't know could fill a thousand honey jars. Didn't any of your neighbours keep bees back in old Petite Riviere?"

Evan shrugged. "All our stuff came from the grocery store. How am I supposed to know?"

Matthew stood, patted Evan's hand. "You'll have some tomorrow morning on toast." He gathered dishes and cutlery.

"Toast from homemade bread," Lansing taunted. "That'll blow your mind."

"Don't be unpleasant, Lansing," Matthew said. "Are you finished with your plate?"

"I'm just teasing him," Lansing said. "Boy knows that."

"I'll help with the dishes," Evan said, eyeing Lansing steadily as he pushed back his chair.

"Kiss-ass," Lansing called after him.

"It seems to me he's getting worse," Matthew said, elbow-deep in sudsy water.

"Oh, I don't know," Evan said. "He's pretty much like that all the time."

"So hostile," Matthew said. "He didn't used to be that angry."

Evan made a doubtful sound in his throat.

"Oh, he was always sharp," Matthew said, "and on the sour side. But this seems—different. Has he said much about it?"

"About what?" Evan asked.

"About how he's feeling, what's to come, what his plan is

for getting through it ..."

"Oh well," Evan said with confidence, "that's where I come in. I do the driving, I keep everything organized and on schedule. I take care of all that stuff, so he just has to worry about being an artist." He rubbed the juice glass in his hand till it was bone-dry. "It's okay with me if he's crabby. He's Lansing Meadows."

Matthew nodded, was quiet for a moment. "He's lucky to have you along."

Evan blushed, the slow red creep moving from neck to hairline. "I'm the lucky one," he said.

They worked in silence for a while, Evan gazing out the window at the expansive yard, a stone firepit flanked by low-backed benches, and nearby the pile of logs Evan had split and neatly stacked.

"How long have you lived here?" Evan asked.

"Born here," Matthew said. "This place has been in my family a long time."

He pulled the plug from the sink, watched the water disappear. "I left for a while, made music in the city for a few years, but this place always pulled me back and eventually I was able to build a little studio in one of the barns. Lansing and I spent some fevered days out there, making records and wasting time." He dried his hands on a tea towel. "It's good to see the old bastard again, just to get a look at him, see that he's alright."

"I haven't been alright since the seventies," Lansing said, suddenly behind them in the kitchen. "And I'll thank you ladies to quit gossiping about me."

The night was crisp and the sky was high and clear, the stars bright pinpoints overhead and the moon so bright and full it threw shadows. Smoke curled from the logs Evan had split. He shivered in his fleece jacket and leaned in toward the fire.

Lansing Meadows was playing guitar and laughing, trying to keep up with Matthew, who raced ahead of the melody on mandolin. Evan took a long pull off a fresh, cold beer and couldn't imagine anywhere else in the world he'd rather be. Lansing's face in the firelight was younger, more alive than Evan had yet seen it, and at the same time was lined with story and past. A face steeped in its own history. Evan thought again of his thirteen-year-old self, so voracious for music and experience, and felt he'd barely aged at all.

The mandolin made sounds that were high and lovely, and Matthew curled around his instrument, fingers flashing in the firelight, pulling sounds that made Evan's heart ache and soar at once. He felt a wave crash over him, a rising tide of emotion and desire for something. For this, yes, but for more, too, a more he couldn't name. He wanted in. He reached for his guitar with trepidation, unsure he could find his way into this tune, not convinced he had a right to be there. Still, he was carried by the wave, and so he played a tentative chord, just dipping his toe in the stream of sweet rushing sound, and then he played another more boldly, and Lansing looked up from his own efforts for a moment and gave Evan a half-smile, then bent again to his instrument and that was enough of a welcome for Evan Cornfield. He leaned into it and played along and he rode the waves of the song into shore.

"Remember that guy—hell of a player," Lansing said. They had put their instruments aside and the crackling fire provided their soundtrack now. "What was his name? Tucker Drew. Guy could play. My God, he could play fast." Lansing lit a cigarette, drew a deep lungful. "Probably because he had six fingers on each hand."

Matthew was using the back of his mandolin to roll a joint. He looked up, caught Lansing's eye and looked down again.

"Really?" Evan said.

Lansing nodded and smoked.

"No, not really," Matthew said. He shook his head at Lansing.

"Jesus," Lansing said. "Remember the time I got married twice in one week?"

Matthew finished rolling the joint, held it up to the firelight to inspect it.

"That was a time," Lansing continued. "I married that one girl—what was her name? Candy? And then plum forgot about it and then the next day, I married her sister!"

Matthew flicked his lighter till the joint caught.

"Really?" Evan said, uncertainly.

Matthew inhaled, held it, exhaled. "No," he said, trailing smoke. "Not really."

Lansing threw his cigarette butt into the fire. "Spoil all my fun," he said, holding his hand out for the joint. "Evan Cornfield, I've never met anyone quite as gullible as you." He drew on the joint, looking steadily at Evan. "Really."

Evan started to speak, but Lansing held up his hand. "Play us one of your songs," he said.

The next morning they stood in the foyer with their bags, repacked with fresh laundry. Evan still felt the tingle of exertion in his shoulders and back, and the smell of woodsmoke lingered in his hair.

Matthew gripped his hand and looked him in the eye. "It was a pleasure to meet you, Evan. Don't let him give you too much guff." He tilted his head toward Lansing. "He's mostly bluster anyhow, but you've probably figured that out by now."

"Jesus, Matthew, I'm trying to maintain a certain degree of mystique," Lansing said gruffly, but he smiled at his old friend. And Matthew turned to face Lansing and grasped each of Lansing's forearms with his big, work-hardened hands. He inclined his head back so he could look Lansing in the eyes, despite the hat. He gazed at his friend a long moment. Lansing rolled his eyes and tried to look away, but Matthew's grip was firm, as was his look.

Finally, Matthew said, "Be good, old friend. Stay well. And when you're ready to let your friends take care of you, you know where I'll be."

Lansing met Matthew's steady gaze and then closed his eyes. When he opened them again, Evan could see that Lansing had once more steeled himself.

"That's enough of that talk," Lansing gruffed. "Thanks for the good times."

Matthew released his grip on Lansing's arms and Lansing stuck out his hand to shake Matthew's. "We'll meet again, if you're lucky."

Matthew smiled at this and clapped his old friend on the back. "Travel well," he said, as his visitors turned to go. "Evan, don't you be a stranger, either. Let me know how you make out. You have my number."

Evan Cornfield nodded, his throat tight with an emotion he didn't understand. As he guided the car back down the drive, Evan said, "He's amazing. What a great guy."

Lansing peered out from under his hat to where Matthew stood in front of the house, watching them recede. He nodded. "He's getting soft in his old age. One more stop, and then we'll head for Toronto."

26

Dacey Brown had made a decision. She would indeed take a westbound bus to Toronto. She spent the morning hours once again roaming the streets of Montreal, filling up on espresso and croissants, and snapping photos of the little streets she'd quickly come to love. By the time she got to the bus station her heart hurt with leaving. This too, she thought, must be what connection is like. It aches to break away. She thought of the various trips to the airport, the long drive to Fredericton first to drop off her brother, and then at regular intervals, it seemed, with successive family members. At last it was just her left behind at Departures, waving as her parents wheeled their luggage through security, then turning away and making the long drive, all alone, back to Grand Falls. It must have hurt their hearts to go, she thought, as it hurt hers now.

She sat in the bus station and waited. How far could she go? She'd left Grand Falls with a little over two thousand dollars in the bank, and Montreal had taken little of it, enough to stay in the auberge a few nights, and then enough to keep her in espresso and croissants. If she was thrifty, it was probably enough to take her all the way to Alberta, if that's where she decided to go. She tried to picture her mother making coffee in the kitchen Dacey had never seen, her father working in the garden she wasn't sure they had. She would decide not to decide any further. She would live in each moment as it came. She would get on the bus when it arrived, and she would see.

27

The day was fresh, the air cool though the sun was high. Evan took direction from Lansing, moving the car along a rutted country road to Michelle's house.

"She an old girlfriend?" Evan asked.

"Eh?" Lansing said. "Something like that. That's all in the past now."

"Will she be as glad to see you as Matthew was?"

"Why all the questions this morning, boy? Can't you let an old man be?"

Evan bit his lip. He hadn't yet asked the question he most wanted answered. What had Matthew meant when he'd said that thing about Lansing being ready to let his friends take care of him? Evan bided his time and drove the Corolla.

Michelle lived much further off the beaten path than Matthew. They'd driven for twenty minutes without seeing another house. Lansing leaned forward in the passenger seat. "Slow down now, boy, see if I can remember which lane is hers."

Evan slowed and breathed in the scent of lilac borne on the breeze from the trees that lined the road.

"Turn here," Lansing said. "This is it."

The lane was even more rutted than the road they'd just travelled. It wasn't even paved, just surfaced with gravel and Evan drove along it carefully. Lansing was pitched forward as if he could somehow make the car move faster by shifting his weight toward the dashboard.

They came to a clearing in the trees where a little cottage stood, with a flagstone path leading to it and a pond just beyond. Ferns grew in the side yard and little white flowers were everywhere, pushing up through the dark soil. Evan parked the car and the two sat for a moment, staring at the house through the windshield. "This it?" Evan said. Lansing nodded. "It's *magical*," Evan said. Lansing nodded again.

"Michelle's like that. Come on, boy." He opened the passenger door and moved toward the house like something was pulling him there. "Michelle," he called, "you here, my love?"

Evan got out of the car too, but he hung back. Lansing had pushed open the front door and Evan could hear muffled voices from inside, Lansing calling Michelle's name, then a pause, then a delighted-sounding shriek and lots of laughter, Lansing's and a woman's.

A moment later, Lansing reappeared, his arm around a tall woman with long, chestnut hair that hung down her back. "What are you waiting for, boy? Get in here." He squeezed the woman and turned her back toward the house. "Kids today," Evan heard him say, and the woman laughed, a high tinkle.

Evan pocketed the car keys and followed them into the house, the sound of their voices leading him to a kitchen at the very rear of the house, with a window that looked out over the pond.

"This is Evan Cornfield," Lansing said to Michelle. "I've taught him everything he knows."

Evan blushed and stuck his hand out, but Michelle took him in her arms instead and hugged him. When she let him go she said, "How nice to meet you, Evan. Any friend of Lansing's is a friend of mine."

"My God, it's good to see you, Michelle," Lansing said. There was a little two-seater sofa in her kitchen and he sat down on it and patted the seat beside him.

"Did you see Matthew?" Michelle asked. She ignored Lansing's invitation and instead turned to the stove and put the kettle on.

"We did," Lansing said. "He's well, it seems."

"This life suits him," Michelle said. She turned and looked at Lansing. "What about you, Lansing? Does your life suit you?"

"Only life I know, Michelle. You tell me—does it?" He stood up and twirled around. Michelle laughed her easy laugh.

"Same old Lansing," she said.

"Is that a good thing?" he asked.

She shrugged and smiled. "A cup of tea, Evan?"

He nodded and pulled out a kitchen chair. He sank into it. He hadn't seen Lansing like this before. Almost manic. He'd do well, he thought, to keep his mouth closed and his eyes open.

Michelle, like Matthew, seemed at home in a kitchen. She moved easily from stovetop to sink to fridge, producing a plate of cookies, a little jug of milk and a bowl of sugar, scones and jam. She laid the things out on the kitchen table, and chatted endlessly while she did, she and Lansing talking over old times, Lansing asking for news of someone named Marie, Michelle's lips thinning and her shaking her head. Lansing went quiet then, and Michelle did too and they existed in silence in the kitchen until finally the kettle whistled and Michelle clapped her hands and turned back to the stove to see to it.

Cups of tea in front of them, the conversation wandered to more neutral ground. They talked a little about the tour, Evan's family back in Petite Riviere, Michelle's plans for her garden once summer came.

Lansing drained his cup and set it down in its saucer. "Read my cards for me, why don't you," he said, "for old time's sake."

Michelle's face changed from open to guarded and she looked down, her fringe of hair falling across, a curtain.

"Hey, my love," Lansing said. "Lay those cards out and see what the future has in store for old Lansing Meadows." He reached a road-rough finger out and placed it under Michelle's chin, lifting her face so that she had to look at him. "Come on, Michelle, you can't still be mad at me so many years later."

Michelle sipped her own tea, clasping the steaming cup in her hands. "I'm not *mad* at you, Lansing," Michelle said, and Evan got the sense this was well-travelled territory between the two of them. "I haven't been mad at you for years now."

"Then what's the problem?" Lansing asked. "Don't you remember how? All those wild fortunes you told for me back in the day. Some of them even came true." He patted his breast pocket. "I keep 'em all right here, even the ones that didn't come to pass."

"I won't do it, Lansing, so stop asking."

"Why not make an old man happy one last time?"

"Oh my God, Lansing," Michelle said, eyes flashing dangerously. "It always took more than that to make the likes of you happy, and you are not an old man, so don't *even*."

"Ah, Michelle," Lansing said quietly. "You're wrong on both counts. Though I may not have shown my happiness then, nor my age now. Please, Michelle." He reached his hand across the table, but Michelle did not send hers out to meet it.

"I don't know why you won't let this go," she said. She pushed her chair back and busied herself at the counter, taking muffins from a tea-towel-lined basket and packing them into a brown paper bag. "I won't read your cards, Lansing."

"But why won't you?" he asked, and Evan couldn't tell if he was truly baffled, or if he was just pushing her to see how far he could.

Michelle kept her back to him. She stopped with the muffins and put her palms flat on the kitchen counter. "I don't want to see myself in your cards, Lansing. That's all."

Lansing laughed, but it was an entirely different sound from the whoops of joy Evan had heard from him at the visit's start. "As far as I recall," Lansing said, "there's no nursemaid card in the deck, Michelle. No need to worry."

Michelle turned from the counter, wiped her hands on her jeans. "I'm happy now, Lansing. Can you understand that? I'm finally happy. Can't you please let me be?" She looked at him, but he didn't look back. He opened his mouth to speak, but no sound came out for a moment. Finally, he cleared his throat.

"As you wish," he said. He tipped his hat to her and turned from the room.

Michelle gathered the teacups wordlessly and piled them beside the sink.

"I'm sorry," Evan said, though he wasn't sure what he was apologizing for.

Michelle shook her head. "He doesn't change," she said, "except for moment to moment. He always was mercurial like that, you'd swear he had a twin." She poured what was left of the tea into a Thermos. "But deep down, in who he *is*?" She shook her head again. "No. No change." She gazed at Evan, seeming to see him for the first time. "You take care with him," she said. "Take care of him if you can. Man's more layered than an onion and twice as likely to make you cry. And I'm too old for that now." She handed Evan the Thermos and the paper bag. "Take these," she said, "and let me get back to my life without him."

Evan took what Michelle offered and whispered again, "I'm sorry," but she had already turned away.

Lansing was already in the car. When he saw Evan emerge from the house, he beeped the horn impatiently. Evan scowled.

They drove in silence for a while, making their way back toward the interstate and then along it, passing factory after factory standing shuttered and dormant.

"See this is the problem," Lansing said, breaking the silence between them at last. He tapped the window with the Thermos. "Used to be these little places could be their own destinations, they were self-sufficient. You could live and work, your kids could go to school and you could buy everything you needed on the main street of town, sold to you by your neighbour. Used to be a sense of possibility in these little places, boy. A silver-screen star could come to town, hell, or come *from* town. Was a time any place could be someplace—and every place was. But then, you know, a big factory moves into town and everyone works there and suddenly there's prosperity and then Walmart or whatever the hell else moves in and puts all the little guys out of business. And then it's all centralized and dehumanized and nothing is for you and me anymore, boy. And so when the bottom falls out and the shareholders start screaming for money and answers, head office shuts the factory down and outsources the work to Bangladesh and that's the end of another pretty little American town. These small places, they don't exist anymore except in their own imaginations. Now they're just places to get out of soon as you can before you knock up your high-school girlfriend and get trapped forever. Only people left living here are losers who have nowhere else to be."

"What about your friends who live here?" Evan asked. "Matthew, Michelle?"

Lansing fumbled with the paper bag, peering inside. "Huh? Oh, Matthew's alright. What are these, bran-raisin?" He pulled out a muffin, sniffed it suspiciously. "Fucking hate raisins," he said and he tossed the bag out the window.

28

Dacey arrived in Toronto hungry in every way. Spring was further along here. In Grand Falls, spring was always a muddy mess, with torrential rains one day and a hard fall of snow the next. In Montreal, that last hot day notwithstanding, dirty crusts of snow had still been in evidence. But in Toronto the mid-April air was soft and fragrant, and the trees were beginning to bud. Stomach growling, Dacey made her way down from the bus station, following her nose and her curiosity as she went. She bought a hot dog from a street vendor and piled it high with chopped onions and pickles, ketchup and mustard. She ate it as she roamed, wiping the grease off her face with the back of her hand.

She found Queen Street West and loped along, happy and anonymous in the steady stream of people flowing along the sidewalk artery. Here was true city life, she thought, bustling, self-important, in a hurry. In Toronto, it seemed, no one made eye contact. This city didn't know who she'd been yesterday and didn't care who she would be tomorrow. It existed in the moment, and Dacey had lately vowed to do that too. So she drifted along, afloat on a sea of beautiful unfamiliar faces, far from who and where she'd been before.

On a whim she turned right at the next corner and began to head north along a street that offered a mix of boarded-up places and new places where the paint was barely dry. It was a collision of old and new—a body shop next door to a record store next door to a Portuguese bar filled with old men next door to an espresso bar filled with people Dacey's age. She felt again the excitement she'd felt in Montreal, the sense of possibility each doorway and intersection offered.

She wanted to try something she'd never tried before, and so she pushed open the door of a Vietnamese restaurant and went in.

The clattering of spoons against bowls and lids on pots soothed her, and the air was heavy with spice and brothy smells. A short, brisk, Asian woman pointed to a chair at a tiny table for one and Dacey sat. She pulled off her scarf and slid out of her jacket. The woman handed her a laminated menu and returned moments later with a glass of water.

"You ready for order?"

Dacey wasn't quite, but she pointed at a picture on the menu of a big bowl of noodle soup. "With fish ball?" the woman asked, eyeing Dacey doubtfully. Dacey shook her head. The woman nodded and took the menu. "I bring you special to drink."

The restaurant was just about full, every table crammed with eaters, their heads bent to wide bowls out of which they slurped noodles and broth. Dacey watched carefully and pressed her belly when her stomach complained loudly.

The woman brought a thick, dark yellow drink. "Mango shake," she said. A wide straw protruded. Dacey raised the straw to her lips. The drink was cold and sweet, with an almost sour edge, alive with the taste of somewhere else. Dacey slurped it greedily, the cold thick shake snaking up the straw and freezing her teeth.

She set it aside reluctantly when her soup arrived, the aromas of garlic, ginger, and star anise displacing the sweet glee of mango. But she dipped her face toward the broth and breathed deeply its heady scent. Then, taking her cue from the diners she'd watched, she dug in with her chopsticks.

The soup was the drink's opposite. Hot and fragrant, dark and mysterious. She spooned up the rich broth and rooted around inexpertly with her chopsticks to pull out thin slices of meat and tendrils of bean sprouts. She grew more bold, drawing out a tangle of rice noodles and jamming them in her mouth with abandon. She ate till she felt she would burst and pushed the bowl away, regretful she couldn't finish it.

Thus fueled, she set out again, up to College Street and then east, through neighbourhoods that changed every couple of blocks: Latin, Korean, Portuguese. She passed a big city park ringed with well-put-together women pushing expensive cantilevered strollers containing babies dressed in the latest fashions. She passed old women, Italian maybe, or Portuguese, their stout bodies dressed all in black, ankles like tree trunks and startled-looking eyes under thick mops of grey-black hair. Bakery windows offered treats Dacey couldn't name. Barbecued meats hung red and glistening in neighbouring windows. And old men drank espresso on the sidewalk, or sat inside dark social clubs, watching faraway soccer games on television.

She walked wide-eyed, open to it all, and not feeling the thousands of steps she'd already taken that day. What the city lacked in connection it made up for in variety. So caught up had she been she'd barely documented the day, had looked not at all through her camera's lens. She'd been propelled along by excitement from block to block till finally she came to a halt where a red light commanded. It was a relief to be forced to stop. The visual information streaming by had made her almost sick it was so rich. She waited for the light to change, but when it did, she stayed still, a log in the stream of other pedestrians. She stared at a poster on a lamppost beside her. The familiar craggy features and unmistakable hat of Lansing Meadows. Thursday night, the poster said. The Cat's Pyjamas. So there was her next move, waiting to be made.

29

Evan and Lansing hadn't spoken since Lansing had thrown the muffins out the window. He'd sat sullen since then under his hat, the heaviness a mantle that threatened to cloak Evan, too. Evan wondered when the time would be right to ask the questions he'd been collecting—questions that had only multiplied in the wake of the visits with Matthew and Michelle. Though he'd seen Lansing in many moods now, he believed he knew him less than the day they'd met. If he tried to map Lansing it would be all prickly parts and unknowns, he thought. *Here be monsters.* All he could do was what he'd been doing. Keep them in motion, get them to the next place on time and on budget, and try to keep his mouth shut and his eyes open.

It was a straight shot from upstate New York to St. Catharines. There'd be a house concert there for them, a home-cooked meal, soft beds. A good crowd. A crowd who would know Lansing's tunes, who'd know all the words to "On My Honour," and who'd know exactly who had written them. There'd be no heckling from this crowd. Just straight-up adulation, and a nice fat pay packet at the end of the night. Evan glanced at Lansing, smiling in anticipation of a better night ahead for them both. To his surprise, Lansing was staring at him.

"What are you so happy about?" Lansing asked.

Evan looked away, studying the road ahead. "Just looking forward to tonight," he said, fingers tight on the wheel.

"Tonight," Lansing rasped. "What about it?"

Evan darted another look at his passenger. "Just, you know. A full house. Appreciative fans. The kind of people you should get to play for every night." He couldn't help it. The gruffer Lansing was, the more tenderness Evan felt toward him.

Lansing seemed to think about this assessment of the evening's promise. He pushed his hat up his forehead, and Evan was struck by the startling dark blue of the eyes beneath. "You remember that wanker doodle dandy Lloyd Crane? Remember him?"

Evan started to speak. He'd never heard of Lloyd Crane, but Lansing didn't wait.

"That sonovabitch was twice the musician I'll ever be," Lansing said. "Had a voice on him that could de-pants a girl three notes in. Oh Jesus, he could sing. And good-looking too. The whole package, Matthew," Lansing said. He stared at Evan with intensity.

"I'm not Matthew," Evan said, fear rising in him, but Lansing pressed on.

"But that frigger lacked two things. He could not write a song to save his life—guy just had nothing to say. And I mean nothing. And he lacked courage. I mean, you could play Ping-Pong with his balls, you know?"

"I—" Evan said.

"Tiny," Lansing said. He curled his thumb and forefinger toward each other in a circle, squinted at the ball they described.

"Seems a pretty average size," Evan said quietly. He didn't know what was required of him in this situation. Lansing seemed to be having an episode of some kind, the likes of which Evan had never seen.

"And average balls just won't cut it," Lansing spat. "You need soccer balls. Medicine balls. Fucking cannon balls in this business. Lloyd Crane just couldn't take the life. You'd have had to ship him back home long before now, weepin' and suckin' his thumb." He reached out and clapped his big gnarled hand on Evan's knee. "But at least he's still playing. Every Saturday night at the Ball and Chain in Pictou. It's him and his guitar and that shitty drum machine, and a steady rotation of covers. Hell, he does a better version of 'Cantina Heart' than I do. And he makes his money nice and regular and sleeps in his own fucking bed every night with his own fucking wife, who doesn't seem to mind those Ping-Pong balls at all. But you, Matthew," and here Lansing's voice grew quiet and he pressed down on Evan's knee. "You just stopped everything. You let it all go. No balls at all."

Lansing reached his right arm up and crushed his hat so far down over his eyes Evan thought the crown would split. When Lansing spoke again, his voice was ragged and almost tearful. "Why'd you do that, Matthew? Why'd you just give up? We were in it together, weren't we?" His hand tightened on Evan's leg as if trying to wring forth an answer, and Evan covered Lansing's hand with his own. He couldn't think, he couldn't make sense of this at all. And so he just reacted.

"I'm sorry, Lansing," he said. "I'm so sorry."

They continued on in silence, the yellow line leading them into the unknown, and finally Lansing released his grip on Evan's knee. But Evan felt the pressure would never lift.

Evan used the BlackBerry to call Crouse. "I think he's cracking up," he said quietly and urgently. They were stopped at a gas station and Lansing had gone into the restroom. Crouse's voice down the line made Evan almost cry with gratitude, so relieved was he to hear a friendly, familiar voice.

"Cracking up how?" Crouse said.

"We had a whole conversation where he thought I was his friend Matthew."

"What happened when you set him straight?" Crouse asked.

"It was more of a monologue than a conversation," Evan said. "I didn't really have a chance to set him straight." He tried to imagine Lansing being set straight by him or anyone else. Impossible. Lansing was a bull. Evan was a china shop.

"Well, so now what?" Crouse asked.

"Good question," Evan said. "I was kind of hoping you'd have an answer."

Crouse exhaled. "Shit, dude," he said. "Where are you?"

"Almost in Rochester," Evan said. "Couple hours from the border. We play in St. Catharines tonight."

"Maybe get him to a doctor," Crouse said.

"Yeah," Evan said. "Listen, he's coming back. I gotta go."

"Let's get at 'er, son," Lansing said, as he got back in the car. "Who you talking to?"

"No one," Evan said, stowing the BlackBerry. "Just checking the email. Guy from the *Globe and Mail* wants to talk to you."

"The less I hear about that, the better," Lansing said. He tipped the seat back and settled his hat over his face.

Evan sat, the car keys dangling from the ignition. "Lansing, I think we should talk—"

"I don't," Lansing said from beneath his hat. "I think I should sleep and you should drive. That's what I think."

"But Lansing—" Evan said.

"I don't hear driving," Lansing said, his voice muffled by hat. "Why is that?"

Evan started the car and put it in drive.

"That's better," the hat said.

But Evan couldn't have disagreed more.

His mind raced as the wheels turned over asphalt. Get him to a doctor. It was obvious but useless advice. He couldn't even get Lansing to agree to an interview. What would be involved in getting him to see a doctor? All he could do right now was drive, and so drive is what he did.

Lansing slept without moving, waking at the border only when Evan poked him fiercely. He handed over his passport and received a desultory "Welcome home" from the border guard, then refiled the passport in the hat and slept again, or appeared to. Lansing slept till the Corolla turned into the driveway of the house he would perform at in St. Catharines.

As the car rolled to a stop, Lansing sat up and took his hat off. He ran a hand through his thick hair, making it stand on end. He rubbed his hand over his eyes and yawned hugely. Then he turned to Evan and said, "How's my hair?"

Evan looked at Lansing, whose hair stood up like a rooster's comb. "Well," he said, "it's good. It's a little—it has character."

Lansing flipped down the little passenger-side visor and regarded himself in the mirror, nodding appraisingly. Then he turned to Evan, looking very much like himself again, lucid, present, and in control. "Jesus Christ, son, you were going to let me walk in there looking like this? What kind of tour manager are you fixing to be, exactly?"

Evan felt relief washing over him like cool water. "Just testing you, old timer," he said.

"Don't call me that, you little Christer." Lansing was still eyeing himself in the mirror, and smoothing his hair down. "I swear you'll regret it."

The gig that night was just as Evan had anticipated. Fifty or more adoring fans, crammed into a giant living room, listening reverentially to every word Lansing sang or spoke. Gracious hosts, a hearty meal, a fine paycheque, and two soft beds at the end of it. Lansing was in fine form throughout—flirting with the women, ribbing them, holding them all in the palm of his hand from the start of the evening to the finish.

After the guests had been seen off and the star-struck hosts had been indulged with a nightcap, and then another, Lansing kicked off his boots and rested his hat on the little table between the twin beds he and Evan would sleep in.

"Now that's how you do that," he said. "Fucking Cornwall can bite me. This is what we should be doing every night, boy. I don't know why I ever play anything but house concerts. Those people couldn't give me their money fast enough."

Evan nodded. "It was a good one, alright," he said. "Hey Lansing, I want to ask you something."

"Aw, not now, son," Lansing said. He peeled off his shirt and tossed it on the floor, shimmied out of his jeans and got into bed. "I'm beat. 'Night, now."

Evan lay in the dark and tried to come up with answers. The stress of the road, maybe, the monotony of it all. The anticipation of Winnipeg and the lifetime achievement award, the attendant media circus. Maybe Lansing's discombobulation came with seeing his old friends again—both visits had had moments of tension. Maybe there was shock at the changes time had wrought on Fulton, the once-bustling stomping grounds of a younger Lansing Meadows. Things change, things fall apart. That was probably it, Evan told himself before he fell asleep. He almost believed it, too.

In the morning, Lansing seemed entirely his old self, and Evan could hardly imagine the episode the day before had been real. Evan packed their gear into the Corolla and returned to the front hall to find Lansing, hat and boots on, looking hale and hearty and not at all like a frightened old man. Ann, their host, gripped Evan's forearm warmly. "You must come back and see us again, whenever you are nearby," she said. "What a pleasure to meet you. And you—" she turned to Lansing "I just don't have the words to describe."

"I can think of a few," Evan said, and Lansing swiveled to look at him with mock sternness.

"I'm sure you can, son, but Jesus Christ, not in polite company."

Hearty laughter all around. There was nothing to worry about, Evan thought.

Evan piloted the car onto the QEW and merged smoothly into what felt like rush-hour traffic, though it was ten in the morning.

"So busy," he said. "Where are they all going?"

"Same place you are, boy," Lansing said. "You're not *in* traffic, son, you *are* traffic."

Evan nodded at this. His previous experience of traffic was four cars arriving simultaneously at the four-way stop signs in Petite and no one being quite sure who should go first. Eventually, they'd worked it out with elaborately polite facial expressions and hand signals, but neither of those had helped him at all on this trip. And now he had other skills to help navigate the endless chain of brake lights that stretched out ahead. He was learning to see past rain drops to the road beyond. He could anticipate now, on a busy highway, when the traffic would slow and when he should speed up. He was less fearful. Still, he thought of the country, stretched out in front of him, tried to imagine the expanse of a Manitoba or a Saskatchewan, the hours of endless driving and the way those hours would all fall to him with no respite. He sighed and squirmed, trying to get comfortable.

"What's wrong with you?" Lansing asked.

"Nothing," Evan said. "I need to go for a run, I think. Too much sitting behind the wheel."

"We'll have a couple days in Toronto," Lansing said kindly. "You won't have to drive again till after the weekend."

Emboldened by this display of kindness, Evan said, "How are you doing?"

"Who wants to know?" Lansing said.

Evan looked around the car. "Just me, obviously. Just, you know, a little check-in."

"Why would I be any different than the last time you asked me, over breakfast? I'm fine."

"If you say so," Evan said.

"I'm not going to talk about my goddamn feelings—" Lansing spat the word out like a scrap of rancid fat—"with you, so don't even try."

Evan nodded at this. "I was only trying to be nice," he said.

"Well, don't," Lansing said.

"You're acting like one of my sisters in a snit," Evan said.

Lansing cut his eyes at Evan. "I swear to God, boy."

"I'm just saying," Evan said.

"And I'm just saying don't say anything more about this."

Evan sighed. "It's gonna be a long tour."

"If you're lucky," Lansing said, and he pulled his hat down with finality.

30

Lansing glared out the window from under his hat as the Corolla slipped along the highway, cutting a swath through greening farm fields that soon gave way to Southern Ontario's other plentiful crop: tracts of suburban houses, hulking and ridiculous, squeezed onto lots too small to leave room for much beyond a swing set in the backyard and a tasteful row of evergreens in the front. Of course, you wouldn't want much land to tend, Lansing thought, given the amount of time you'd be spending in your car. And you'd need a house big enough to contain your wide-screen television, not to mention all the giant-sized stuff you'd bulk-buy at the big box stores that anchored each new suburban development. He thought of all the people driving into the city each day in order to afford the gas for the cars that got them there, not to mention the killer mortgages on these big suburban monstrosities they'd return to each night. Once there they'd plate some takeout in their gleaming, state-of-the-art kitchens and collapse in front of those wide-screen televisions that waited like sleek, one-eyed gods in their empty temples.

Lansing remembered when all this was farmland, verdant and rich. When the little towns were like pearls in a necklace, laid out across that farmland, each with its own personality and possibilities. He and Marie had lived in one of those little towns in Southern Ontario, after things had fallen apart for them in Fulton. After the pastoral farm scene turned on them. The seventies had been all about dissolution for Lansing. Matthew and Michelle were the only friends who remained from that period, and even those relationships were fraught now in many ways. The recent visit had proved that to him. But it had been important to see them now, while he was still lucid. Among the many thoughts that dogged him about what was to come was the idea that the people in front of whom he'd been strong would someday see him weak and there'd be nothing he could do about it. He'd be helpless as a baby to hide it or to change it. He scowled. This was the worst kind of cruelty. To be aware of a future in which he would be utterly unaware. All his faculties dismantled. Fuck that.

Where had these episodes of forgetfulness begun? Could he trace it back? He used to drive all the time, had driven between and within every little town in Southern Ontario and beyond, getting himself to gigs and back with aplomb, without even thinking about it. Even sometimes with a couple of drinks in him. Nothing he couldn't handle and nothing he'd ever been caught doing. A few close calls, maybe, but those were due more to inattention than to alcohol.

But perhaps that was the beginning. Moments of inattention. Episodes of forgetfulness. Did one become the other?

One night, driving home from a gig, tired and adrenalized, he'd steered his car full of gear through the unfamiliar streets of some small town, music dogging his thoughts as it always did. Even the voice of his beloved Marie could barely make it through the music in his head most days, and some days it didn't at all. Which is why she was his ex-wife, he knew. He had driven several blocks without noticing them pass by, at first looking for late-night coffee for the drive home, and then just needing to be in motion while a song wrote itself in his head. He was winding through the narrow streets of a residential neighbourhood, and he had just figured out the pre-chorus, when the car came to a halt with a sickening crunch. Lansing's attention snapped back, along with his head, and he was horrified to discover his car had nosed into someone else's. The car was parked and there was no one in sight. Heart beating an uncomfortable rhythm, thoughts of money with wings flying away, and Marie's voice loud and clear lamenting, *Oh Lansing*, a mix of love and exasperation. All of that pushed him out of his car in a panic of limbs.

He inspected the damage. It wasn't terrible, but it was enough that the car's owner would notice. Colonized by panic and dread, Lansing crept back to his own car, re-versed gently. He looked around, but the sound of collision had brought no one to the sidewalk. He put the car in drive and slunk off.

Two hours later he glided to a stop in his driveway and sat in the car, stinking with shame and fear. He should have been paying attention. He should have left a note. The damage wasn't really all that bad—and yet the damage was there and he had caused it. He should have been paying attention.

His own street was quiet, asleep. He thought of Marie, asleep in their bed, tired of waiting for him, her curls tumbled on the pillow where his own head should be. The song in his head had gone quiet. Determined to do better, he put the car in reverse, and then headed back the way he'd come.

The car was gone when he got back, or else he was on the wrong street—that was possible too. The sun was coming up and everything looked different in the light.

And so he turned his wheels for home again, wondering whether he'd tell Marie. He'd never been unable to trust himself before. This new mistrust became a wedge between them till finally she couldn't trust him either.

Not long after that, he'd stopped driving altogether. Bad as it was then, it would be so much worse now. The moments of inattention were getting so long the space between them was beginning to disappear.

He felt bad for the boy, but there was nothing he could do about it, not at this late date. It was better for both of them if he just rode shotgun.

31

Dacey Brown had not come to feel about Toronto the way she felt about Montreal. She was not sure this would be a place in which she could belong. She was used to feeling like an outsider, a rare anglo in francophone Grand Falls. In Toronto, it seemed, everyone was an outsider. The mix of cultures was rich and heady, but there seemed to be fewer opportunities for connection. No one made eye contact at all, unless they wanted something from you. It was never flirtation; it was transactional. They wanted money, or information, or furtive sex. This would be a place to stay if you wanted not to connect at all. But Dacey had been doing that just fine, and what she wanted now was the opposite.

She had experimented with connection on the subway. She'd ridden the Bloor line from west to east and watched the ridership change every few stations. A young woman with a baby on her hip, the baby's hands grabbing at the woman's earrings and necklace. A couple of kids in hoodies and baggy pants, hands deep in their pockets and their headphones on, together but separate. She remembered the intimacy of sharing earphones with Nicholas in high school and knew these kids didn't know what they were missing. She rode alongside small clusters of people, families perhaps, speaking in soft susurrating syllables of unfamiliar languages, neither French nor English. The languages and the look of the speakers seemed to change as the train headed east. Midtown, young men in business suits and loosened ties boarded, voices loud with entitlement, the smell of spirits subtle but noticeable.

As the subway moved east, people fell away till finally the car was almost empty but for Dacey and one tie-loosened man. He sat at one end of the subway car, a few rows away, facing her. He was nice-looking, Dacey thought. Slimly built beneath his suit, his well-cut shirt only a little rumpled. His hair was dark and curly and it fell across his forehead. His face looked friendly.

"Hello," she called, across the subway car. "I'm Dacey."

He nodded at her. "Hello."

"You're not going to tell me your name?"

The man looked away, out the window at the blackness of the tunnel, a spot of red burning in the cheek Dacey could see.

She got up and moved unsteadily, wobbling as the train did, and sat down just a few seats away. He looked at her then.

"What do you want?" he asked. Then, quickly, "I'm not interested."

"I don't want anything," Dacey said. "Just, it was awkward and I thought it would be less so if I introduced myself. But that didn't really work out."

The man looked out the window again, but he smiled a little. At this proximity Dacey could see his eyes were a blue so dark they seemed black.

"It's just," she said, "where I come from, people say hello."

"Well," the man said, turning slightly toward her, "this

isn't there." He seemed to relent. "I'm Eric. Where do you come from?"

Dacey told him that in Grand Falls, everyone says hello, partly out of friendliness, she guessed, and partly out of a desire to catalogue, to know the small-town news. It had kind of driven her mad when she lived there, she told him, but after a few days in Toronto, she missed the Grand Falls way.

Eric laughed and responded with a list of all the things he'd seen on public transit that stoic Torontonians had pretended weren't happening.

"A man playing strip poker," he said, "with himself. So he was naked really fast. There was a woman I used to see all the time when I lived near the lake, who would kind of sweep through the aisle of the Queen streetcar, proclaiming she was the czarina of Russia, and that the Queen car was under her command. That was a good one. Once, on the subway, a man waited till the train was almost at the station, and then ran through the subway car, snatching everyone's hats off their heads as he went. He bolted out the doors when they opened. I lost my favourite tuque that way."

"And people just pretend it's not happening?" Dacey said.

"Listen," Eric said, "I've been on a subway car three times now where someone was actively taking a dump on the floor and everyone else just casually moved to the other end of the car and got out at the next stop to change cars, sometimes without even warning incoming passengers. We're really dedicated."

"To being indifferent?"

"To self-preservation," he said. "The city is right up in your face all the time. There's all kinds of misery on the streets and on the subways. If you don't develop a middle-distance stare and the ability to disengage, to tell yourself, *not my problem*, you'll go nuts. And the next thing you know, you're the one shitting on the subway. So."

Dacey nodded. "That's intense," she said.

Eric laughed. "Absolutely," he said. "But I love this city. This is where things are happening. Everyone comes here eventually." He reached out and tapped Dacey's knee. "Even the Grand Fallsers make it here before too long. And I know how to survive in it. It's probably ruined me for other places." The train slowed, approaching the next stop. "Hey, do you want to go out for a beer?"

Dacey smiled at him. He seemed like a nice guy. "Are you secretly crazy?" she asked.

He raised his eyebrows and looked to the side. "Does it show?"

"I think I will say no to your offer. But thank you. And it was nice talking with you." She stood as the train lurched into the station, and stuck her hand out to him.

"Nice talking with you, also, Dacey. If I'm ever in Grand Falls, I'll look you up."

She grinned. "I probably won't be there. But it's not a bad place to be."

And she whisked out the doors just before they closed. Not a bad first attempt at connection, she thought.

32

The city traffic was worse than the highway. Here there were surprises every block. Parked cars where none had been a metre before, pedestrians, cyclists, and stalled streetcars. There were people in ragged clothes who behaved erratically, and Evan drove slowly, fearful one of them would dart out in front of the Corolla and be crushed beneath its wheels. Guys on expensive-looking bicycles, carrying bulging packs strapped across their bodies rode aggressively, shouting at drivers and pedestrians alike, occasionally thumping a car on the hood for some transgression Evan couldn't parse. At least here he could read the road signs. In Montreal, it had been city traffic just as thick, but all in French.

Lansing was upright, his seat at ninety degrees for the first time since they'd crossed the border into the States. Lansing had his hat pushed back and he was staring out the window. "It's all changed," he said, pointing with a tilt of his head, "except for the parts that are the same."

"I wouldn't know," Evan said, gripping the steering wheel. He was glad his passenger was alert. It would be up to Lansing to direct him through this urban maze. The driving alone required all of Evan's effort and attention. He couldn't spare a single thought for navigation.

But Lansing seemed to know just where they were going, and his navigational notes came with bits of local history and conjecture about the changes he saw now. "This whole area was derelict last time I was here," he said, sweeping his arm to include everything in the view around them. "Boarded-up storefronts, the odd rub-and-tug upstairs."

"Rub and tug?" said Evan.

"Boy, you really don't get out much, do you? Massage parlour, son."

Evan rolled his shoulders. "I do feel a little tense," he said. "Any of those still open?"

Lansing laughed. "Kinda massage parlour your mama wouldn't want you in, boy. Kind where they give you a happy ending."

Evan was quiet, shimmied his shoulders again.

Lansing looked at him beneath lowered brows. "You do know what that means, dontcha boy? A happy ending?"

"I can guess," Evan said quickly. He could feel his face get hot.

"Then drive on, son. Looks like they cleaned those all out of here, anyway."

The chairs were stacked on top of the tables and the bartender was dressed in ripped jeans and a stretched-out T-shirt, opening fridges and assessing her supplies for the night. "Want anything?" Her tone suggested the answer had better be no.

Evan shook his head, but Lansing said, "I wouldn't turn away a draft."

She scowled and drew the beer, pushed it sullenly across the bar. "There's a key here for you," she said, slapping an envelope down after it. "For the apartment upstairs. Let yourself in right next door."

"Well, that's handy," Lansing said. He took the beer and drained half of it, leaving the envelope for Evan. "Why don't you load our stuff in upstairs while I get set up here, boy."

Evan took the envelope gladly and made his way out to the car. It had been washed by the recent rain, but it still looked a little worse for wear. There were streaks of highway dirt and vestiges of road salt on the doors and body. Loaded up with their bags, he unlocked the door next to the club. He climbed a long, narrow staircase to an apartment that was small and sparsely furnished. There were two bedrooms, a rare treat. A little kitchenette with a kettle and toaster, and a fridge for the snacks that remained in their cooler. He'd bring the cooler up from the car, along with his guitar. The apartment would more than do for their two nights in town. A room of his own, and the whole city before him.

33

Dacey Brown had spent the afternoon in a café in the Junction, a scrappy neighbourhood in Toronto's west end, clicking through the photos on her laptop and trying to formulate a plan. Having been turned away twice, she was prepared to give it one more shot. Third time, she thought, might be the charm. Or not. And if not, well, she'd just keep on moving. Out to Alberta and then who knew where.

She felt compelled to be part of Lansing's story, though. He'd been absent from the stage for several years—long enough that some people probably thought he was dead. But the lifetime achievement award and this tour leading up to it, a tour that seemed to be taking him to every town along the Trans-Canada Highway, well, she had been a reporter long enough to know a story when she heard one.

And she couldn't forget the feeling of connection. How, from the first notes of his music she had heard, she felt at home in it, in a way she rarely felt at home anywhere.

Her face went warm as she remembered the graceless way she'd tried to get him to take her along on this tour, and the speed and conviction with which he'd turned her down. Dacey didn't spend much time on regret, but she wholeheartedly regretted that moment, coming as it did so swiftly on the heels of what felt like a moment of connection. He'd beckoned her closer, let her in a little on his true feelings about belonging himself. And then she'd gone and wrecked it by being too intense.

This was the way things often ended for Dacey. Relationships were rocky in the beginning as she struggled to feel what was required or expected of her, struggled to feel anything like the emotion the other person might be feeling. And then she'd turn a corner, she'd *get there*, eventually and wholeheartedly. Too wholeheartedly. It had happened with her high school boyfriend, Nicholas, and every one she'd had since.

She looked to her siblings. They seemed normal. They had friends, they understood social cues, they moved easily through the world. But not Dacey. She ran hot or cold, and never the right one at the right time.

She found her place in photographs, though. In photography she was fluent. The visual language and all its shades of meaning were obvious to her. Unfortunately, that fluency did nothing to smooth her way in the world.

She sighed and drained her coffee cup. Time for one more, and then she'd screw up her courage and walk to the Cat's Pyjamas and give it one last try.

34

Evan lugged the cooler and his guitar up the stairs. He moved quickly, wanting to get into the venue again to make sure sound check was going alright and that Lansing didn't need him for anything. He loped down the narrow wooden stairs, taking them two at a time. Then he lost his footing and the floor dropped away from him. He reached for a railing to steady himself but there was nothing, just smooth plastered walls on either side. And so he fell, sliding down seven or eight stairs, gaining speed as he went till he was expelled out the open door to the sidewalk below.

Like some cartoon character who has come to misfortune, he swooned, his head a riot of pain and ringing, with stars and birds circling. He was surprised to discover he felt a ridiculous need to laugh. He crouched on the sidewalk throbbing in pain and howling with laughter.

It was in this condition that Dacey Brown happened upon him.

Evan sat with his right foot stretched out on a chair in front of him, while Dacey carefully balanced a bag of ice wrapped in a damp bar cloth on his ankle. He was nursing his second-ever glass of bourbon. His first-ever glass he'd shot down without flinching—much—a few minutes earlier.

Several metres away, Lansing Meadows leaned against the bar, muttering darkly. "It's all a plot," he said, shooting a look Evan's way. "He did this on purpose."

The bartender wiped glasses absently and put them away. "No doubt to inconvenience you," she said, sounding bored. "Why else would he bother?"

"Exactly," Lansing said, pointing a finger in the air in triumph. "Exactly my point." The bartender balled up the towel and tossed it in the sink. "Remind me," she said, "why exactly he would do that."

Lansing looked at her to see whether she was mocking him. It was getting harder and harder to tell. But her back was turned, so he pressed on. "Oh, he's been mooning after that girl since Grand Falls. And complaining about doing all the driving. As if I hadn't made the role of tour manager perfectly clear at the time I agreed to take him on. Ridiculous," he said darkly. "Ridiculous," he repeated loudly as Dacey approached.

She squinted at Lansing, then leaned across the bar. "Excuse me," she said, "could I get a glass of water with no ice?" The bartender pointed to a plastic beer jug and a collection of cloudy plastic glasses. Dacey helped herself and said to Lansing, "He's going to be fine, I think."

Lansing grunted.

"Looks like a strain, is all. Probably not even a full sprain. But it'll take a while before he's walking properly. Saw strains all the time when I worked the ski hill in Edmundston the year between high school and university. RICE is what's needed."

Lansing roused at this. "What the hell does he need

rice for? Some kind of airy-fairy New-Age treatment?" he rolled his eyes.

"Oh no, RICE—rest, ice, compression, elevation." She turned to the bartender. "Is there a drugstore around here? He really should have a compression bandage."

"Up the street," the bartender said.

"I'll be right back, Evan," Dacey called. Evan hoisted his half-empty glass in response. "I'll be right back," Dacey said to Lansing, and she was out the door.

"I'll be right back," Lansing mocked, screwing his mouth up and nodding his head grotesquely from side to side. "Got yourself quite the nursemaid, my boy," he called across the room.

"She's not my girlfriend," Evan said, the edges of his words blunted by bourbon.

"Nursemaid, I said," Lansing grouched. "Ah, fuck it." He strode toward Evan. "Think you're pretty smart, I guess, cooking up something like this." He stood in front of Evan glowering down at him. "You're supposed to be working for me, son, paying attention to me."

Evan knocked back the rest of his drink. "Firs' of all," he said. "I didn't fall down on purpose." He carefully replaced his empty glass on the table. "Seconuvall, I am paying 'tention to you right now. I put all the stuff upstairs. I drove us here in the rain and traffic. I drove us everywhere we needa go. I just need a day or two and I'll be fine again." He picked up his glass and held it up to his left eye, inspecting it. "It's empty," he said sadly.

"Get ahold of yourself boy. What are we gonna do?"

Evan looked at Lansing, one eye squinted shut, the other unwavering. "You're gonna play your show tonight and tomorrow night," he said. "If my ankle's not better

Saturday, we're gonna press Dacey Brown to come with us."
Evan held up his hand. "I know what you're gonna say, but
I already asked her. She has her license."

Lansing wiped a hand across his eyes and bumped up
his hat so he could rub his forehead. Then he settled his
hat back down over his eyes, pinched the bridge of his nose
hard between his thumb and forefinger and sighed deeply.

"Alright, I don't have time for this. She followed you
home, I guess you can keep her. But she's paying for all her
own meals and half the gas."

"Fine," Dacey said. Lansing started at the sound of her
voice. She held out a Tensor bandage to Evan. "Here, put
this on." She held out a package of chocolate-covered ginger
to Lansing. "This is for you," she said. "Your favourite."

Lansing frowned. "What are you, a witch?"

"Just a really good researcher," Dacey said. "Do you
need help with that?" she said to Evan, who had extracted
the bandage from its wrapping and was looking at the
metal clips that came with it in confusion. She took it
from his hands, moved the melting ice pack to the side
and wrapped his swollen ankle tightly. She stood and
brushed her hands together. "Alright," she said brightly.
"We've got a show to put on."

The Cat's Pyjamas was a supper club, and by far the nicest
venue Lansing had played on this tour. Every seat was occupied, every white-tablecloth-covered table crowded with
people, the air soft with the gentle clacking of cutlery on
plates, of a couple hundred people raising drinks to their
lips, murmuring to each other between songs.

Lansing played that night with an intensity Evan had
never seen. Even through the fog of his whiskey hangover

and the dull throb of his ankle, not to mention the complicated feelings stirred by the sudden presence of Dacey Brown, Evan could feel the energy steaming off the stage. Lansing played his instrument hard one moment, cradled it the next. His voice rang and growled, climbed and fell, and through it all his eyes flashed from the stage. Anger, Evan thought, or something else. Whatever, Lansing was alive in a way he hadn't yet seen.

Dacey sat beside him, bristling with energy of her own. Her eyes were large and shiny, reflecting the spotlight she gazed into. Her straight chestnut hair across her face was a glossy curtain that fell and parted, fell and parted. She tucked a hank behind her ear, but moments later it would start its inevitable slide, drawn back toward the center of her heart-shaped, open face. She watched the stage, rapt, and would occasionally turn to him, her face an exclamation point, big eyes bigger, eyebrows raised, smile beaming. He knew the feeling.

35

There was a new world order in the Toyota Corolla. Despite Dacey's ministrations, Evan's ankle remained puffed-up and painful. The swelling meant he couldn't point his toes, so pressing a gas pedal was out of the question. And sitting with his foot on the floor for any length of time hurt enough to make him long for whiskey. And so he was installed in the car's back seat, stretched out across the bench with his foot propped on Dacey's knapsack. In the front seat, Lansing muttered under his breath. Dacey was relaxed, her hands loose on the steering wheel.

Evan could see her forehead in the rearview mirror and wished, too late, he'd thought to orient himself the other way so he could see the side of her face, at least, as she drove. Instead, he had an unobstructed view of Lansing. Same one he'd had from the driver's seat, pretty much.

Lansing was grousing about not being able to tip his seat back.

"What's stopping you?" Evan said.

"Your precious ankle."

Evan rolled his eyes. "Doesn't bother me," he said. "Plenty of room back here."

"I wouldn't want to intrude on your sick bay."

Dacey flicked a glance over her shoulder. "Don't be ridiculous," she said brightly, like an efficient teacher in a class full of slow youngsters. "You've got all kinds of room. You two should get comfortable. I'll have us in Parry Sound in no time." She turned her attention to the road again, navigating through dense city traffic with ease, it seemed to Evan.

Lansing waggled his head side to side and Evan could see his lips moving in exaggerated mocking. But he tipped his hat down and his seat back and soon enough he was asleep.

Dacey clicked the radio on and fiddled with the knob till she found a station that promised hits of the fifties, sixties, seventies, eighties, nineties, and beyond. She straightened up in her seat till she caught Evan's eye in the rear-view. "Well, that's pretty much all of them, then," she said. Evan wished he had something funny or smart to say back, but his throat was suffused with a knot of warmth and all he could do was grin and nod like an idiot. She said, "You go ahead and get some sleep too. I've got this."

For all he'd longed for weeks to hear someone say those words, he believed he'd never sleep. The car was a perfect capsule of privacy. With Lansing conked out between them and the rest of the world at bay beyond their windows, it was just him and Dacey. His heart pounded at the thought, and he felt a corresponding throb in his ankle. But he was tongue-tied around her, and anyway, she was her own perfect capsule of privacy. She'd dealt with him, issued the directive for sleep, and moved on. He knew the feeling exactly, of open road and possibility, when the sun was shining and the radio offered every hit song from the entirety of rock and roll.

His dream of camaraderie with Lansing and whatever else with Dacey was a dream dissolving, if not already dissolved. Evan could see that now. That wanting something wasn't enough to make it so. And also, that possibly the promises sold by every one of those hit songs issuing tinnily from the Toyota's stereo were built on some impossible lie of brotherhood or perfect romance. It was all mythology, and he'd spent his whole life thinking it was true. He sank back into his seat.

He did sleep, he must have, for the sound of voices brought him back to the surface and for a terrible moment he jumped, guilty and horrified, thinking he had been driving and had fallen asleep. But he was safely in the back seat, free to sleep or wake, or to wake and pretend to sleep, which is what he did.

"Have *you* ever been in a fist fight?" Lansing was asking Dacey.

"Once," Dacey said slowly, "and it wasn't much of a fight, really. One shot and the guy went down. Don't know if that means he had a glass jaw or I happened to hit him just right or what. And I'm not sure who was more surprised, him or me."

"Him," Lansing said with confidence. "I'm gonna go out on a limb and say he was definitely more surprised." He looked at Dacey and seemed to see her for the first time. "What happened?"

"It was at Grand Falls Days one year. I was maybe fifteen." She turned to Lansing. "You know Grand Falls Days?"

"Not intimately," Lansing said. "Where I grew up it was the Windsor Junction Jamboree. Beauty contest, a pie-off, a coupla crummy local bands, the town warden in the drunk tank—"

Dacey Brown smirked. "Yeah, but you don't know it intimately."

Lansing doffed his hat. "So you were saying," he said.

"Yes, right," Dacey said. "Grand Falls Days, final concert. April Wine was headlining."

"Big deal for them," Lansing said.

"Big deal for Grand Falls, definitely," Dacey said. "Must have been everyone in town at the fairgrounds. Which was a baseball diamond most of the time. This girl Kinnie and I had waited all day in the sun to see the bands. She had a crush on the bass player from Out and About, this band from Edmundston we totally thought was the shit. But all these other people started crowding in around us, jostling and pushing."

"It really was a big deal for Grand Falls," Lansing said.

"You've been to Grand Falls," Dacey said. "Nothing happens there. And all these people had come in from God knows where, so instead of seeing the same couple hundred people we'd seen all our lives, suddenly there were all these strangers too."

"Heady stuff for a couple teenaged girls," Lansing said.

"Yes," Dacey said. "Up to a point."

"This must be the part with the fist fight," Lansing said, his voice warm and eager. In the backseat Evan opened one eye, suspicious of the vibe evolving between the driver and her passenger.

"Kinnie and I found ourselves in the thick of this mob scene and before we knew it we could barely see the stage at all. A crowd like that gets a mind of its own. We were getting pushed and moved and carried further away from the prime spots we'd staked out. I had my camera, because I was taking pictures for the *Examiner*, and it was, like, my prize possession. And of course Kinnie was trying to catch this bass player's eye. And then one of those waves went through the crowd, there was this ripple, and this sketchy older guy we didn't know bashed into us hands first." Dacey took her hands off the wheel and held them out in front of herself, as if copping a feel of the space between her body and the dashboard. "You know what I mean," she said to Lansing, who nodded gravely.

"Well, he got a good squeeze on Kinnie with one hand and the other was headed my way and I thought he was gonna grab my camera."

"You wouldn't have minded a grab of what was under your camera?" Lansing asked.

"It's par for the course," Dacey said. "But the camera, you know, was practically brand new."

"Right, of course," Lansing said, laughing. "So?"

"So all I remember is the sight of my own puny white fist rising out of the crowd and connecting with the guy's jaw. Pow." She paused, smiled. "Dropped him."

"Dropped him, eh?" Lansing said. Evan tried to place the emotion in his voice. Pride? Admiration? Evan had never heard it directed his way, that much was certain.

"Sucker went down," Dacey said, "and he did not get up again." She nodded and gazed into the middle distance, remembering. Trees and trucks flashed by in silence for several moments.

"I mean," she said. "I assume he did eventually, but I grabbed Kinnie's hand and we ran."

"So you missed the show entirely," Lansing said, totally caught up in the tale.

"Not so fast," Dacey said. "We plowed almost headlong into the sound guy for Out and About, who was a friend of Kinnie's older brother. He took us backstage. I got amazing photos, we saw the show, Kinnie got to hang with the bass player." Dacey smiled and drummed her fingers on the steering wheel. Then she turned her heart-shaped face toward Lansing and beamed. "Best Grand Falls Days ever," she said, and Evan could see the teenager she'd been.

Lansing grinned back. She was irresistible, Evan thought. Of course Lansing grinned. Evan closed his eyes again and ached.

36

When Evan awoke again he perceived a shift in pitch and momentum. A ramping-down of speed, individual rotations of wheel on road becoming discernible. He blinked, waiting to remember where he was. The back seat of his own car, and it was coming to a stop.

In the front seat, Lansing's hat was low. The radio was on, playing a Steely Dan tune, and Dacey Brown was singing along.

"The werewolf goes, the fine coat running, make tonight a wonderful thing, say it again," she sang.

Evan smiled so hard he gritted his teeth. He felt a heart-squeezing affection for her, for this moment, for himself, as vulnerable as he'd ever been, and Dacey blithely stepping in, making everything better. He wanted to be in this moment alongside her, not separate and apart.

He shifted, careful to make some noise. "'Hey Nineteen.' Great song," he said.

She lifted her eyes to see him in the rear-view. "What is this song about, anyhow? I could never figure it out. What does a werewolf have to do with Aretha Franklin?"

"I think it's about an older guy having a relationship

with a much younger woman," Evan said, sidestepping the question.

"But how does the werewolf figure in?"

Evan looked at her eyes in the mirror, so guileless and brown, pools he could swim in. He shrugged.

Lansing's voice was muffled, his chin tucked down toward his chest.

"Tequila," he said, referencing the lyrics Dacey had mistaken. "Cuervo Gold. And cocaine. That part's about debauchery."

Dacey seemed to think about this a moment, then sudden understanding illuminated her open face. She laughed, a free shout of hilarity. She pulled the car to a stop at last, at a one-pump gas station nestled in the trees. "Cuervo Gold," she said. "Coke. Oh my God." Her delight was infectious.

"Did you really think it was about a werewolf all this time?" Evan asked.

"I don't know what I thought," Dacey gasped between shouts of laughter. Her eyes were dancing and the silk curtains of her hair slid across her forehead, obscuring her face till she brushed them back. Evan laughed too, eagerly in the moment with her.

"Is anyone going to pump the gas?" Lansing asked. "Not that I want to interrupt you two."

Evan said, "You could do it. Your leg's not broken."

"Neither is yours," Lansing said pointedly, but he wrenched the door open and got out, slamming it behind him.

"You shouldn't let him talk to you like that," Dacey said, catching Evan's eye in the mirror.

"It's okay," Evan said quickly. "He's probably just tired." He twisted to look at Lansing, who was working the gas pump with one hand and caressing an unlit cigarette with the other, letting it roll through his fingers. "Don't worry about him. He'll settle down."

Lansing slapped the gas tank door closed and, barely throwing them a glance, rubbed his fingers together in a way that connoted money. He stalked off to lean against the gas station wall where he lit his cigarette.

"I guess that's my cue," Dacey said. She slid out of the front seat, all fluid grace. She made her way to the building, raising a hand in greeting to Lansing, though he barely acknowledged her. Evan felt his stomach tighten. Lansing lit a second cigarette with the end of the first and began to pace, his face broody, his shoulders set. Dacey emerged from the gas station with a bottle of juice and a packet of beef jerky. She jammed the jerky in her back pocket and approached Lansing. Evan watched with trepidation.

After a brief exchange, Lansing pulled out a pack of smokes and shook one out for her. She took it with slender fingers and Lansing leaned down to light it for her, his hat and the lighter's glow making an intimate tableau.

Evan's heart jumped in his throat and he swallowed a taste like ashes. He stared intently as the two conversed, at first casually and then with increasing animation. At last Lansing shook his head and pulled his hat down, turned and stalked back to the car. He pulled the door open with enough force to rattle Evan's teeth, and sank heavily into the front seat. "That woman will be the death of me," he blazed.

"Dacey?" Evan said. "If anything is going to be the death of you, I'd think it would be chain-smoking."

But Lansing wasn't listening. "She's intransigent. All I want from that woman is a little compassion. I said, Michelle, I'll ask you once more, lay out those cards for me. Why won't you look once more into an old man's future?

She's a cold woman, that one."

Evan's stomach shrank. "Lansing, that's not Michelle," he said quietly, but Lansing scowled and sank further into himself. Outside the window, Dacey had ground her cigarette out and was shaking the bottle of juice as she made her way back to the car. She slid into the front seat, as serene as ever. She turned the bottle of juice upside down and spanked its bottom, then righted it and popped the cap off easily. She leaned forward to retrieve the jerky from her pocket and held it up. "Anyone hungry?" she said. Lansing glowered silently out the window. Evan reached for the packet and brushed her fingertips with his in what he hoped was a comforting and knowing way. She met his eyes in the rear-view and he did his best to send her a message. Her own gaze burned for several beats till she broke the connection, tipped her head back, and drained the juice bottle. One eye squinted closed for a moment and her whole face seemed to pucker, and then she was back.

"All ready?" she said. "We should be there in about ninety minutes."

Lansing grunted.

"Don't hog that jerky," Dacey said. "You'll spoil your dinner." She held a hand out and Evan obediently passed it to her. She put the car in drive with a surprisingly forceful jerk, turned the radio up loud enough that conversation would be impossible, and pulled away from the gas station with a lurch that threatened to spill Evan to the car's floor.

37

Evan Cornfield longed to run. He imagined the wind parting his hair as he parted the air. The feeling of blood charging through him, the sensation of every molecule at attention and alive. The hard work of uphill, the reward of down. Feet and breath and purpose united. He drew in a lungful of air. He wanted the sweet seaside air of his adolescence, but was met instead with a load of stale motel air, the faint taste of cigarette smoke, a whiff of spilled beer, and an after-note of despair.

He lay on the shiny polyester bedspread with his ankle propped up on his guitar case. It felt strange not to be with Lansing, preparing for the night's show. Dacey had been firm, installing Evan in the motel room with strict instructions about taking the night off.

But he found he could not relax. He remembered the chummy way Dacey and Lansing had talked in the car, the way Lansing seemed to awaken to Dacey's charms. Evan's blood percolated a little at the thought of them together, of smooth, practiced Lansing finding out all Dacey Brown's secrets before Evan even had a chance to try.

And then there was the more troubling behaviour Lansing had shown lately. The episode in the car when he'd railed at Matthew. And that afternoon, when he'd mistaken Dacey for Michelle. Evan thought again of Matthew's parting words to Lansing, about letting his friends take care of him. He thought again of Matthew's offer of help any time. And Crouse had said to get Lansing to a doctor.

But there, too, was Lansing's determination. The big award show was a week away. There were only a handful of shows to play before they'd be in Winnipeg, with a day off on either side. And there was the crowning jewel of this recognition Lansing seemed to be so keyed up about. Maybe it was just nerves, Evan thought. He tried to imagine what Lansing might be feeling as he prepared to finally be recognized for his contribution to Canadian music history. And Dacey Brown joining their little gang—that change seemed to have rattled Lansing, too. It would probably all even out in a few days, he thought. Because on stage, with a guitar in his hands and a crowd at his feet, Lansing Meadows was golden. It seemed to Evan that Lansing got better every night.

He shifted on the bed, kicked the melting ice pack off his swollen ankle with the other foot. He flexed and pointed. Pain both ways, and he still couldn't walk on it with ease. And the rest of him, he feared, was beginning to atrophy. A couple of weeks in the car, and now these motionless days. He imagined again the wind in his hair, his long stride smooth and unbroken, his legs taking bites of landscape, pushing him forward with his blood beating in his ears. He stuck out his ankle and turned it in a circle. He winced. It would be some time before he'd be running again.

Lansing had made him tour manager. It was up to him to make a decision. He could see that Lansing's work wasn't finished—and Lansing himself had said it a number of times. *I'm not done yet.* No, Evan wouldn't be calling a doctor. And he wouldn't be calling Matthew either. He would do what he had to for Lansing, to make sure Lansing Meadows got everything he had coming to him.

Evan would stop short, though, of giving him Dacey Brown. He sat up and dragged the guitar case closer, undid the clasps and drew out his instrument. He'd had dreams, forever, it seemed, of performing alongside Lansing Meadows, his hero. Evan strummed. But there he was in a room in the second-cheapest motel in Parry Sound with a bum ankle and an out-of-tune guitar while Lansing was across town no doubt charming the pants off Dacey Brown.

Not literally, Evan thought. Please, God, not literally. He twirled the tuning knobs and listened to the sounds the strings made, bringing them back into tune. "Can't think about that," he said aloud. "Nothing to be gained in thinking about that."

He held the guitar across his lap. His fingers soon found a melody and he lost himself in the playing. He thought about the old house in Petite Riviere, loading up the wood stove and blowing long and steady on the embers till the satisfying moment of full ignition. He thought about the river itself, wide and graceful and forever on the move. He'd spent days watching it and wondering where it would take him, if he were to cast his fortunes in with it. The sea, he guessed. And he'd been there before. Instead he'd cast his fortunes in with Lansing Meadows's, and he had to admit he had no idea where this highway was taking him. He could see the places on the map, read about the gigs in the tour bible. But it wasn't about geography, this trip. How much better it was, he thought, to be rolling on this asphalt river, to be on this adventure. How much better, even despite the setbacks of twisted ankle, ornery employer, and dream-girl who was both within his reach and just beyond it.

As for Dacey Brown, he knew he needed a plan. The palms of his hands itched when he thought about her, and he felt like all his blood had been replaced by ginger ale. She was friendly, brisk, and efficient, though he could see she burned as he did for motion and momentum.

For all that she was easy in herself, she kept herself apart. Her face was open, but her gaze could be unfocused, one minute with you, the next in the middle distance. Her camera was never far from hand and in quiet moments, or in times of great activity, she'd raise it to her face and stay behind it, her finger working always, capturing and collecting. Later he'd see her bent over her laptop, clicking through the photos she'd taken, till the world in pictures was the one in which she lived. A world unto herself, a perfect capsule of self-sufficiency.

Evan wanted to step inside that world. But he didn't know the way in. The only conduit that had ever served him to enter anything was song. In music he was most himself.

He bent low over his guitar now and let his fingers find a melody and bring it to light. He played for a while, his mouth hanging open, listening to the tune unfold, and aching. It hurt his chest, this music. He felt a tingle of tightness in his jaw. The tune was dark and mournful. It broke his feelings wide open and he tipped his head back to get away from it for a moment.

But you couldn't back away, not if the song was really what you wanted. You had to go right up to it, press yourself against it. And so he put everything he had into it. His longing to be like Lansing. His fear about the future. His desire for Dacey Brown. The way he both missed and didn't miss

Petite Riviere. He was a young man on a lumpy bed in the second-cheapest motel in Parry Sound and he was breaking his own heart on purpose.

38

Dacey sat in the back row of the theatre in Parry Sound, her feet up on the seat in front of her, rolling one of Lansing's cigarettes along her thigh, back and forth, while she thought. Lansing Meadows could try the patience of a saint, and she was certainly no saint. She didn't mind his gruffness with her, but it was clear Evan Cornfield deserved better.

Lansing was on stage, tuning his guitar, his hat pulled down against the house lights. The hat itself was a disgrace, Dacey thought, grubby and well thumbed. He used it against people. Against Evan, mostly. She wanted badly, she realized at once, to figure Lansing out. He had a gift, obviously, but equally obviously he was acting like a dick.

She wondered at the impulse that had made her urge Lansing to take her along in the first place, the impulse that had pushed her along after them. The way he'd leaned forward during their interview, the way he'd said *this'll be my last tour*. Dacey was accustomed to missing out—to staying behind while everyone else moved on. There'd been an intimacy. An invitation. A challenge, maybe. It said, *pay attention. Don't miss this. Connect.* Already she felt herself a comrade. The conversations in the car—she felt at ease in a way she'd rarely experienced. More at home among these two virtual strangers than she'd been among her own family.

On stage, Lansing strummed his guitar fully twice and stepped toward the microphone. He raised his face till it was bathed in the lights and Dacey thought she could see a glimpse of a younger man, a man who had nothing but possibility before him. There was a trace of a smile on his face and a look of pleased surprise in his eyes.

"Alright," he said, his voice amplified in the empty theatre. "Guitar sounds alright. Let's see what we can do about this voice."

He nodded toward the back of the room and Dacey twisted to see the sound man nod back at him. Lansing took a half-step back from the microphone and breathed visibly, his chest lifting with the inhale, his nostrils flaring slightly. He leaned his head back and opened his mouth and sang. It was a song as pure and sweet as Dacey had ever heard. He accompanied himself on the guitar sparely, a finger-picked melody both calming and haunting, with words about the sorrows of the past and about his guarded hope for the future. It was short, it rose and fell in a matter of minutes, and at the end the theatre was silent. Of course it was, Dacey thought, there was no one in it but herself and Lansing and the sound man. But the spell had been complete, and it was all she could do not to leap to her feet and stamp and applaud wildly and whistle for more. She could see how someone like Lansing could be allowed and excused his bad behaviour. How there might easily be a different standard of conduct for such a one as he. How someone like Evan could leap to his defense even while reeling from his cruelty. Dacey didn't like it, but she could see it.

In the green room, Lansing was pacing furiously when she arrived, devouring the length of the room with a few long strides, then turning and retracing. When Dacey broached the door, Lansing halted mid-stride, his head snapped up, his face expectant at first, then crestfallen when he recognized her.

"You were expecting someone else?" she asked. She held up the cigarette. "Thought you might light this for me."

"Where's the boy?" Lansing said, pacing again.

"Evan, you mean?" Dacey said.

Lansing rolled his eyes. "Yeah. Obviously."

"He has a name," Dacey said. "That's all. And at the gas station you were ranting about someone named Matthew."

At this, Lansing turned to Dacey, who arranged her features in a semblance of cool innocence.

"Did I now," he said softly. He seemed to consider this possibility with sadness. "I must have been confused."

Dacey nodded. "That can happen, I suppose."

Lansing narrowed his eyes at her. "What do you know about that?" he said.

"I know a little," Dacey said. "My grandmother was prone to confusion, and after she died, my Granddad often said he wished he had her ability to forget."

"A terrible thing to wish for," Lansing said with feeling. "No one should ever wish for that."

"He had a lot of sorrow," Dacey said.

"Don't we all," said Lansing.

"Not all of us," Dacey said, "not like that, in any case. But I guess we all deal with what we've got in our own way." She looked at him hard.

Lansing nodded, the corners of his mouth tugged downward. "That's right," he said.

Dacey took a step into the room. "What I've got right now are two vouchers for dinner, and a cigarette that needs lighting. You coming?"

"The boy gonna meet us there?" he said, shrugging into his coat.

"Evan's taking the night off, Lansing. What's the matter, you don't want to have dinner with me?"

"A night off," Lansing said. "From what?"

"Don't you worry about Evan Cornfield," Dacey said, threading her arm through his. "Tonight you're all mine. The soundman says there are two diners worth checking out in town. He says The Stem has the best burger and that the hot turkey sandwiches are to die for at The Vic. What's your pleasure?"

Lansing seemed to puff his chest out a little when Dacey took his arm. His sadness slipped away and he was once again the strutting bantam. "Lady's choice," he said, and he patted her hand where it lay in the crook of his elbow. "Lead the way, lovey."

39

Evan caught a glimpse of himself in the mirror. His eyes were wild with writing and his hair stood out in uneven tufts where he'd been pulling at it. He'd eaten all the ripple chips in the snack bag and had gotten up to see about another beer and something more substantial.

The song was almost finished, he thought, and it felt like a good one. He couldn't always tell right away but in this case the melody he'd written was unmistakably a winner and the lyrics that presented themselves astonished him. He couldn't say for sure where they'd come from. The road, maybe. Endless long drives with nothing to do but imagine. Freedom from the workaday world of Alley Oop, the inscrutable expectations Colleen had for him, the more pedestrian but no-less-limiting expectations his parents had.

He hopped to the bar fridge and stooped to peer inside it. There wasn't much left. A few baby carrots turning white in a ripped plastic pouch. A skiff of hummus. A triangle of cheese wrapped in foil.

He limped along the side of the motel to the office. Inside, a skinny red-haired girl was watching hockey with the sound down and texting without looking at her phone.

She barely looked up when Evan banged through the door.

"There a diner nearby?" he asked when he finally got her attention.

"Huh?" she said.

"Is there a diner around here?" he gestured to his bandaged ankle.

"I'll call you a cab," she said and picked up the phone.

The streets were wet with rain. "Worse than home," he said, looking out the window of the taxi, "all this rain."

"Spring," the cabbie grunted. The car rolled to a stop in front of a well-lit diner, its neon sign reflected on the rain-shiny pavement. Evan leaned forward, digging in his pocket for change.

He was tired of being alone, and the lights in the diner beckoned him. He could see that there were just a few tables occupied. Old men with coffee cups stared at nothing. A woman tried to convince a child to take a bite of something. And Dacey Brown and Lansing Meadows sat, heads together in close conversation, at a counter that ran the length of the open kitchen.

Evan's heart leapt to see his friends, so unused was he lately to being on his own for any length of time. He had his hand on the door to the diner, but what he saw next made him pull it back as if it had been burnt. Dacey had her hand on Lansing's arm and was squeezing. She threw back her head, her silky brown hair a tsunami, her heart-shaped face open and laughing and Lansing Meadows, that old double-crossing dog. Lansing Meadows seemed to look right at him with a face that said *mine, all mine*.

Evan turned away from the door, tears already gathering. "Taxi," he gasped, as he hopped back to the curb. He wrenched the door open and fell once more into the back seat.

"No good?" the cabbie asked.

"My girl," he said, "my best friend." The words were funny in his mouth. Neither description was true, but he wanted both to be.

"Okay, pal," the cabbie said. "The other diner?"

Evan nodded dumbly and the cab pulled away from the curb, delivering him a couple blocks later to the second diner.

"Good luck, buddy," the cabbie said, waving off Evan's proffered handful of money.

"Yeah," Evan said miserably. He pulled himself out of the cab and turned to limp into the restaurant. His ankle throbbed. His appetite was all but gone. And after a promising start, spring had stalled again. It was cold and wet. Pathetic fallacy, they had called it in English class. It was exactly right, he thought.

And then he heard her laugh and it was too late, there was nowhere to go on this wet street.

"Evan Cornfield," she said, pulling her arm from Lansing's and reaching for Evan. "You're supposed to be hanging out with yourself." She squeezed his arm and smiled merrily, turning to Lansing, "Look who's here."

"I am hanging out with myself," Evan said coolly. "I'm going to get some supper."

"Second-best diner in town," she said, gesturing toward it.

"Out of a field of two," Lansing said, drawing even with them.

"We ate at the other one, down the street," Dacey said.

"The best diner in town," Lansing said.

"Out of a field of two," Dacey said, and she laughed like music, her eyes dancing along. "You didn't hop all the way here," she said to Evan, a mixture of concern and admonition.

"No," he said. "I took a taxi. Look, I'm hungry," he lied. "And you've gotta get to the theatre, so."

"No, no," Dacey said. "Lansing doesn't need me once I get him back to the venue. You get your supper and I'll come get you in thirty minutes and run you back to the motel, okay?" She didn't wait for an answer. "Alright, gotta get this one on stage now." And she tugged Lansing's hand and they continued on their way. Evan grimly hobbled to the diner's door, feeling too sick to eat anything.

He hunched over the table, alone at a booth for two. His ankle was pulsing. He scowled into his coffee. He thought about going home, just leaving Lansing and Dacey and pointing the Corolla back east. But to what would he be returning and to what end? He'd be someone who'd gone away and done nothing, and come home with nothing to show for it. Worse, he'd come home to nothing. Lou would have given away his job. No way Colleen would want anything to do with him. And so then what? Not much to do in Petite. Move to Halifax and start again, he guessed, and try hard not to be the guy who tells lame stories about the time he'd spent on the road with Lansing Meadows, like it was something to brag about, some kind of claim to fame.

The server brought the coffee pot and filled his cup. Evan barely looked up. "Just a minute more for that cheeseburger platter," she said.

"Thanks," Evan muttered. He pulled his little notebook and a pen from his pocket and sat staring ahead, waiting to know what he wanted to write. He didn't have the words yet, just the feelings of longing and disappointment. He could feel it coming the way you got tight in the throat when tears were coming, a haze of what was to come. Before it could coalesce, the bells above the door jingled and Dacey Brown strolled in.

"Fancy meeting you here," she said cheerfully.

Evan capped his pen and slid the notebook off the table protectively.

"Oh," she said, "I didn't mean to interrupt you. I might be a little early. You know how Lansing gets before a show. I had to get out of there."

As a matter of fact, Evan did know how Lansing got before a show. He knew it much better than Dacey did, that much was certain. Christ, what a mess. He swallowed it down as best he could, gestured to the seat across from him.

"Not at all," he said, "you're not interrupting. If anything, I felt like I was interrupting earlier."

"Did you eat yet? I think I want a milkshake."

"You know," Evan said, "on the street. You and Lansing."

Dacey looked at him blankly. He held her gaze a beat or two, then flicked his eyes to the open kitchen where a cook with an unlit cigarette between his teeth was sliding a cheeseburger into a bun and onto a plate piled high with fries.

"Me and Lansing on the street," Dacey repeated.

"Forget it," Evan said, as the server delivered his cheeseburger platter. "You know what, I'm in a weird mood. I'm not as hungry as I thought I was. Maybe I can get this to go instead." The server started to lift the plate again.

"No," said Dacey, "I'll help you eat some of those. I think we should stay here." She put a hand on the woman's arm. "Could we get some vinegar? And a chocolate milkshake?"

"I don't know," Evan was saying, but Dacey was on a roll.

"You think there's something going on with me and Lansing."

"I don't know," Evan said. "Yes, kind of."

Dacey took a french fry off his plate, put it to her lips, then set it back down. "What if there is?" she asked. "What's it to you?"

Evan scraped relish off his burger as if it were his life's work, trying to look nonchalant about what he was hearing. "Nothing," he said, feigning earnestness. "Just, you know, it changes the dynamic. You know, Lansing and I have been travelling and we kind of have a groove, you know, and then you come along—"

Dacey picked up the french fry again and this time bit into it. She chewed and bit again. "Oh my God," she said. The server brought the vinegar. "Thank you," Dacey said. "Oh my God, you're jealous." She picked up the vinegar cruet. "Vinegar?" she said. She didn't wait for an answer before she sprinkled it over the fries, then added salt. She tasted the finished product.

"Eat your burger," she said, "it'll get cold."

"I'm not jealous," Evan said, "and you're not my mother."

"Whatever," Dacey said. "Look, it doesn't matter to me. I don't care. I was just trying to give you a night off from the old bastard. But if that's not what you want, no problem. Don't worry, I'm not trying to eat your lunch." She grasped a handful of fries and transferred them to her mouth.

Evan looked at her pointedly, her hand as it moved from his plate to her mouth. "Despite evidence to the contrary," he said and smiled at her in spite of himself.

Dacey laughed her musical lilt and wiped the back of her hand across her mouth.

"God," she said, "yes. Ha! That wasn't exactly the right expression to use. I am eating your dinner. Where is that milkshake? You can have half."

It was late and Evan was asleep when Lansing lurched into their shared motel room. Evan stirred and came to the surface briefly. He thought he heard a muffled feminine giggle, but when he turned over, there was just Lansing alone, silhouetted in the light thrown by the clock radio, shaking off his cowboy boots one at a time before falling otherwise fully clothed onto the bed. Within moments he was snoring and Evan Cornfield turned again and found his own way back to sleep.

40

Lansing's dreams had always outrun his reality, but even so, he thought, he hadn't done too badly, when all was said and done.

Not much had been expected of him by anyone in Windsor Junction. Even his own mother had modest hopes for her only child. But Lansing himself had dreamt early and large. He dreamt of untold riches, though had to be content, even in his salad days, with just a few extravagant nights. One of the most memorable was with Marie in New York City. They ordered both the shrimp and the scampi, just to be sure, once and for all, what the difference was between them. The salad days hadn't lasted long. He had enough, but only just, most years. "On My Honour" had made plenty of money since he'd written it three decades earlier, just most of it didn't end up in his pocket.

He'd dreamt of fame, of his name on the lips of great leaders and beautiful lovers alike. That hadn't quite worked out either. Lovers, he'd had a few, and about as many regrets, but the latter lingered while the former tended not to. As for leaders, he'd yet to even be named to the Order of Nova Scotia, and what were they waiting for? To make it a posthumous honour? They wouldn't have much longer to wait, he reckoned. Perhaps he'd have to be content with this lifetime achievement award, though whenever he thought of it, he got squirrelly. Some stupid ceremony and a big speech, and everyone content to think his day was done, that would be Lansing Meadows, sorted and on the shelf. Fuck that.

And women, oh, he'd dreamt of women. Still did. His Marie, wherever she was. He remembered Marie when she was happy, those curls bouncing. She loved the hayloft at their place in Fulton, she'd lie in there for hours, reading, and emerge with bits of straw stuck in her hair. "Doesn't it itch?" Lansing would ask, tenderly pulling straw from her hair. "Not if the book's good enough," she'd say. And her laugh, good God, her laugh.

A half-dozen other women haunted him still. Michelle was only the most recent to break his heart.

He'd had glory days, he surely had. Days in upstate New York, engaged in serious camaraderie and hard work and *sweat equity* they called it, building something for the future with Matthew and that crowd. But that had fallen apart for Lansing, or else he'd dismantled it. More likely the latter. But Matthew was still living that dream of self-sustaining peace. And Lansing Meadows, soon to be honoured by his peers with a lifetime achievement award, drifted in such reverie as he could on a sagging mattress in the second-best motel in some Podunk Ontario town while one bed over, a callow, jealous youth pretended to be asleep. Where were his glory days now?

He'd had rivals in the game. Lloyd Crane, he thought again of Lloyd. Lloyd had had dreams too. He knew it. They'd talked of little else those childhood years and even as they grew to musical maturity. Lloyd had hitchhiked alongside Lansing to Toronto when they were still teens, but the stage had never set Lloyd on fire the way it had Lansing. Lloyd became too fond of creature comforts and his indulgent wife, ultimately, to venture too far from home. No sagging mattress, no callow companion for Lloyd. Lloyd was a coward, Lansing knew, unwilling to take the risk, to step off the edge of the known world and stretch his arms out in the hopes the wind would lift him.

Lansing lit a cigarette. Damn the rules. He lay on the bed and smoked it gently till a slender column of ash replaced the paper tube entirely. Thing was, Lloyd Crane was happy. And Lansing? Lansing was alone for all intents and purposes, alone in the world and in the moment, with a guitar, two virtual strangers, and a past he could barely remember.

Dacey Brown could see that, in some way, these relationships—with Lansing, with Evan, with Lansing and Evan—were like the dream she'd had in that dry winter landscape. Drive one car forward twenty metres, run back for the other and drive it to catch up. The first, the next, over and over. It was the slowest kind of progress she could imagine. She had a strong sense that a car on the Trans-Canada highway heading west was a place she could belong. It wasn't a place she'd been born into, like Grand Falls. Or a place she fell into, like Montreal. It was a place she'd chosen, decided on, pursued. The connections were there, she thought, two ends almost touching. A spark going back and forth between those ends, perhaps.

She had started looking to her photographs for answers and information, clicking endlessly through slide shows she made on her laptop, slide shows organized by the colour of the objects the photos showed, or by their shapes, or by whether they showed motion or stasis.

She sat on the double bed in her motel room, limbs tucked in as if it were a raft and she were at sea, and in a way she knew she was. The days that had led her to this suspiciously damp motel room, where even the carpet expressed humidity, were days that blurred together behind her, though stasis was their defining feature. A jumble of mismatched clothes discarded on the floor, shoes that pinched and never got worn-in, half-read novels she just hadn't been able to find a way into, a cellphone without signal. Flotsam and jetsam. Her little house in her little town, the job she'd never wanted and rarely excelled at, the friends who'd moved or fallen away. Her family, transplanted wholesale, but for her.

What did it amount to, the kilometres she'd crossed, the decision she'd made to hit the road, the jumble of life behind her, that job, her house. Even Lansing and Evan. The things she saw when she pressed a camera to her face, the way it let her see what was right there in front of her, yet obscured always by her own—Daceyness. She was too fast always, or else too slow to see what was really going on. Her shutter speed was jammed one way or the other at exactly the opposite of what it should be for maximum clarity. She reached for her camera now, her movements careful as if a sudden jerk might startle it and dispel the power it had to bring order to her thoughts. What did her thoughts amount to after all? She raised the camera to her eye and gently swung her head, surveying the room patiently, waiting for it all to become clear.

41

Dacey Brown was getting it done. The long drives made her feel better; chasing change all down the highway was invigorating. And she liked being with Lansing and Evan. She felt like she was part of something in their company, and it was clear they needed her. That gave her energy focus, and that was good. Sometimes she couldn't see the forest of the world for the trees of her own mind. It was good for her to be needed.

She hadn't felt herself needed much; there weren't very many people who brought it out in her. She wasn't partial to babies. She hadn't really looked after her own little brother, and she had chosen summer jobs like shooting photos for the *Examiner* or lifeguarding at the local pool over babysitting the kids in her neighbourhood. But during university in Sackville she'd worked at a vegetarian restaurant, and though mothering the customers got old in a hurry—some were picky to the point of bringing their own special bread and requesting that she make them a sandwich on it—one of her co-workers caught her attention on their very first day together.

Tara Lea Jones was a work-in-progress, a tough angel

in eye makeup and combat boots who smoked endless cigarettes while she waited for everything to become clear. Dacey had recognized an instant affinity, though Tara Lea was almost ten years older and spoke of her past only enough to give Dacey the impression it had lacked the middle-class comfort and banality of Dacey's own. What Tara Lea and Dacey had in common was a willingness to look for cosmic hints, to read coincidences as proof that the universe was taking care of things.

"Surround yourself with white light," Tara Lea would urge Dacey when times were tough. And when Tara Lea herself was feeling particularly broke or lovelorn, she'd say, "I'm just trying to attract what I need. I've put it out there to the universe and I'm trying to draw it toward me."

Back then, Dacey was chronically broke, a nineteen-year-old know-nothing from Grand Falls. She'd never seen an avocado nor had fresh squeezed orange juice till Tara Lea introduced her to both one eye-opening brunch. Dacey always had money on her mind—specifically her lack of it—but she didn't notice that focus doing much to draw more toward her. Or did her paycheque and the tips she earned at the restaurant count? Was that the universe providing, or just Dacey's own sweat, patience, and aching feet? She couldn't tell.

For all of Tara Lea's sophisticated knowledge of the arcane—she'd read Dacey's Tarot cards, pulling out the oversized Rider-Waite deck whenever Dacey expressed a moment's confusion or indecision—and despite the difference in their ages, Dacey felt a strong compulsion to take care of Tara Lea, who was forever late getting to work, having become engrossed in the study of maps of energy channels or Bach flower remedies or some similar. Tara

Lea would fast, drinking only a vile mixture of cayenne, ginger, maple syrup, and hot water, and she'd flake out on her tables at the restaurant. Dacey would willingly step in to cover for her. And when the universe didn't serve up an extra helping of money in times of need, Dacey would help Tara Lea get by till payday, once by giving her a couch to sleep on for a month when Tara Lea got booted out of her apartment for not paying her rent.

There was something about the way Tara Lea moved through the world. As if her actions had no consequences, and as if the universe would indeed provide for her. And Dacey had to admit that thanks to people like herself, it must have seemed very much to Tara Lea that the universe was always providing.

Dacey thought now, as the endless tableau of rocks and trees threaded past, that if wanting something could make it so, Lansing Meadows would have much more than he did. There was, in fact, one point of contact, one connection Lansing wanted more than just about anything else, and Dacey had agreed to help. Dacey knew it wasn't going to be easy to find the person Lansing wanted. Anyone could disappear if they were motivated enough. Even with the Internet and her small-town-newspaper-reporter skills, if Lansing's daughter wanted to stay hidden, she would.

Dacey had lived through this kind of thing before, and she knew how it ended. She thought of her Gran, the last days of her life a whirl of wrong names and hot tears, and then at last the oblivion that was cruel to everyone but her grandmother. Dacey remembered those days, the way memories and abilities had slipped away, one by one at first, and then in faster succession till her Gran's slight decline became a free fall. Gran had lost some of her vocabulary first, *whatchamacallit* becoming her most-used noun, until she even used it in place of people's names. Gran had regularly mistaken Sam for their father, and Lily for their mother, and when Gran's sister died, Dacey remembered having to explain, every time she visited, that Aunt Bette had passed on, and every time, Gran burst into tears as if she'd just heard the news. Because, Dacey thought now, every time, she had. Dacey would have done anything to help bring peace to her Gran's heart before the storm took over and took her away. Perhaps here, with Lansing, was a second chance to do that.

The steady thrum of highway under wheels had become a kind of music to her ears. It hadn't taken her long—was it three days on the road, maybe four?—to feel at one with the moving vehicle and to crave that forward motion. The inhalations and exhalations of her companions were part of that thrum, only occasionally breaking free and rising above the white noise. A ragged snore from Lansing, a surprised *oh!* from Evan in the midst of some dream, or a more perturbed sound if the car jolted his ankle and raised him out of sleep.

At the moment, her passengers were quiet. Their warmth and breath fogged the windows and Dacey fiddled with the various dials and knobs of the dashboard to try to keep the windshield clear. She twisted the one dial, and the car emitted a high-pitched drone. The steam along the bottom of the windshield quickly disappeared, sucked into some invisible vacuum.

She became aware that she was hungry when she caught a whiff of curry simmering. She glanced in the rear-view mirror to discover Evan awake, clutching a copy of *Rolling*

Stone with Bob Dylan on the cover.

"Smell that?" Evan said.

Dacey nodded. "I do, yes. Unusual?"

"I'd say," said Evan. He put aside the magazine, carefully dog-earing his place. He inhaled deeply. "What is that?"

"Curry," Dacey said. "Well, not curry, but smells like."

Evan nodded. "Where's it coming from?"

Dacey gestured to the dashboard.

"Well, that's not good," he said.

"No."

He leaned forward, sucked in a breath when he put pressure on his ankle. "No engine light on?"

Dacey shook her head. "Just the smell. I turned on the defogger and it whined a bit and then the smell."

Evan sat back. He was equally at sea with girls and machines. "It's probably nothing," he said.

"You think?" Dacey said.

Evan shrugged.

"What's for lunch?" Lansing asked, coming suddenly awake. "Smells great."

"I'm pulling over," Dacey said, the road stretched out empty before them and behind. She signaled to no one and guided the car to a stop on the shoulder. "There's no lunch, Lansing."

"The smell's coming from the car," Evan said.

Lansing breathed deeply in, holding the breath in his lungs and then slowly letting it out. "It's probably fine," he said at last. "But I am starving. We should get some lunch."

42

"Where are we supposed to be next?" Lansing asked. They were in the restaurant of a motel in Wawa, waiting for the local garage to fix the Corolla. He pulled a cigarette from an almost-empty pack and tapped it three times on the table.

"You can't smoke in here," Dacey and Evan said in unison. A glance between them. Dacey smiled. Evan looked away and then down to his open notebook. He picked up his pen and pretended to study it.

"I'm not smoking," Lansing said.

"Thunder Bay," Evan said, "two days from now, and Winnipeg after that. We could cancel Thunder Bay—though my sister lives there, and if she finds out I came all this way and didn't stop to say hello there'll be hell to pay—but we can't cancel Winnipeg."

"So we have a bit of time," Lansing said.

"But only a bit," Evan said. "We don't have a plane."

"We barely have a car at this point," Dacey said.

Evan looked at Lansing steadily. "My foot is feeling better. I think I'll be able to drive again soon."

"Great," Lansing said, putting the cigarette in his mouth. "About time you stopped malingering, give poor Dacey a break."

"Yes," Evan said, "or if Dacey wants to get on her way she can, and I can take over from here." The words hung over their little group and for a moment Evan wished he had tested them inside his head before saying them aloud. But now that they were out and he could see the effect they were having—Dacey looked as if she'd been punched in the gut, which was exactly how he'd felt when he'd seen her and Lansing looking so cozy—he felt their power as a positive and decided to let them stand.

Lansing raised his eyebrows. "Don't be ridiculous, boy. We're all in this together, and we'll wait it out together."

"*You and I* are in it together," Evan said.

Dacey pushed back her chair and it made a skittering sound against the linoleum floor. "I'll be right back," she muttered, and she scurried away toward the restroom.

Lansing put the cigarette in his mouth and leaned forward.

"You can't—" Evan said.

"Goddamn it, boy, don't you think I know that? In fact, don't you think I know more than you about just about everything?"

"You seem pretty sure of it," Evan said.

"Any idea why that might be?" Lansing asked, the cigarette stowed in the corner of his mouth.

"Because you're Lansing Meadows," Evan said quietly in an exhale of frustrated breath.

Lansing laughed, a bark of genuine glee. "It's okay, son, you can say what you really think. It's because I'm a pompous windbag, sure." He took the cigarette from his mouth and tapped it on the table, filter, end, filter, end. "But I also have a lot of years under this hat, a lot of miles in these boots. From long before you were born, back when we still called them miles. So don't worry about sassing me. I don't give a good goddamn what you say to or about me. I may be losing my mind, but I have not yet lost my wits."

At this Evan looked up and Lansing continued.

"Much as it pains me to admit it, boy, I need your help. And I need Dacey's too."

Evan narrowed his eyes. "What do you need her for?"

Lansing sneered. "It's none of your damn business what I need her for, son. All you need to know is that I cannot do this alone, so if you have any love in your heart for old Lansing Meadows, listen to me well. I can see that you and Dacey Brown are in some kind of trouble with each other. I don't know what kind, but I guarantee you, whatever it is, I've been in it before too, three or four times in my life." He leaned back. "It passes son, don't you get that? It all passes."

He took his hat off and passed his hands over his hair as if trying to soothe it. He put the hat back on and patted it gently, then reached across the table and tapped his finger hard in front of Evan. The cigarette was back in his mouth. "You can worry it all you like, it won't change. Feel fucked up about it, go ahead. Doesn't matter, son. It passes. Whether you're ready or not. Whether you do it right or not. Whether you're wrong or not."

Evan tapped his pen against his teeth. "So then, what? he said. "What's the point if it passes and it doesn't matter what I do?"

Lansing laughed again. "It matters what you do, of course it does. It's your life and it's piling up all around you. I'm just saying you can choose to be happy is all." He nodded his head toward the restroom door, and Evan's gaze followed, to see Dacey emerging, her eyes bright and her hair mussed as if she'd splashed water on her face. "Choose not to be a dick."

"Is that what you did, Lansing?" Evan said, swiveling his head back to look at him.

"No," Lansing said, standing. "That's not what I did. And this is how it's gone for me. Stranded in Wawa of all places, trying to convince you not to fuck up the way I did. This is what it's led to: a short list of people I can count on. Myself, most days, and maybe—or maybe not—you." He looked at Evan, who looked down at the table.

"So let me know how that goes for you." He had the cigarette lit before the restaurant door swung shut behind him.

"Where's he going?" Dacey asked, a note of fear in her voice.

"Don't worry about him," Evan said.

"Actually, Evan, I am kind of worried about him," Dacey said.

"He doesn't need your help," Evan said. He was a stew of confusion, unable to take in what Lansing had said and now confronted with Dacey Brown. When he looked at her, he saw her open face tipped back, laughing, her silky hair cascading freely down her back. He heard her silver laugh, he saw her hand on Lansing's arm. "He's fine."

"He needs somebody's help," Dacey said. "A doctor." She pulled out a chair and sank into it. "Evan, he's not well. Surely you can see that?"

She's trying to drive a wedge, Evan thought. He shook his head. "He's fine," he repeated. "We have to keep on going. He wants to keep going."

Dacey reached her hand across the table, but Evan pulled his arms back and crossed them on his chest. "We owe it to him to help him, Evan."

"And that's what I'm trying to do," Evan said. "How does

it help him to stop the tour? How does it help him to see some doctor who could prevent him from getting to Winnipeg and getting that award? *That's* what he needs, Dacey. He's tired, that's all."

"But Evan, he's forgetful. He called me Michelle the other day. He referred to you as Matthew. It's not normal, it's not okay." Dacey looked like she might cry. Her eyes were glistening and her open face was turning pink.

Evan closed his eyes for a moment. He thought back on the weeks he'd spent alongside Lansing Meadows. They felt like years, in the best possible way. The communication that had begun when Evan was a kid had only deepened since the fateful night they'd met in Petite Riviere. What had been the simple admiration of a fan had evolved into something much more complex. Lansing's struggle—for acknowledgement, for acclaim, for approval, and esteem—had become Evan's struggle. The rest of the dates on the tour, Evan thought, didn't matter. But come hell or high water, he would get Lansing Meadows to the stage of the theatre in Winnipeg to receive the adulation that was his due.

He closed his notebook and put his pen down. "I'm the tour manager," he said. "What I say, goes. We'll be in Winnipeg in a matter of days. We're not stopping now." He stood up. "If you don't like that, you are free to go any time."

Dacey started to speak and then stopped. She shook her head once. "I can't," she said, and her voice quavered. "I can't be part of this, and watch him fall apart."

Evan shrugged. "You don't even know him."

Dacey stood up now too. "Maybe neither do you," she said.

They stared at each other for a beat. Dacey's eyes were luminous and Evan felt the intimacy of the moment, a strange and backward experience of intimacy. This was everything he wanted in reverse, and the intensity of that realization swept over him and he almost wavered. But then he thought of Lansing, rising above the indignity of a thousand terrible gigs, keeping his eye on the prize that was always just out of reach. "I think you should go," he said quietly. And when Dacey Brown did, he felt he'd never be the same again.

43

Lansing began to see that making it all the way across the country was a fantasy. His big idea that somehow he could wrap it all up with one last show of bravado. That he could give them all something to remember him by. His critics, his fans, his friends and family even, or what was left of that rarified group.

He was shocked, in some ways, that it had come to this. Him an old man, let's be honest about it, he thought, still folding his weary bones into a different strange bed every night, still chasing after the spotlight. And all that stood between him and the end of the line was a kid who, Lansing feared, was in over his head.

He touched the packet of letters in his shirt pocket and felt their comforting bulk. My God, he thought, the mistakes I've made could fill a book. He thought of the neatly lettered fortunes he carried among those letters, and how he wished now he could rely on some kind of directive from anywhere else. It wasn't just his bones that were weary. It was exhausting lately to be Lansing Meadows.

But Lansing Meadows he was. And there was nothing to be done about that.

He needed a plan, something concrete he could turn to when the wind blew in earnest between his ears the way it had started to do. He sat on the bed in the motel room and made a list, chewing a pencil end till he tasted wood in his mouth, wondering if this lifelong chewing habit had in some way led him to this place, introduced insidious poison that was steadily running down his clock. He shook his head, stuck out his tongue and plucked a fleck of paint off of it. The list read:

Lloyd Crane telephone
Matthew
Michelle?

He folded it into tighter and tinier squares and put it in the sound hole of his guitar. He would go as far as he could. He would go all the way if he could.

Evan sank back down onto the chrome-and-vinyl chair after Dacey disappeared through the restaurant's front door. He breathed in the enormity of what had happened. He felt like he'd watched his heart walk out the door and now he sat without that vital organ, a shell of a man. He corrected himself: a boy. Lansing had called that one exactly right, for weeks now. Evan Cornfield was a boy. He had never felt it more keenly. And yet it had never felt more important that he be a man. He knew that what Dacey had said made sense. But he had to believe that Lansing could hang on, that they could get to Winnipeg and make it through the ceremony, and then there would be time to get Lansing whatever he needed, whatever he wanted. And if Lansing couldn't hang on? No point thinking about that.

In the short term, he'd set himself up for another lecture. He was going to have to tell Lansing that they were parting ways with Dacey. And so he would have to listen to Lansing berate him—but he would tune it out, he decided. Lansing was maddening, and Dacey wasn't much better. How had it happened, exactly, that he was in this lousy motel in Wawa half-in-love with Dacey Brown and half-in-love with Lansing Meadows and wholly unable to sort himself out?

He was nothing but longing. And it seemed very possible that was all he'd ever be. Longing for who and what he didn't have, who and what he had no idea how to be.

Dacey Brown let the door of the restaurant fall closed behind her. She stood outside for a long moment, in a town spring had barely touched. It was cold, but Dacey was colder. Evan was making a mistake, a big one, she was convinced of that. But maybe he was right about one thing. Maybe she didn't know Lansing Meadows at all. Here, perhaps, was another example of her tendency toward inappropriate intensity and the way it couldn't help but undo her in the end.

She reached reflexively for her camera. It was jumbled in her shoulder bag and she rooted blindly till she put her hand on it. She exhaled. Before she could let herself disengage completely, there was someone she had to see.

She walked down the length of the motel making note of tableaux and angles she might like to come back and shoot later. It made her feel calm to think of photos she would take. And calm was necessary. She was in the middle of nowhere and her resources were few. She stopped at Room 17 and knocked on the door.

"Lansing," she said. "It's me, Dacey. Can I come in?"

The door swung open. "Well now," he said. "This can't

be good."

Dacey ducked her head, her brown hair swinging. "Can I come in?" she said again. Lansing stepped back and swept his arm, ushering her into the room.

"What's going on, lovey?" he asked. He leaned against the room's low chest of drawers, his arms crossed against his chest, his hat pushed back.

Dacey squeezed her eyes shut and pressed her lips together till they reddened. She shook her head. "I've got to go," she said. "I think it'd be best if I get on my way." She opened her eyes and looked at him with trepidation. "I'm sorry," she said.

Lansing looked at her with warmth. "You should do what you have to do, lovey. But I gotta ask, are you sure this is what you have to do?"

Dacey thought about her desire to be part of something larger than herself, to find a place where she belonged. She once thought she'd found that place, but then she remembered Evan's intransigence, the way his eyes blazed at her. She didn't have the skill to navigate connections that didn't come easily. She smiled sadly at Lansing and nodded.

He stepped toward her, put his hands on her shoulders. "You'll be alright, lovey," he said, his voice a road strewn with gravel. "You remind me of my girl. She's about your age. A good girl, like you."

Dacey almost broke down then, her knees swayed, but she steadied herself. "I can still help you look," Dacey said. "If I find her—"

Lansing shook his head. "Don't you worry about that no more," he said. "You need to worry about your own self."

"Still," Dacey said. "I know where to send her if I find her."

"Don't you worry about that now," Lansing said again.

"You take care of Dacey Brown."

"I'll be watching for you, Lansing Meadows," she said.

"I know you will, lovey. I know you will."

She put a steadying hand once more on her camera and then she said, "Okay."

And Lansing said, "Alright."

Dacey said, "I'd better go."

And Lansing nodded.

She rose on her tiptoes and brushed his old cheek with her lips, and then she slipped out of his arms and out the door.

44

Evan limped along the streets of Wawa—the main one and the other one—barely stable in his sneakers on the town's old crust of snow. Past the middle of April. Wherever spring was, it wasn't here. His ankle was complaining about the protracted exertion, but after all Evan had said it was feeling better, and now he had to prove it. He was struck by the pure idiocy of all that he'd undertaken, starting with the vain idea that somehow he and Lansing Meadows would forge some unbreakable road-bond, that they would become peers and more than that, friends.

Things were complicated and Evan was simple. He'd been the kind of kid who thought dogs were boys and cats were girls. Who thought good eyesight was something you grew into. Who was fooled every time by his sisters' taunts that his epidermis was showing—and that he should be ashamed. He was ashamed now, of his own ignorance. Once things were explained to him, he got them right away. But it seemed there was no end of the things that needed to be explained to him. A lifetime of that should have produced some skepticism, but it never had. He remained credulous. Embarrassingly so.

And then there was Dacey Brown, into whose arms he'd almost literally fallen and who was so tantalizingly close and yet so entirely far away. At this moment perhaps also literally. Because of him. Because he couldn't for one minute stop being a jealous baby. All longing and all misery both.

When his own storm clouds cleared he tried to think about what was best for Lansing. Lansing had said he needed Dacey. And so he'd set out to try to find her, to apologize, to bring her back.

There was a diner in town. There was a bus stop and a bookstore and a movie theatre with one screen. The diner was empty and the box office wasn't set to open for a half-hour. Evan tried to steady himself, inside and out. If he couldn't find Dacey. If the car were not repairable, if he actually couldn't drive after all. He had to find Dacey and apologize, make some kind of deal with her to get her back.

His ankle throbbed, unused to so much work and such uneven terrain. At the end of town he saw a squat brick building with the lights still burning. The Wawa Public Library. He pushed open the door.

The library was almost empty save for a couple of women shelving books from a cart and a couple of old men in overcoats, one drowsing and one holding an old issue of *Life* magazine upside down. Evan made his way further into the library and stopped when he heard a familiar voice.

"How far back do these go?" Lansing Meadows had his hat in his hand and was using it to gesture at a shelf of thin phone books.

"We keep them for five years," the woman standing with him said, "though they don't change much from year to year."

"Thanks," Lansing said. "Mind if I pull them all?"

"Sure," the woman said. "I'll help you." She drew three of

the phone books from the shelf and handed them to Lansing, then pulled the remaining two and carried them to a table. "Now, what are you looking for?"

What indeed, Evan wondered. He'd tucked himself into the stacks where the magazines were archived. He could peer through the shelves at Lansing and his stack of Wawa and District telephone directories.

"Carrie or Caroline Meadows," Lansing said quietly. "Though she might be going by Carolyn O'Ray or Carrie O'Ray." He flipped through one of the books. "Of course, she could have a different last name altogether."

"That's the trouble with women," the librarian said.

Lansing looked at her a long moment. "Lady, you don't know the half of it."

The librarian blushed and bent to the directory in front of her. "Nothing here for any of those names," she said. "Are you quite sure she lives or lived in Wawa?"

Lansing let the pages of the phone book sift through his fingers like sand. His face was long and craggy, his eyes more guarded than Evan had ever seen them.

"Honestly," he said, "I'm not sure of much. But nothing would surprise me." He stared straight ahead and Evan blanched, sure he'd been spotted. "But I check wherever I go," Lansing said, "just in case."

The librarian closed another phone book gently and added it to the pile by Lansing's hat. "I'm afraid there's nothing in any of these," she said. "And the name doesn't ring a bell." She stood. "Anything else I can do for you?" she asked kindly.

Lansing sat for a moment more and then, as if a switch had been thrown, he said, "do you have anything on Lansing Meadows?"

"The folksinger?" the librarian said. "I think there's something in the latest issue of one of the music magazines. *Penguin Eggs*, I think? In the latest issue or maybe the one before. Our music magazines are just through here—" she waited for Lansing to rise.

Evan didn't, though. He scurried deeper into the stacks, then retraced his steps to leave the library, chasing a glance at Lansing bent over a story about himself in the magazine. Lansing's face was creased in confusion or dismay. Evan didn't stick around to find out which.

45

Dacey Brown was as alone as she'd ever been. With a heavy heart she'd taken her things from the Motel 6 they'd all checked into together, and moved them to the older, dumpier Wawa Motor Inn near the highway. With her camera in hand and no plan in mind, she locked her little motel room and set out into the streets of Wawa.

She felt there was no fixing it now, that continuing to shadow Evan and Lansing in the hopes of reconnecting was a zero-sum game. She knew no one in northern Ontario. There were twenty-five hundred kilometres between herself and her family, she'd looked it up. She walked to the bus station in town and inquired about a ticket. There was a bus leaving for Calgary at two in the morning. It would only cost a couple hundred dollars, but it was a two-day bus ride and she thought back to the pent-up feeling she'd had on the bus between Grand Falls and Montreal and knew she'd never make it. She pocketed a paper schedule in case she changed her mind and pressed on.

There was a car rental place nearby and she stopped in to inquire. She could rent a car and drive it one-way to Calgary—"I could put you in a Toyota Corolla—" the man behind the counter said, but it would cost just about every cent she had left.

She needed to think. Just off the main street there was a little tavern. She pushed open its door.

The smell of a million cigarettes hung in the air, though it had been illegal to smoke inside for as long as Dacey could remember. Maybe the air retained the particles, hazing the light from the cold beer sign, making a dusty halo around the VLTs. Inside, it was just like Grand Falls. Two old guys and a young guy, all three in foam-and-mesh ball caps. A woman behind the bar with dyed blonde hair and eyeliner that looked tattooed on, the ring of dark blue around each eye as if it had been drawn on with a ballpoint pen, a little dogleg under one eye where perhaps the tattooist had lost her steady hand. The woman's body was shaped like a box, and she had dressed it in a blue-and-green flouncy top that did nothing to hide that boxiness. Her ass was non-existent. Her jeans were tight. Her laugh was harsh and Dacey Brown felt instantly at home.

"What can I get you, hon?" the woman said.

Dacey tucked her hair behind her ear. Immediately it came untucked. She smiled, but before she could answer, the call was taken up by the older-looking of the two guys. "What can I get you, hon?" he cackled.

His companion roared with laughter, a direct hit that mocked both women at once.

"Frig off," the bartender said, and flicked her bar towel in their direction. "Frig right off, the both of you." She rolled her eyes elaborately. "Don't you mind them," she said to Dacey. "Pair of idiots. Useless as tits on a bull."

They snickered at her language and again she flicked the towel. Dacey smiled gamely. "A rum and Coke?" she said.

The woman nodded.

Dacey turned to choose a table in the otherwise empty bar, but the young man stuck his arm out and blocked her path. "I apologize for my acquaintances," he said. Again snickering from the older two. "I hope you won't judge all Wawaites by their conduct."

Dacey raised an eyebrow. "Okay," she said. She made again to move, to choose a table.

"Sit here," the young man said, pulling out a bar stool and sweeping his arm grandly in its direction.

"Oh," said Dacey, "no thanks."

He didn't let her pass. His jaw flickered, or maybe Dacey had imagined it. "Come on," he said, "let me show you we're not all like that."

"I don't think you're all like anything," Dacey said, "but—"

"Then come sit," the young man said. "I'm just trying to be friendly." He put a hand on her arm. "What's the harm in acting friendly?"

And Dacey didn't have an answer for that, or at least not one she could articulate. So she held on to her camera and mounted the stool he offered.

46

Evan sat propped on his pillows on one of the motel room's single beds. He adjusted the ice pack on his ankle. After a day spent peg-legging around Wawa, he regretted from yet another angle his harsh words to Dacey and their effect. It was ridiculous, the way it was falling apart. He had the tour bible out, open on his lap. If the car was ready, if he could drive, if nothing else went wrong. These seemed like insurmountable ifs.

Lansing was on the other bed, remote control in hand, watching a nature show in which a honey badger and a deadly snake were battling it out. "See this?" Lansing said, gesturing to the TV with the remote control. "This is crazy."

"Yeah," Evan said absently. "Lansing, why did you fire your tour manager?"

"That honey badger doesn't give a shit about anything," Lansing crowed. "Never seen anything like it."

"Lansing," Evan said. "Answer my question. Why did you fire your tour manager?"

"Oh, son," Lansing said. "Really? You want to get into that?"

Evan nodded. "Really, Lansing. I really do."

Lansing clicked off the TV and tossed the remote onto the night table between their beds.

"We had a disagreement about the tour and how it should go," Lansing said.

Evan waited but nothing more was forthcoming. "And what was the substance of that disagreement?"

Lansing sighed. "This is old news, boy. No need to rehash this."

"It's new news to me," Evan said.

"It was a pretty fundamental disagreement," Lansing said.

"In that?" Evan prodded.

"In that he thought I shouldn't do the tour. He thought Lansing Meadows was too old to travel this country one last time by car, playing every little shit-ass town that would have him. He thought that, in my condition, I would just be asking for trouble. Thought I'd be throwing away an opportunity to go out on a high note if I didn't just fly to Winnipeg, accept their stupid award, and gracefully bow out."

"Your condition?" Evan said.

"But see, this is where he don't know me, really. First of all, I don't intend to go out at all. Where there's life, there's hope, boy, and where there's Lansing Meadows, there's a tough old son of a gun who doesn't give a shit about anything. Like that goddamn honey badger. Bring me your poisonous snakes, boy. I will fight those fuckers with my bare hands and win."

"You're not tired though? I mean, don't you sort of wish you'd taken his advice?" Evan thought of the scene in the library, Lansing's evocation of Matthew, of Michelle, of past wrongs.

"Of course I'm tired, boy. Don't be ridiculous. But this is what I do, son, don't you see that? This is who I am. I didn't do this, what would I do? Rot away somewhere reminiscing with myself about my glory days? As long as I've got words I'll write them and as long as I've got breath I'll sing them, boy. And long as I've got sense, I'll get up on stage more nights than not, and I will leave not a dry pair of panties in the house. Don't forget that. This is what I am here to do. And I intend to do it till they take me off stage feet-first."

There was no mistaking the vigour, Evan thought. Maybe he'd been seeing it all wrong. Maybe this was just life on the road. You just accept a certain amount of crazy behaviour because that's what it takes to get the job done. He looked across the valley between their beds. His hero was lit up from inside.

"You with me, boy?" Lansing's face was ablaze.

What could he say but yes?

47

Dacey Brown had miscalculated. There *was* harm in acting friendly, if friendly wasn't what you really were. She'd had a rum and Coke and then another. The young guy—whose name, it turned out, was Tyler—had been persistent, asking her questions about herself. Where she was from, how she'd ended up in Wawa, where she was staying. What her plans were. The story felt long and complicated even to Dacey, and she glossed over its details. There were more drinks. Time melted away inside the tavern. With no windows and no clock it was perpetual evening, though there had still been daylight when Dacey pulled the door open to enter.

Now she was tired, and she'd batted Tyler's hand off her knee so many times the motion began to feel meaningless. Its effect, at least, was utterly meaningless, as each time she batted it off, the hand found its way back in a matter of minutes.

"Leave her alone now, Tyler," the boxy bartender said, flicking her bar towel at him. "Poor thing is falling asleep."

"Better take her home," one of the older men said, and Tyler said, "Good idea."

He guided Dacey off her bar stool. "Come on now, girl,"

he said, and Dacey let herself be led.

"My camera," she said urgently, feeling for the bag that held it.

Tyler dangled it. "I've got it here," he said. "Nothing for you to worry about." His voice was soothing, but it made the older men laugh, and Dacey wasn't sure why.

Tyler's hand on the small of her back was insistent, and so they were soon out the door.

He steered her along the streets of Wawa till Dacey recognized the light of the Motor Inn. "My place," she said, and pointed.

"Let's not call it a night just yet," Tyler said, and guided her away from the motel's door.

"I wanna go home," she said, and started to pull away from him. He had her camera still, and she didn't like that at all. She reached out a hand to grab the bag. "Gimme," she said.

He held it up just above her reach. "Nuh-uh," he said. "Not yet."

"Come on," she said. "Give it back. I need my camera. I need to go home."

He dangled it so she could almost reach it, then snatched it back out of reach again. He held it over the space between them like mistletoe.

"I'll give it back," he said, "if you give me something first."

"I don't have anything else," Dacey said dumbly. "Everything's in that bag."

Tyler closed the space between them in an instant and Dacey could smell liquor and feel his breath hot on her face. "Not everything," he said. "Not what I want."

He dropped the bag on the ground beside them and put his arms around her. Dacey wanted to scream, but she wanted her camera more. Tyler pushed his face in close to hers and she felt his hands on her back, trying to get under her layers.

She brought her knee up hard into his groin, and when he dropped to the ground she grabbed her bag with its precious camera and she ran. She palmed the motel room key out of her pocket as she ran and the sound of her own breath almost drowned the angry shouts coming from Tyler behind her. She fitted the key in the lock and slammed the door shut after her, throwing all the locks on it into place. She left the lights off, finding her way to the bathroom in the dark, patting the air in front of her with both hands. With the bathroom door shut tight and locked, she ran the water as hot as she could stand it, and got beneath the shower's spray. She stood there a long time, letting the water beat her down.

48

It was going to be another day before the car would be ready. The part had to travel down from Thunder Bay. "Couldn't I just travel up to it?" Evan asked, but the mechanic sucked his teeth balefully. "I'm going there anyway, is all," Evan said, but the mechanic shook his head.

"Not a good idea," he said.

"It seemed like a good idea to me," Lansing said consolingly in the motel diner, a space they'd come to think of as their own. "Bastards don't even know what's wrong with it really, so what's the big deal? What's it to them?"

Evan sighed and swirled his coffee around so it sloshed dangerously against the sides of his cup. "The price of the repair, I imagine," he said.

Lansing smiled and tapped the side of his nose. "You're learning, son."

The BlackBerry buzzed on the table where it lay. "This goddamn thing," Evan muttered, peering at it. He rolled his eyes. "What can I tell this guy at the *Globe*, Lansing?"

"Tell him to fuck himself," Lansing said cheerfully. He picked a french fry off Evan's plate.

"Already did that," Evan said, "in not so many words. He

is undaunted. What's the big deal? Just say yes, and he'll stop hounding you."

Lansing tipped his head back and laughed loudly. "That's a good one," he said. "Ha, stop hounding me, oh boy, you've no idea what you're talking about. You say yes to one of them, and the hounding's just begun. They want to know everything, boy, and they'll stop at nothing. What you had for breakfast, the duration and timing of your last orgasm, what side you dress on."

"It's not a tabloid," Evan said. "It's the *Globe and Mail*."

"All that means is that they'll dig a little deeper, son. After he's done with me, he'll talk to Matthew and God help us, Michelle— he'll even talk to Caroline if he can find her." At this he fell abruptly silent. He pressed a finger to his mouth, then snapped his fingers for the bill. "Well," he said.

"He's already talked to Matthew," Evan said. "Who's Caroline?"

"None of your beeswax, son. Are you going to eat that sandwich or am I?" He reached for it, but Evan picked it up first. He chewed steadily and stared at Lansing.

"Cut it out, boy," Lansing said. "Tell him fine, yes, he's worn me down. Tell him he can have one hour of my time in Winnipeg, if we ever make it there. Tell him not to push for more. And tell him to show up with a bottle of rye whisky."

Evan raised an eyebrow as he lifted the BlackBerry and began to type.

"Might as well get something out of it to ease my pain," Lansing said. "God, I can't wait to get the fuck out of Wawa."

49

Dacey Brown woke with a mouth like the desert and a mind that was already racing. She'd slept with all her belongings in the bed alongside her. The knapsack that held her clothes she'd placed between herself and the edge of the bed, and covered it with the blanket so it would look like a sleeping figure to anyone who might see.

Of course, there was little chance anyone would get in the room to see, as Dacey had pulled the room's table in front of the double-locked door, and stacked its two wooden chairs on top.

It seemed only a little ridiculous in the light of day. But the fear that had pushed her the night before was replaced this morning by the deep need to make a plan. She moved the knapsack aside and planted her feet on the floor. Good first step, she thought. No shower this morning. Her skin still felt raw from the night before. She dumped the contents of the knapsack out on the bed. After almost two weeks on the road she had nothing to wear that passed for clean anymore. So, that would be a good next step, she thought. A laundromat. And then what? And then she'd have to call her mother, she guessed. She would put that off for as long as she could.

She got dressed in her least offensive-smelling clothes and crammed the rest of her belongings back into the knapsack. She disassembled the furniture barrier she'd made in front of the door, and with the knapsack on her back and the camera safely hung around her neck, she let herself out into the Wawa morning.

It was cold and dry and she hurried to the nearest diner and ordered coffee and breakfast. She sat at the counter and read the little local paper, and there was nothing in it for her.

She thought longingly of a younger Dacey who would be content to wait till some sign or symbol presented itself. A younger Dacey would have had her cards read two or three times by now over this kind of crossroads. Tara Lea would have unwrapped her Rider-Waite deck from its fringed scarf and handed the oversized cards to Dacey to shuffle till they felt ready or till Dacey's forearms ached, whichever came first. Then Tara Lea would lay them out one by one, looking for the through-line in the story they were telling. Two of Swords. Indecision, a stalemate, avoiding the facts, hiding distress. Dacey saw that one a lot. She pictured the blindfolded woman, her dark hair divided evenly on either side of her oval face, arms crossed against her chest, in each hand a sword. Yes, Tara Lea might as well have had a deck full of Twos of Swords.

She'd have laid out all the cards and contemplated them while Dacey looked eagerly on, awaiting insight and an instruction manual for living. Tara Lea would have consulted her worn paperback guide for a deeper look at each card's meaning. She'd have rolled a homemade cigarette and let it burn in her hand, hardly drawing on it. In the end, she'd give Dacey advice so open-ended as to be meaningless, and

Dacey would have done what she wanted anyway, citing whatever shifting wisdom the cards had offered up.

But there was no Tara Lea here, and no deck of Tarot cards. Dacey felt inadequately equipped to make any kind of decision about her life, so long had it been since she'd done so. The last decision—the one that had pulled her out of her existence in Grand Falls and onto the road to this point—couldn't properly be called a decision, could it? It felt more like an impulse gone wild.

She paid for her coffee and breakfast and pushed back out to the sidewalk. The wind in Wawa was cold and sharp, and Dacey tucked herself into her hoodie and set her face against the bluster. She made her way down to the triangle of grass where Wawa's most recognizable resident, the giant fibreglass goose, resided. It held its wings aloft, ever-ready to take off, but never quite achieving air. Beyond it, the lake beckoned. Superior was vast and moving, a muscle that constantly flexed and released. It pulled Dacey to its side and she stood and stared. It was at once like the ocean and not. She remembered Parlee Beach where her parents would rent a cottage for a week in the summer, and on the bad-weather days, the ocean was upfront about its menace. Superior was vast like the ocean, but subtle, its intentions harder to understand. For all its movement it was smooth and glassy, with none of the tumult and danger of the ocean waters she'd seen back home. And yet, Dacey remembered a snippet of lyric. Superior, it is said, never gives up her dead. Dacey stared at the shoreline, all dark thoughts and unease.

"Beautiful, hey?"

Dacey turned her head toward the voice, but met only the inside of the hoodie. She pushed it aside and saw the man.

"Don't be fooled," he said. "It's a complete pain in the ass.

Fickle as a woman."

Dacey recognized him from the tavern. The older of the two old guys. Ed, she thought his name was, or maybe Ned.

"Uh-huh," she said, wanting very much to get away, but pinned by politeness. "I don't know about that. Seems to me it comes on more like a man. Pretending to be all strong and silent, but inside there's always a temper tantrum going on."

The man nodded and narrowed his eyes. "Hell of a generalization," he said finally.

Dacey raised an eyebrow in disbelief. "But your thing, about women being fickle—"

"Just teasin' ya, darlin'."

"Not your darling," Dacey said. Her hand was on her camera around her neck, and she felt her every molecule alert to what might happen next.

"Geez, you're a touchy one," the man said. "Well, drop by the tavern later, I'll buy you a drink, make it up to you."

Dacey raised her camera to her face and turned back toward Superior.

"You might just want to consider being less standoffish, is all. You know, think about who your friends are. Small town, word gets around."

Dacey shrugged and pressed the shutter release. She heard the camera freeze the moment and store it in its memory.

"Alright," the man said and he turned away. "Bitch," she heard him add under his breath.

Dacey stared at the lake a while longer, but found she no longer had any patience for its steady muscular way, and so she turned away and headed back toward the motel, which she no longer thought of as home.

50

Lansing and Evan were back in the motel room, having quickly determined that there was not much to do on a Monday afternoon in Wawa. The BlackBerry lay between them on the little night table. It had been buzzing all morning. Requests for interviews in advance of the award show in Winnipeg. The venue manager in Thunder Bay inquiring about technical details of the gig there. It buzzed again now.

"That goddamn thing," Lansing said.

Evan glanced at it. "It's the garage," he said. He hopped off the twin bed and clicked the phone on.

"The car's ready," he said to Lansing. "We can pick it up anytime."

"Hallefuckinglujah," Lansing said, barely looking up. "Let's get out of this no-horse town."

"I'll go get it," Evan said. "You pack up."

"Yeees," Lansing said, drawing out the vowel. "I'll get right on that." He picked up his guitar by the neck and swung it on to his lap.

"Okay, good," Evan said, then shook his head as Lansing settled against the headboard and started picking.

"Oh, go on, Nancy," Lansing said. "I'll be ready."

He played for a few minutes after Evan left, feeling the solitude fall over him. The moments he spent alone were few and far between and the times of confusion were coming thicker and faster. The episodes of forgetfulness were evident, he knew, to Evan, even if the boy wasn't ready to admit that something wasn't quite right. But there were cracks growing and the boy was beginning to peer into them. There was an urgency now about what had to be done. He tore a little sheet of paper out of Evan's notebook and uncapped the pen that lay nearby on the night table. He made a list.

Lloyd Crane telephone
Matthew
Michelle?
Caroline
Marie

He tapped the pen against his teeth and had a flash of déjà vu. He turned the guitar over and tapped its back lightly. He could hear a rustle within. He shook the instrument and something bumped against the strings. He turned it over again carefully and fished a little wad of paper out of the sound hole. He unfolded it, already knowing what it was. How many times had he made this same list? He balled up the older one and pushed it down between the mattress and the bedframe. The new one he folded and put in his shirt pocket, along with the letters and fortunes and the other bits he carried. The pocket was starting to bulge. He carefully drew out the wad of papers and shuffled through them. Marie's handwriting looped across creamy stationery, creased with age and wear. It had been some time since anyone had sent him a love letter. Michelle's tidy handwriting described his future. All those fortunes he should have learned something from. And there was the old photo of Caroline, her face just like her mother's. He bundled the papers into his shoulder bag, secured them with a rubber band he found at the bottom. He took the tour bible from the night table and fitted that into his shoulder bag as well. He almost took it out again, but finally he patted the bag and looped its clasps shut.

Things were going to happen now, he imagined, things he wouldn't be able to control. He knew he should make more than a list so that the boy would have some idea what to do if things went a bad way, but he just couldn't bring himself to do it.

Just a little more time, he thought. He picked the guitar's strings. Just give me a little more time. He sang a melody to match the chords. Just a few more miles, and I will meet you down the road.

He leaned into it, even though he knew he should stop, he should pack, he should try harder not to be a disappointment to the boy. But the songs had always come first, and that was part of the problem. Part of his problem, and Marie's, and certainly Caroline's. But the songs had never let him down, not once. They'd had an understanding, he and the songs. And who knew how many he'd have left. And so he leaned into it and lost himself again, by choice in the song, instead of the many ways he'd lost himself in the past, by circumstance and cruel fate, by inattention and avarice.

51

Dacey didn't love the quality of one-hour photo processing, but the truth was she needed to see where she'd come from if she was going to figure out where to go. And she needed to hold the pieces in her hands. She'd taken her camera to the Wawa Plaza and found a photo-processing place. She left her camera's memory card with the woman behind the counter, and then she walked through the mall, killing time.

There wasn't much to see. An Orange Julius stand, the old kind, free-standing and shaped like an orange with a deep wedge lifted out of it. A tightly packed magazine store with racks of glossy tabloids and a rainbow of chewing gum options. A dry cleaner, a dollar store. There was no food court, but beside the Orange Julius was a Tim Horton's and Dacey ordered herself a large black coffee and a Dutchie. She took her purchases to a bench and sat down. The coffee was steaming hot and she sipped it greedily. The doughnut was a fine accompaniment, juicy little raisins studding a landscape of sweet fried dough. The taste reminded her of early mornings with her parents, going to the Madawaska rink for skating practice, bleary-eyed but eager for the simplicity of bending and pushing, gliding. She missed that simple equation. The physics in a sharp blade on slick ice, the force coiled in warm muscles, those moments when she had her parents' full attention. Connection, motion.

At the photo store, the woman slid a fat envelope across the counter, and Dacey's fingers itched to open it, but she knew she needed space to lay them out and ponder them. She bundled them into her jacket and made her way from the mall to a laundromat on the main street.

She was hurrying along the sidewalk when a blast from a horn broke her concentration. She looked up, expecting to see perhaps the old guy from the tavern in a pickup truck. Instead she saw the Corolla and Evan at the wheel. He was waving eagerly. She approached the car with caution and he rolled the window down.

"You're still here," he said.

She breathed deeply. "The car still smells like curry."

"I know," Evan said "They put in a new part and all and they say it's not dangerous and we've got to get going, so."

"Right," Dacey said. The envelope of photos was heavy against her chest. "Okay, well, see you."

"Wait, what are you doing?" Evan said. "I mean, what's your plan and stuff?"

"Laundromat," Dacey said.

"And then?"

"We'll see after that."

She looked at him and he looked back. There was an offer of conciliation on his face, she thought, or something like it. She struggled to come up with the right combination of things to say and do and finally she said simply, "I gotta go," just as Evan was saying, "Why don't you come with us?"

"We'll see," she said.

"We're leaving today," Evan said.

Dacey nodded. "Okay, well. Good to know." She gave a little salute with her takeout coffee cup and then stepped back from the curb. Evan looked at her out the window and Dacey couldn't read his face. He nodded, and put the car in gear again.

"Okay," he said. And he drove away.

The laundromat was warm and muggy, and Dacey gratefully peeled off her leather jacket and the hoodie beneath it. She put all her clothes, hoodie included, into a washing machine and filled it with warm water and soap. While it churned, she sat at the scratched wooden table in the laundromat's front window, her coffee at her elbow. She flicked open the envelope and drew out a fat stack of photos.

Bus-window views of snowy Quebec landscapes, the mighty St. Lawrence a current that ran through it all. Neon signs and flashes of bare legs at night in Montreal, despite the temperature. A smoked-meat sandwich on a plate. She'd eaten half of it and found the other half two days later in her knapsack in Toronto. Southeastern Ontario sameness, the ribbon of highway, long fields, a tide of brake lights.

She laid the photos out on the table as if she could divine some insight, the way Tara Lea had over a Grand Cross of Tarot cards. She studied the images, what remained of what had brought her this far. She looked for meaning. She looked for patterns. She wished there was a book to consult.

She tried to find the story in the shots of the stage at the Cat's Pyjamas, Evan's foot elevated, endless plates of french fries, guitars head-to-toe in the trunk of the Corolla, rocks and trees, rocks and trees. A lineup of fans waiting to talk to Lansing after a show in Sault Ste. Marie. The fibreglass goose. Lansing's hat. If there was a story, she couldn't see it. If there was meaning, she couldn't get it.

She sighed and pushed the photos away.

She moved her clothes from the washer to the dryer, jeans and socks all tangled up together. She pulled the cellphone from her pocket. She had put it off long enough. She jabbed the numbers on her phone, then pressed it to her ear and imagined it ringing in the kitchen she'd never seen, and when her mother said hello, Dacey held her breath.

The word came a second time and Dacey exhaled.

"Is that you," her mother said, "Dacey?"

"Hi, ma," she said.

"Where are you, Dacey?"

"Doesn't matter," Dacey said. She watched her clothes tumble in the dryer and felt lonesome.

"If it doesn't then just tell me. They called from the newspaper about you. Phil did. He said you took off. We've been worried."

"I'm okay," Dacey said, but her voice trembled.

"Oh, Dacey," her mother said.

"I'm *fine*," Dacey said.

"Of course you are," her mother said.

"Do you think there might be something wrong with me?" Dacey said. "I feel like there might be something wrong."

"I don't know about that," Dacey's mother said. Dacey could hear her chopping something, the sound of a knife against a cutting board. "You've always been that way, Dacey. In your own world, somehow. You were sensitive, that's all." Her mother's voice down the line was both comforting and distant, as it was in person.

Dacey inhaled in two stages, a big breath and a small one, and swallowed a sob. She *was* fine, was the thing, but making the connection, familiarity, and hearing her mother's concern, that was undoing her. Had she always been like that? Her own little world? Just sensitive? There were questions she wanted to ask, but instead she just said, "I'm in Wawa, Ontario. In a laundromat. I am okay. I'm with friends."

"Are you coming this way?" her mother asked.

"I don't know, honestly," Dacey said. "Maybe I'll come see you."

"I'd like that," her mother said. "Your father would too."

"Okay, ma," Dacey said, feeling an urgent impatience. "I gotta get going now." And she clicked off the phone without waiting for more.

52

Evan pulled right up to the motel room door and threw the car in park. He banged open the door to find Lansing leaping guiltily off the bed, guitar in hand. Nothing was in order. Lansing hadn't packed a thing.

"You're back," he said, eyes wild. He held out the guitar to Evan.

"What the fuck, Lansing?" Evan said, taking the guitar. "Why aren't you ready? Jesus, I ask you to do one thing for me." He tossed the guitar gently onto the bed and grabbed its case. He pushed the instrument into place and snapped the case shut. He felt like coiled springs, like lightning itching to strike. He turned to face Lansing, all energy and impatience. "Let's get going."

Lansing cowered, his face a map of confusion. "Don't be mad," he said. He put an arm up to shield his face. "Don't hit me."

Evan shook his head, his face creased in annoyance. "Jesus, hit you? What on earth is wrong with you? Of course I won't hit you." He took a step toward Lansing, who took a step away.

Evan put the guitar case down slowly, careful to make his

movements fluid and deliberate, without a hint of threat. "Are you okay?" he asked. A tide of panic swelled in his chest. Lansing was staring at him, eyes wide in his pouchy face.

"You're okay," Evan said, changing tack. Questions were superfluous, he saw at once. They did nothing to help. Answers were more useful. "You're fine," he said, and Lansing nodded. The old man's face relaxed a little and looked less old, less frightened, and for an unguarded moment gratitude suffused his features. Then the moment passed.

"Shall we get on the road now?" Evan asked carefully.

Lansing nodded.

"What happened there? Do you want to tell me what just happened?" He kept his voice low, no note of accusation, just curiosity and concern.

Lansing shook his head and Evan watched him arrange his features again, the guard back up. "Lost track of time," Lansing said quietly. "You know how I am with a guitar in my hands."

"Lansing, is there something—" But Lansing was at the doorway now, gesturing out at the idling Corolla.

"Fixed, is she?"

"Still smells like curry, actually," Evan said. "But somehow, six hundred dollars later, it's roadworthy, according to the mechanic." He picked up the guitar case again and moved toward the door. "But Lansing, seriously, maybe we should—"

"Get on the road?" Lansing said, taking the guitar from him. "Absolutely." He shouldered the case and pulled his hat from the foot of the bed. He tipped it end-over-end up his arm, then flipped it up onto his head. "I'll be in the car."

Evan stabbed at the BlackBerry's keypad with shaking fingers. He listened to the phone ringing, imagined the farmhouse as he'd last seen it, an oasis of tranquility. It rang five times before it went to voice mail. Matthew's voice gave instructions for leaving a message. He glanced out the door to see Lansing settling himself into the front seat of the Corolla. He clicked off the connection without saying a word.

Evan pulled the door closed and jogged down to the motel office, turned in the keys and used Lansing's credit card to pay. He jogged back to the car, mind racing, distracted. He had a nagging feeling he was forgetting something. He pushed it aside. Things were getting out of hand. They'd see his sister Elaine in Thunder Bay. She was a doctor. He'd ask her for help. Lansing was working too hard, he told himself. The stress of being on tour, the buildup to the lifetime achievement award, the added pressure of this newspaper reporter talking to all of Lansing's old friends.

Evan pulled open the driver's side door.

"Jesus, boy, I thought you'd taken off on me. Let's get the fuck out of here. Good riddance, Wawa."

Same old Lansing, Evan thought. He's just the same as ever. He nodded and started the ignition.

"Where's the girl?" Lansing said, as Evan eased the car out of the motel's driveway.

The girl indeed. "I saw her," Evan said, his voice almost breaking with excitement. "She's still in Wawa."

Lansing nodded. "Well, is she coming with us or what?"

Evan pulled out on to the street and picked up speed. "I don't know," he said. He remembered her on the sidewalk, hunched in her hoodie and her leather jacket, her usually bright eyes dull. Her hair raining down either side of her face and pooling in her hood. "Let's go find her."

53

Dacey had asked the clerk at the motel about hitchhiking out of Wawa, and the clerk rolled her eyes.

"You've got to be kidding," the woman said. "This place is, like, the worst place in the world for hitching out."

"Really?" Dacey said. She could feel the warmth of her just-dried laundry in the knapsack on her back, the comfort of her camera around her neck.

"Officially the worst," the woman said. "People get stranded here for days."

Dacey thought about the bus schedule she'd pocketed. Perhaps a bus that left in the middle of the night and took two solid days to get to Calgary wasn't such an unappealing choice after all.

The office door opened, and a neatly-put-together woman entered. She had sleek blonde hair and her leather jacket looked buttery and rich where Dacey's was cracked and old. She was wearing slim-fitting dark jeans tucked into brown leather boots and Dacey unconsciously stood up a little straighter when she saw her.

"Where are you trying to get to?" the motel clerk asked Dacey.

"Calgary, probably," Dacey said.

"Probably?"

"Well, west of here, anyway," Dacey said.

"Need a ride?" the blonde woman said, as she slid her room key across the counter to the clerk.

"I do," Dacey said, without hesitation.

The blonde woman turned and pointed out the office window. "I am driving that family sedan to Thunder Bay on behalf of a client. I'm bored out of my mind. Can you tell a good story?"

"I worked as a reporter," Dacey said.

"Welcome aboard," the blonde said.

The blonde slid behind the wheel and they were off.

The music's gone back home again
nowadays we're playing in
the parlours like the way they used to do
the big-times they are a changin' fast
the only thing that's gonna last
is that folks like us sing songs for folks like you
there will always be a small time
keeping a roof over our head
there will always be a good time
when the nine-to-fivers go to bed
there will always be a grapevine
where everybody brings a friend
there will always be a small time
just come and see us now and then

—"There Will Always Be a Small Time"
(Corin Raymond/Jonathan Byrd 2007)

54

"Son, I think you should accompany me in Thunder Bay," Lansing said, after a long period of silence.

They'd gone to the laundromat to look for Dacey, but all they'd found there was a mess of her photos on a long wooden table. Evan gathered them up greedily and stowed them inside his jacket. They'd made a sweep of the town's main streets, then asked at the Motor Inn. She'd checked out, grabbed a ride with another departing motel guest. Evan had fallen silent at that and Lansing had just let him be. He wasn't one for jollying or being jollied and anyway, he had the sense that things weren't quite right between himself and the youngster he'd press-ganged on the road.

Lansing tried to feel regret about that. He knew he should at least be remorseful about the lies he'd told—continued to tell. But there was too much at stake. God willing, there'd be time in the future for feeling bad and feeling sorry. For now, there were too many entries on his list as yet unchecked, and without Dacey Brown's help, there was no real plan for making any of it happen. The boy would get over it and meantime he'd thrown him a bone.

"You should accompany me," he said again.

"I am accompanying you," Evan said, but all the fight was out of him.

"No, you gearbox," Lansing said, giving the boy's shoulder a light punch. "Not escort me, chaperone me, supervise me. Accompany me on *stage*—play alongside me."

Evan darted his eyes toward his passenger, then fixed them again on the road. He turned pink in a slow tide from shirt collar to scalp. Lansing watched the tide rise with something like admiration.

"I don't know, Lansing," Evan said after a while.

"Why not?" Lansing blustered. "You certainly know the songs—almost better than I do. You're a very decent guitar player. Are you much of a harmony singer?" The lad's face showed no signs of paling. "Well, never mind," Lansing said generously. "Harmony doesn't come naturally to everyone."

"I don't know," Evan said again.

"Look," Lansing said. "We've been through a lot together. You've been through a lot. And you're a real trooper, kid. Let's have some fun for once." He said this last as if Evan were a stick-in-the-mud, a taskmaster who'd so far kept any fun from happening.

The boy was by now chewing his bottom lip and staring fixedly out at the road. He gripped the wheel at ten and two, looking more tense than he had even on the highways around Toronto.

"Jesus, son," Lansing said, "grip that wheel much tighter you'll turn it into diamond. What's the matter, boy?"

At this, Evan flinched, flicking his gaze to Lansing and holding it a moment longer than was usual. "What's the matter?" he said. "What's the matter." He thought for a moment. "Honestly, Lansing, I don't even know how to answer that. I just—" He stopped abruptly, gripped the wheel with renewed force. "Is there anything you think you should tell me, Lansing?" he asked at last, his voice low and fighting to be steady.

Lansing thought about this. He sucked his teeth and turned away to look out the window. The endless pattern of rocks and trees repeating. Little heaps of stones and rock, inuksuk left by travelers of all kinds. Was a time, was a place those little heaps were meant to guide, to wayfind. But now they were just a rite of passage for those who drove this northern highway, so common their traditional messages of guidance were meaningless. They seemed to be saying *you are here you are here you are here*, but they offered nothing about where, exactly, *here* was. Lansing wiped a hand across his face, resettled his hat.

"My boy, there's likely no end of things I should tell you, but where would I start? It'll all become clear in the end, son." He felt his pockets. "We'll have to stop for cigarettes soon."

Evan remained silent.

"Come on, boy, quit playing hard to get. I've never had to beg someone to share the stage with me and I'm not likely to start now. Will you or won't you?"

Evan pressed his lips together and Lansing could see the boy didn't totally trust him. "I'll do it," Evan said at last, letting all his breath out in one slow deflation.

Lansing grinned wolfishly, gratefully. "Jesus, son. You'd think I was trying to cadge a loan or something. Plenty of young fellas who'd jump at the chance I just practically had to force you to take."

"I said I'll do it, Lansing," Evan said, "unless you'd rather find one of those other young fellas?"

Lansing hooted at this, knocking his hat off his head as he did. "Call my bluff, will you. My God, the cheek." He nudged Evan in the ribs and Evan began to smile, in spite of himself, Lansing thought. "You've changed, my boy. Become road-hardened. Well, watch yourself, lad. Did you know Woody Guthrie once made me a similar offer and I turned him down, too cocky to take his sloppy seconds? Imagine where I'd be now if I hadn't been so callow."

"Really?" Evan said. "Woody Guthrie?"

"No," Lansing said, crowing anew. "There's the gullible lad I know and love. No, not really. Woody Guthrie! Ha! As if I'd share a stage with that hack." He laughed merrily into his sleeve.

"Woody Guthrie—you think he was a hack?" Evan said.

"Hoo, got you again, son."

"I hate you, Lansing," Evan said, though there was love in his voice.

"I know you do, son, I know you do."

55

Dacey took her role seriously. She regaled Shara with tales of the chicken-and-egg derby in the streets of Grand Falls, in which chickens raced each other, pulling little carts that held eggs they had laid themselves. She talked about her recent travels with Lansing and Evan and how she came to find herself in Wawa.

"I thought for a while there I was going to be stuck in Wawa long enough to need a job," Dacey said. "Thank God that didn't happen." She stole a quick and guilty glance at Shara.

"Doesn't bother me," Shara said. "Not my town."

"Right," Dacey said. "It came to me, during a conversation with one of the charming locals, that Wawa is Grand Falls, just north and west, and fuck *that*. I realized that if I want to live in a tiny town where nothing happens and everyone already knows—or thinks they know—what I'm about, I might as well go back to Grand Falls. I already have a house there. And a job." She was silent for a beat. "Or I did. I assume I don't any longer." She laughed.

Shara laughed too and Dacey felt glad. She felt at ease in this comfortable car with this generous woman.

"Thanks for the lift," Dacey said. "It feels really good to be on the move again." Perhaps this *was* the story she'd sought in her photographs. A modern voyageur tale. She was on the move, crossing the Canadian Shield, exploring, making discoveries. Experiencing further arrivals. This was what she'd left Grand Falls for, and also why she'd left Toronto, and even Montreal—a place she could have stayed. Maybe it was for this feeling of always moving away from where she'd been.

56

They'd been lucky so far, dodging spring snowstorms as they went. Their closest brush with one had come just a few days earlier between Parry Sound and Sault Ste. Marie.

"God takes special care of special people," Lansing had said as they happened upon the remains of a sudden squall, the only evidence of which was a feathering of snow clinging to the sides of the roads and the wide ditch littered with less fortunate cars.

"Seriously, Lansing, that is a fucked-up thing to say," Evan breathed, his stomach swooping like all-seasons with no traction on a slippery road, even though Dacey was driving and seemed to be fully in control.

"Kidding, son," Lansing said. "Don't lose your sense of humour on me now, boy, or we'll be in trouble." He gestured widely across the scene. "God had nothing to do with any of those, nor fate. It's all random, boy. Anything can happen to anyone at any time. There are two ways to approach this. You can either be prepared—somehow—for every unknowable eventuality, or you can say to hell with that and just live exactly the way you want to, everything else be damned."

"How's that going for you, Lansing?" he asked, after a time.

Lansing rolled his shoulders back and stretched his neck from side to side. "I feel alright," he said.

They'd made it through that squall with ease, and now Evan could see that perhaps, even here in northwestern Ontario, the worst was over. Just ahead there was lushness in the endless stretch of roadside trees, and Evan's heart lifted to see leaves filling in and life returning. But perhaps it was illusory. As he drew closer, the early spring sparseness was revealed, the teasing lushness seemed to be just out of reach, always slightly further down the road. Meanwhile, the deadfall from autumn and winter was not yet consumed and composted. Exhausted trees that had given up the ghost some months before sagged wearily in the arms of their brothers, waiting for time and nature to do their work.

What Evan wanted was always just out of reach. There was the dizzying offer to accompany Lansing; but it was coupled with the suspicion that there was something more at play, an uneasy feeling that when the other shoe dropped, he would discover the hard way that the shoe was made of cement. There was the moment of seeming détente with Dacey, the discovery she'd waited in Wawa; and then there was the confusion of discovering she hadn't been waiting for him and the devastation of knowing she'd made the decision to travel on without them.

There were the songs that teased around the edges while he drove; but hid completely when his guitar was uncased and his notebook lay open. There was his feeling that he didn't know the half of what was out there to want; and that the more he knew, the harder he'd yearn. Finally there was his despair that desire could never be slaked, and so what was the point.

God, he was sick of himself. He clicked the radio on and turned the dial till he found the CBC. Some Hollywood type was being interviewed about his long career and extreme fame. Evan nudged the volume higher.

"I don't give a rat's ass about the fame," the Hollywood legend said. "I'm not in it for the fame. If I want to make an obscure little art film I just go ahead and do it. I haven't spent the last fifty-odd years putting every ounce of myself into my craft in pursuit of fame. Fuck that."

Evan flinched at the language. Certainly it was nothing he hadn't heard on a daily—hourly—basis from his passenger, but hearing it on the public broadcaster was shocking. He imagined the blistered ears of a million listeners, including his mother. But the radio host glided smoothly over it. "You obviously feel passionately about that," she said. "But surely fame has some benefit."

"Sure," the Hollywood legend said. "I can say *fuck* on the radio and get away with it. Seriously though, of course there are benefits. The Weinsteins always take my calls, I don't need a reservation at the best restaurants in the world, and I can say what I want with impunity. But that's got nothing to do with my body of work over the last five decades, nor with why I act in the first place."

"That is total bullshit," Lansing said from beneath his hat. "Utter and complete bullshit." He sat up, pushed the hat back. "Fame is the reason this jerk-off has been *able* to pour every ounce of himself into his *craaahft*," Lansing stretched the word out derisively, "instead of having to pour his precious self into bagging groceries or working at a bank. Or a bowling alley." He nodded at Evan. "Right? I mean, I get that Mister Hollywood Wanker here is a Very Important Thespian, but he's also a grade-A shitheel if he thinks fame has nothing to do with it. Fame has everything to do with it. Without fame, he'd have nothing. Jesus. He's the worst kind of liar." He jabbed the radio off and they rode in silence again.

"The thing about fame," Lansing said, a few kilometres down the road, "is that it's slippery."

"What do you mean?" Evan asked. He was glad to have something to focus on that wasn't his own misery.

"I have a certain amount of it," Lansing said, "among a certain kind of person. There are some people—yourself, for instance—to whom I am tremendously famous."

Evan felt his face get hot. Lansing glanced at him and laughed. "Chrissakes, son, it's alright, nothing to be embarrassed about. Without folks like you, hell, *I'd* be working at the Alley Oop. These are the fans who can't believe there's anyone who doesn't know who I am. God love those fans; I know I do." He looked out the window. "But it's all relative, right? There are the people who know all the words to 'On My Honour,' but they think Love Conniption—"

"Love Allergy," Evan said.

"Stupid name," Lansing said. "They think Love Allergy wrote that one. They would only be disappointed to hear me sing it my way. Think of that young thing at that godforsaken gig in Cornwall. Loved my stripped-down version, my *ass*."

Evan laughed at this. Lansing was remarkable in every way.

"But most people, son, they don't have the foggiest fucking clue who Lansing Meadows is."

"They should," Evan said.

"Ah, yes," said Lansing, "but see, you only think that because you're in that rarefied first group."

"No," said Evan. "I think it because it's true. What could

be more important than what you do and how you do it?"

Lansing shook his head. "Just about anything, boy. I could be saving someone's life. Inventing some device that would make the lives of future generations easier and better. Bagging someone's groceries *just so*. All, ultimately, would be more useful than what I'm currently doing. What I've been doing since the age of fifteen, well before you were born."

"You don't really think that," Evan said.

"Sure I do," Lansing said. "Some days that's all I think. Why didn't I make something of myself?"

"It's not your fault you're not more famous," Evan said.

"Ah," Lansing said, and here he leaned toward Evan. "But that's just it. Making something of myself and being famous—not the same thing. Not the same thing at all."

He jabbed the radio on and leaned back.

57

Dacey Brown was back at the wheel. Shara had begun to yawn, and Dacey was only too glad to drive. She had grown to love the feeling of being in charge at the wheel, of chewing up the kilometres beneath the rhythmic whirr of rubber over asphalt.

They'd stopped at a gas station to fill the tank and Dacey dipped into her savings to buy snacks. Nibs, mini peanut butter cups, three boxes of Nerds, and a bunch of bananas.

"Want some?" she asked, thrusting the bag toward Shara, who surveyed the contents doubtfully and finally chose a banana. Dacey herself drew out the bag of peanut butter cups and tore it open.

"Don't get chocolate on the upholstery, please," Shara said.

"I'll be careful," Dacey promised. "So what's your story?"

Shara neatly bit off the last of her banana, then folded its peel carefully and tucked it into an empty paper coffee cup and replaced the lid. "Not much to tell," she said mildly. She yawned, stifling it behind her hand. "I'm going to take a nap."

"You go right ahead," Dacey said. She put the car in drive and nosed it back out onto Highway 17.

58

"A hundred kilometres," Evan said. "We'll be there soon."

"Not soon enough," Lansing said. "On this road that's still ninety minutes at least. I can't wait to get out of this goddamn car. I am too old for this shit."

"We can stop any time," Evan said.

"Nah, fuck it, let's just get there," Lansing crabbed.

"No, I mean we can take a break. Cancel a few shows. Rest and then see how you feel about continuing." Even as he felt the words leaving his mouth, he couldn't believe he was suggesting it.

Lansing's voice was low and steady with a current of menace. "Don't talk nonsense, boy."

Evan pushed on. "It's just, you really don't seem yourself lately, Lansing. And you said my job is to look after you, and that's what I'm—"

Lansing interrupted, a growl now in his voice. "First," he said, "you barely know me, boy, so don't tell me I'm not myself. Second, your job is not to look after me like I'm some helpless baby. Your job is to keep this show on the road, not to derail it the second you're a little tired, or a little homesick, or whatever the fuck it is you are." He paused. "You never should have let that girl go. We're both fucked without her. You screwed that one up good."

Evan pressed the gas hard as if he could out-drive it all.

"Fuck you, Lansing," he said.

"There you go, boy," Lansing crooned. "Let it all out."

Evan pursed his lips and narrowed his eyes. He imagined turning all his fears and feelings and desires on Lansing full-throttle. It would be the force of a firehose, an irrevocable eruption.

"Fuck you," he said again instead. He rolled the window down and sped up. The wind was an opponent, punching him repeatedly in the head. It was bracing, numbing, and entirely preferable to the alternative. With the wind roaring in his ears, he couldn't hear Lansing anymore. He could still hear the timbre of Lansing's voice and, at a glance, could tell Lansing was still talking—railing at him or mocking him, probably—but the words were lost in the highway roar. He turned the radio up.

Evan had emailed his sister to say that he was coming and that he'd have Lansing Meadows with him. If she was impressed, she hadn't let on. He hadn't mentioned Lansing's episodes. He lived in hope they would just stop on their own.

He hadn't seen Elaine in years. He'd been a little kid when she left home and she was rarely back in Nova Scotia. If they had anything in common, it would be news to him. He thought maybe it would be nice to see her, but then he glanced at Lansing and thought better. How could he arrive on Elaine's doorstep, an adult in name only, with a car that was surely on the verge of breakdown, and a snarling passenger on the same brink? And how could he dream of taking the stage alongside Lansing Meadows? His volatility seemed to increase with each passing kilometre and Evan's scant confidence degraded alongside. So far, the stage had been the only place where Lansing seemed entirely at home. But Evan wondered whether past performance was truly an indicator of future performance. He was beginning to think perhaps not.

He couldn't shake the feeling that he'd forgotten something in Wawa. Their leaving had been such a shambles, he'd packed so hastily, hadn't done the usual final check of the motel room. And then beyond that nagging feeling was a low-frequency dread that hummed beneath his thoughts. They just had to hang in till Winnipeg. Two more days. He wanted so badly to go toward the things that were perpetually out of reach, but everything within him urged: slow down, stop, go back.

Evan was almost hypnotized by the stream of traffic pouring toward him. Where were they all going, the transport trucks and pickup trucks, the rusted sedans in worse shape than his. He took his right hand off the wheel, brushed the hair out of his eyes. Perhaps he'd get a haircut in Thunder Bay, so he'd look good for the gig. He tilted the rear-view mirror so he could see the top of his head in it. Definitely overdue.

The car waggled sickeningly then, a sudden pitch to the right. Evan snapped out of it in a hurry. "What the fuck," he yelled. Lansing had both hands on the steering wheel, wrenching it toward himself. Oncoming traffic whined like hornets, a higher pitch than the wind. Evan fought for the wheel, pushing Lansing's hands off. Lansing was wild-eyed, determined and frighteningly silent. There was a kind of fight in his face Evan had never seen. He eased his foot off the gas and leaned his body protectively around the wheel, using his right elbow to keep Lansing at bay. What felt like minutes passed as he guided the car to the shoulder, yelling at Lansing before they had even come to a complete stop.

"You get out of this car, you fucking crazy asshole!" he yelled. "Are you fucking crazy? Fuck!"

Lansing was backed against the passenger door, as far away from Evan as he could get. He was shouting back, but the words had no form that Evan could divine.

The car at last came to a halt, and Evan jammed it in park and cranked the ignition off. "Fine!" he said. "If you won't, I will." He wrenched open the door and leapt from the machine, every part of him awake. He paced alongside the car as traffic whipped by, flapping his shirttails and pushing his hair back. Adrenaline jangled every nerve, making him feel sick and high. He chewed the distance along the length of the car and beyond, then turned and strode back, then turned again and strode the other way.

"Christ!" he yelled. The wind took the word and flung it across the highway and over the embankment. He stopped and leaned in his own open window. "Fuck is wrong with you?" he hissed, then moved on before Lansing could answer. He kicked at a big rock, missed, and kicked again. He stopped and dropped to his knees in the last scrap of dirty snow by the side of the road, yelled "Fuck!" and burst into tears.

He cried briefly but whole-heartedly. He forced himself to stop, to stand up. He could taste grit on his tongue and beyond that a metallic bitter disappointment. He looked through the windshield at Lansing. "You're an asshole!" he shouted. He kicked the gravel at his feet and then he ran down into the ditch, through the reeds and into the bushes beyond. He needed to pee, and he needed to be nowhere near that man.

When he emerged, he'd made a decision. He would

confront Lansing once and for all about these episodes and together they would make a plan. He wanted to help Lansing get to Winnipeg, he wanted to see him get the recognition he deserved, but not at the expense of both their lives. He clambered back up the slope to the highway and peered through the windshield. The car was empty. Lansing was gone.

Evan felt the crushing weight of every mistake he'd ever made lift, only to make room for the crushing weight of what he could barely begin to understand.

"You had one job," he berated himself uselessly, the wind taking these words as readily as it had taken the others and flinging them far, far away. He sank again to his knees, but only for a moment, like a marionette in the hands of a demented puppeteer. He bobbed back up, on his feet and wild, swiveling, searching. The landscape was as it had been. Rock and trees and road, the steadily unfurling ribbon of traffic on a curving road drowned out now by the thunder of Evan's heart. He'd lost the godfather of Canadian folk music, his own hero, en route to a lifetime achievement award and who knew what other honours. He'd lost him here, on the 17, two-thirds of the way between Wawa and Thunder Bay, he'd lost him. He strained to see Lansing's figure in the distance, but the road curved away and there was no figure to be seen.

"Lansing!" he roared, pushing all that was in him out with the name. "LanSING!" But it was beyond useless. And for a second time, Evan Cornfield wept on the side of the highway.

Maybe Lansing was cowering in the car, having another spell of whatever it was he'd been having. Evan bulleted up and threw open the passenger door. The car was empty.

He threw his head back and wailed again, "Laaaaa-aannnnnsssiiiing!" and nothing answered but the heedless river of traffic rolling by.

"Okay, think," he commanded himself. He'd often wondered what he'd be like in an emergency and now he knew. He couldn't say he was surprised. He slapped the gravel dust off his pants and pulled the BlackBerry from his pocket. He dialed Matthew's number and left a message. He called Michelle. He stood for a moment with the phone in his hand and he took a deep breath. Without thinking about it any further he dug Dacey's card out of his pocket and jabbed out a message to her. Then he jammed the phone back into his pocket and gently closed the passenger door.

Again a deep breath and he got back behind the wheel and put his hand to the ignition. The keys no longer dangled there. He put his hands to his pockets and dug. He checked the floor. He raised his hips and felt around on the seat. Cold fear was shouldered aside by hot rage.

"Lansing Meadows, you poison bastard!" he shouted. "There's a name I hope I never hear again!" He pulled the phone from his pocket and dialed again. "I've lost him, Crouse," he said. "And he took the fucking car keys. I'm on the side of the road a hundred kilometres from Thunder Bay and I don't have a sweet clue what to do next. What kind of asshole—"

"Did you call the police?" Crouse asked.

"I—no. Do you think I should?"

"That's where I'd start," Crouse said. Crouse was the sort who was good in an emergency.

"What do I tell them?" Evan asked.

"Just what you told me," said Crouse.

"That I lost the godfather of Canadian folk on Highway

17 a hundred kilometres from Thunder Bay?"

"Give them a call, Evan. Let me know how it goes." Saxton hung up.

Lansing Meadows had always had a feeling it would come down to this, in the end. He just hadn't thought the end would come so soon. But clearly his bridges were charred masses smoking in his wake, and all that was left were his own two feet and his heartbeat, and the latter was by no means a sure bet for very much longer.

His boot heels made little coronas of dust around him as he walked and the whiz of traffic threatened to take his hat from his old head. He shouldn't have pushed the lad, that much was clear, but he hadn't meant to push as hard nor as far as he had. He just—well. He wasn't himself. The boy was right about that. But then, the boy was right about quite a lot. More than he had a right to be, his age.

Lansing sighed heavily. He'd left the guitar and taken only his shoulder bag and its precious contents. His lists and his letters, his fortunes and photos. He needed a pack of smokes, and to find the girl, and if this was the only way to get that on the go, then this was what he'd do. But it wasn't going to be easy.

59

Dacey Brown became aware of her pocket buzzing. She felt the vibration separate itself from the general vibration of the road. She glanced at her passenger. Shara was awake.

"I'm going to pull in at the next stop, okay?" Dacey said.

"Pit stop," Shara nodded. "Great."

On the right, a road sign. "Seventy-six to Thunder Bay," Shara said, "and a gas station coming up."

Dacey eased the car off the 17 and into the gas station's little parking lot. Shara had her seat belt undone before the wheels were still. "Need a pee?" Dacey said.

"Do I ever," said Shara, and she was out the door before Dacey had it in park.

"Take your time," Dacey said. She pulled out her phone and read the text.

She had the car turned around and idling when Shara emerged from the gas station.

"Hurry!" Dacey yelled. "We have to go back."

"What?" Shara said. "No we don't. I have to get this car to Thunder Bay."

"It's urgent," Dacey said. "Come on, get in. It won't take long."

Shara stomped her foot. "Dacey, *no*. It's not my car. And I've been driving for days. I just want to get there, get paid, and get on with my life."

Dacey put the car in gear. "Shara. It won't take long and it'll be a whole lot faster if you just get in the goddamn car now. Please, Shara."

But Shara wouldn't. She had her hands on the roof of the car, her face in the passenger window. Dacey took her foot off the brake and the car started to roll. "Shara, make it easy. You could make it so much easier for both of us."

Shara started to jog alongside the car. "You stop it, Dacey Brown. You just stop this right now."

But Dacey Brown couldn't stop it. She knew that for sure. And as Shara became smaller in the rear-view, as the sound of her voice fell away, Dacey felt that glorious freedom again as she moved down the road.

There would be consequences, she was sure, but then there would be either way. And she was convinced it wouldn't take long at all. If Shara had just listened, she'd have been on her way again within the hour, maybe ninety minutes. But now that they were doing it the hard way, who knew how long it would be before Dacey could get back to that gas station.

Well, she couldn't worry about that now. Shara would have to sort it out on her own, just as Dacey would.

60

Matthew was sore all over. Spring time meant work from sunrise to sunset and even though the farm didn't produce much anymore, there was still plenty to do. And he was the man to do it. More and more it was all he wanted in this life, effort and exertion, and the satisfaction of a job well done.

What he was left with from his time in music was a feeling that all that effort added up to not much in the end. Whatever he'd accomplished was ethereal, the achievement made of sand, and it shifted beneath his feet. Cultural currency was unstable, gold standard one day, worthless the next.

Here's what he'd loved: the chemistry of musicians meeting for the first time and getting right down to the business of playing. He loved the discovery in that, the feeling of being on a tightrope, but with the most generous, complete, comfortable net imaginable strung underneath. The community of musicians. He'd loved it when the community was literal—when they'd lived together in a few buildings dotted over rolling farmland in Fulton, nearby his family's place—and he'd loved it when the community was more abstract, a fellow feeling, a warmth and willingness to go to the wall for each other.

Matthew hadn't felt connected for some time. The music industry could do that, he reckoned. Not music—music took you in right away. It didn't care where you were from or what you looked like or how you styled your hair. But the industry, well, it cared very much about those things. And the minute Matthew got a taste of that, he started to withdraw. He watched from the sidelines as friends dipped their toes in. He tried to find the logic in who got ahead, who evolved and adapted as an artist, and who was forever preserved in the amber of changing public taste, thereafter consigned to C-list ridicule, forever wearing some absurd haircut or asymmetrical shirt.

He'd made a sideline study of it. It was bad to get famous too fast, he saw, especially if you were famous primarily among teenaged girls—though, conversely, teenaged girls bought more records, concert tickets, and T-shirts than any other segment of the population. So what was an artist who wanted to make a living to do?

And what was an artist who wanted to make *music* to do? Matthew hadn't had the stomach for it. Even from the sidelines it pained him. Lansing had stayed immune to all that, it seemed. Of course, Lansing had found a few hundred people in just about every town or city across the country who would come out and pay to see him play, and who would buy a new record from him every couple of years. And that's all it took, Matthew mused, to stay in it. Or at least, that's all it took for Lansing. But he couldn't do it. He found himself hating the life, and then hating music. And *that*, he couldn't live with. He played by wood stoves or firepits now, and that was it.

It had been both good and bad to see Lansing. Lansing was cool, sweet water that slaked Matthew's thirst for that community of musicians. To sit before a fire with Lansing and play was, for Matthew, the purest expression of himself. But in many other ways, Lansing was grit under his tongue.

That young fella had his work cut out, and Matthew didn't envy him at all. Or hardly at all. It might be a lark to be on the road with Lansing once more. For a day or two, he thought, and laughed out loud. Matthew rolled his shoulders back, feeling every one of the logs he'd split that afternoon. The spring evenings were cool and these days he could make a night's entertainment out of feeding the fire and watching it burn down.

He had let Marie know about Lansing. Called her after Lansing's visit. Lansing wouldn't like it, but there it was. Soon enough, Lansing would be the only one unaffected by the changes he'd undergo. Marie had put up with plenty at Lansing's hand and she had as much right to know as Lansing had to keep it from her.

Matthew ran water into the cast-iron sink, listening to it thrum against the basin. He put his hands under the stream and splashed it up, into his mouth and over his face, gasping at the contact. Eyes full of water, he groped for a tea towel and passed it first over his face and what was left of his hair, then wrung it in his hands. He chucked it into a basket on the floor near the basement door and noticed the light flashing on his phone. A message. Likely the part he had ordered for the tractor was ready. He glanced at the clock. Too late to call back now. He put the kettle on and headed upstairs to the shower.

61

Michelle hung up the phone and sank down into a kitchen chair. It was worse than she'd thought. She reached mechanically for the deck and shuffled, concentrating on Lansing's face in her mind's eye as she poured the oversized cards from one hand to the other and back again. She lost herself for a time in the comforting, familiar rhythm of the shuffle, and finally something drew her attention back to the moment and she began to lay the cards.

She turned each one over with trepidation. She'd been reluctant to do this with Lansing in the room, and no less hesitant with him at large and in mind now. It had taken her so long to shrug off his hand. She shrank from the possibility of feeling it again in her life.

The cards were inconclusive. A number of journey cards. The Five of Wands, the Knight of Swords crossed with the King of Cups, the Page of Wands. And then the Major Arcana cards that inspired the most fear: the Tower, the Devil. Lots of sound and fury, but Michelle couldn't see what it signified. The Page was certainly Evan. She shook her head, unsure what she could do for him. She left the cards where they lay and put the kettle on. She stood at the stove and stared at the little flame licking at the bottom of the kettle till, thinking better of it, she turned abruptly to the cupboard where she kept the Scotch. She poured two fingers and knocked the liquid back. She poured two more and swirled the Scotch in the glass. She picked up the phone and dialed Matthew and as his answering machine picked up, the kettle came to a boil, sounding for all the world like a man in terrible pain.

She hadn't seen herself in his cards after all.

62

Lansing Meadows began to think perhaps he'd made a mistake. Nothing looked familiar and his boots were pinching his feet in a most unpleasant way. "You've grown soft," he growled to himself, his voice lost to the sound of traffic. "All this travelling by car, too many days off in a row, the endless diner meals." He raised his head, squinted into the sun. "If I never see another grilled cheese it'll be too goddamn soon," he bellowed, then instantly felt hungry.

What the fuck. The boy was never going to come after him. He'd treated him too badly. Evan was probably delighted to be done with him. It was only a matter of time before even his most rabid fans threw him to the side, an old goat like him. He couldn't prance, he didn't preen. He wrote songs with actual words, that expressed ideas, that explored emotions beyond lust. There was no Auto-Tuning his old voice, no Photoshopping his grizzled features into something a little more pleasing to the eye.

He'd done the boy a favour, that was all. Fuck the award. Fuck his list, even. Fuck the whole stupid idea. It would be better all round if he just hopped on the next available ice floe and drifted away from it all.

He stopped walking and shook his head. What a god-forsaken hash he'd made of it all. He couldn't remember the last time he'd felt like he was getting it entirely right. An hour or two a night if he was lucky, he could at least forget himself in the give and take of stage and audience. In the spotlight he was golden. But if he was being honest, it wasn't really him. It was a certain alchemy, a particular chemistry, collaboration between the audience and his best self. Together they were magic, and without them he was tired, bitter, a confused old man. He'd done a perfect job of pushing away everyone who could love him. He knew there was nothing he could do at this late date to make it up to Marie or Michelle. Or Caroline, especially her. But he hoped, he still hoped that she would find it in her heart.

He patted his pockets for a smoke. An empty package. Well, that was another of his problems. His bag was heavy on his hip. He opened its flap and the empty cigarette package succumbed to the wind, flying from his fingers away down the highway. It was all falling apart, he thought. Maybe he should just let it go.

He drew out the packet of letters and lists, fortunes and photos. No point now in any of that. This was where the dream would die, with him alone by the side of the 17. A broken man on a northwestern highway. He dug through the packet for the photo of Caroline, wormed it out and tucked it back in his shirt pocket. He removed the rubber band that bound his pages together. The corners flapped in the wind. He could feel his eyes watering, the highway's grit.

He held tight to the bundle for a moment longer. Then with a deep breath he loosened his grip and let the wind do its work.

He regretted it instantly as the first pages lifted off the

bundle and fluttered away across the highway. He could go after them, but there they went, caught in the slipstream of the cars that passed, and then they were gone. He'd been holding on too tightly, and too late. He opened his hands further and the wind peeled another few pages. All of it, what he'd tried, and what he'd kept, and what he'd hoped to never forget. He let it all go, and he closed his eyes as it flew down the highway and disappeared, a flock of birds.

63

Dacey Brown had almost made it. She could see the Co-rolla a hundred metres or so down the road, when she became conscious of the red-and-blue flashing lights out the back window.

"Shit." She slowed the sedan and pulled over. A squad car screeched to a halt behind her, and pair of officers leapt from it. They approached the driver's side with guns drawn.

Dacey put her hands up and smiled winningly at the woman who arrived first. Officer Grisdale, her badge read. Grisdale threw a glance at her partner, who eased the door open while Grisdale kept her eyes locked on Dacey's.

"Come on out of there, slowly," she barked, and Dacey smiled again, less broadly. She was so close. Still, she slid out of the car and let herself be turned and pressed against it. The so-far silent partner patted her down aggressively and thoroughly.

"It was a simple misunderstanding," Dacey began. "Wait, can anything I say be used against me in a court of law?"

The silent partner snorted. "You're not on TV. And you're not under arrest—yet." She put her hand on Dacey's shoulder and moved her toward the squad car, ducking Dacey's head and inserting her into the back seat. Dacey watched through the shield as the two women examined the sedan. They wouldn't find much beyond snack wrappers. She could see that she'd made a series of bad decisions since arriving in Wawa. She didn't count this latest escapade with the sedan among them. Shara should have listened to her, that's all, and if the cops would just finish sorting through the drift of snack wrappers, she'd tell them the same thing.

Dacey had her cellphone in her hand when at last the cops returned to the car.

"Do I get a phone call?" she asked.

"No," Officer Grisdale said, "not right now."

"That's cool," Dacey said, "I'll just text him." She pecked out a short message and pressed send.

"Oh, for the love of —" the other officer said. She was tall with long chestnut hair tied back and secured under her hat. She reminded Dacey of her sister.

"Sorry Officer—" Dacey peered at her badge. "Parsons. It's just, my friend is responsible for driving the godfather of Canadian folk across the country, but things aren't going well, and my friend is stranded just up ahead, and time is kinda of the essence because there's a gig tonight in Thunder Bay, and then this thing in Winnipeg, that's kind of a big deal and Lansing's sick, but Evan won't admit it and—oh. Here he comes now." Dacey pointed out the window. Evan was loping toward the squad car with relief and dismay mingled equally on his face.

He stood across the two-lane highway bouncing from foot to foot, waiting for a break in traffic.

"Who's this joker?" Officer Grisdale said as Evan darted across.

"Cripes," Parsons said. She was out of the car in one fluid

motion with her gun drawn, while her partner called for backup.

Evan Cornfield dropped to his knees at the first sight of the revolver and put his hands on his head. "Don't shoot," he wailed, "I'm a folksinger."

"You're a drama queen is what you are," Parsons said. "Stand up, don't be such a baby."

Evan stood. "This is highly unorthodox," she said. Parsons gestured to the squad car. "You know that woman?"

"Sure," Evan said. "That's Dacey Brown."

"What's her deal?" Parsons asked.

Evan shook his head. "I don't know exactly," he stammered.

"What do you mean? You said you know her."

"Well, I do, I guess," Evan said. "We've been travelling together. Or we were."

"In what? The gun dangled from Parsons's fingertips and Evan was uncomfortably conscious of it. "The stolen car?"

"*Stolen* car?" Evan said. "Did Dacey? No, not in a stolen car. In my car." He jabbed a thumb toward the Corolla sitting down the road on the opposite side.

Parsons shook her head. What a waste of time. "How'd she end up with the sedan?" She sheathed the gun, but drummed her fingers impatiently on the holster.

"Oh, we had a stupid argument when we were stuck in Wawa, where we had to wait because the car was smelling like curry every time you turned the defogger on—and then they didn't end up fixing it, just charged me six hundred bucks, and I guess we didn't even really have an argument, I just acted like a dick—" he put his hand over his mouth. "Sorry ma'am."

"Don't patronize me. I've heard worse from better people.

I can't imagine where this is all going." She slapped her hand to her forehead and looked down the road, with a sigh of exasperation. "What's wrong with your car now?"

"Ah. My passenger and I had a disagreement and he seems to have taken off with my keys."

Parsons took this in. "Have you considered getting some help for your anger, sir?" she said at last. "You know what, don't answer that. What do you need?"

Evan shifted from foot to foot. "To find Lansing Meadows and get my keys back and get him to Winnipeg by tomorrow night."

"Uh-huh," Parsons said. "Okay." She looked back at Grisdale and at Dacey, who was gesticulating wildly in the back seat. She leaned her head in the passenger window. "All okay here?"

Grisdale shrugged. "She's going nuts." The radio was squawking and so was Dacey.

"Evan," she was shouting. "Evan, it's Lansing!" Evan looked confused.

"What's Lansing?" he shouted back.

"On the radio," she called.

"Being interviewed?" he asked. He tried to peer into the car past Officer Parsons.

"Creating a disturbance," Dacey said. "Can my friend get in?" she asked Grisdale. "We know that man and he's not well. He's confused. If you take us there, we can help him." She motioned to Evan to get in the cruiser, and he did.

"This is highly irregular," Officer Grisdale said.

"Sir, I'm going to have to ask you to step out of the car," Parsons said.

"I can't do that," said Evan, emboldened. "This is very important. A matter of life and death."

Parsons rolled her eyes. "Such drama," she sighed.

There was another burst of static from the radio and the sound of sirens.

"Please," Evan said, "please. He's not well, he's all by himself, and he's a Canadian hero."

"What's his name?" Grisdale asked.

"Lansing Meadows," Dacey said. "He's getting a lifetime achievement award this week."

"For what?" asked Grisdale.

"Please," Evan said, "can't we talk about this on the way?"

"I don't see how he can be a national hero if neither of us has even heard of him," said Parsons.

"And yet," Dacey began, but Evan elbowed her. "You know that song 'On My Honour'?" Evan said urgently.

Grisdale nodded. "Sure, by Love Allergy. Big hit. I love that song."

"I don't think I know it," said Parsons.

"Sure you do," Grisdale said, and she began to sing. She fumbled the verse a little, but when she got to the chorus, Parsons joined in, nodding, and Dacey did too, adding sweet alto harmonies.

"That song," Evan said. "A great song, right?"

The officers both nodded.

"Lansing Meadows wrote that song and a thousand more just as good or better," he said. He leaned forward and pressed his face against the Plexiglas divider. "He's a genius and he's not well and we're responsible for him. Help us," he said. He looked into Parsons's eyes and then into Grisdale's. "Please."

The women looked at each other and finally Grisdale waved Parsons into the car. She put the siren and lights on as she pulled back out onto the 17.

64

Lansing Meadows felt lighter without the papers. It was good, sometimes, to let go, he thought. He felt he could walk much faster, but something nagged at him as he went and he couldn't think what it was. He'd need to get some cigarettes, that much was clear. He walked briskly, with hands jammed in his pockets. His bag bounced against his hip. He could feel questions tugging the corners of his mind. Questions about where he'd been and what was next, but he pushed those down and away, and in their place came lines and verses that attached themselves to a melody he'd been worrying lately. He wished he had his guitar handy, but he figured he'd get it when he got there. Wherever that was.

Push it away, keep walking.

Before long he saw a truck stop. If he were younger, he'd have broken into a run. As it was he picked up his pace, his bag bumping, keeping the time of the tune he'd almost finished in his head.

The truck stop was busy. There were a few cars at the gas pumps and the attached restaurant was crowded, a happy buzz in the room, servers dancing around each other and the sounds of sizzling from the grill mixing with country music and the din of chatter. Lansing smiled. He was at home among these strangers. They were his family and the road was his hometown.

The convenience store next to the restaurant had none of the diner's nostalgic charm. It was cold and newfangled, with muffins posing as homemade and coffee posing as drinkable. He'd wait and take a seat at the diner counter when one opened up. But for now, cigarettes.

He waited in line and the nagging that nibbled at the edges of his mind started to take bigger bites. He smoked a certain kind of cigarette, but he couldn't quite get his tongue around the name. It'll come to me, he thought. He tried to picture the package, but all that came to mind was the damn warnings the things were plastered with these days. He moved his tongue around inside his paper-dry mouth, but the name did not shake loose. He was next in line.

He looked wildly around the store. Didn't they used to display the cigarettes in rows behind the cash register? But here there were just thick, putty-coloured shields and more of those cursed warnings.

"Some cigarettes," he said when it was his turn. He was stabbed with instant fear at the sound of his own voice.

"What kind, hon?" said the woman behind the counter. Carla, her name tag said. He'd known a Carla, hadn't he?

He stared at her, trying to muster some authority. "Cigarettes," he said again.

"Yes, hon," Carla said, "but what kind?"

The lineup was growing behind him. "I'm not sure," he said, struggling to sound more certain. "Perhaps if you could just show them to me."

"Can't do that, hon. The panel snaps shut on me, can't show them all."

Lansing could feel a storm gathering at his temples. He needed a smoke.

Carla smiled kindly. "Tell me what colour your pack is."

"Red?" Lansing asked.

Carla nodded and turned to the panel, opening and shutting it several times. Each time, Lansing tried in vain to catch a glimpse of the rows.

Carla laid out a handful of packages on the counter. The packs swam, a red sea rising before Lansing's eyes. He could feel the lineup behind him, a sinister unpredictable tail that snaked into the shop, shifting and sighing. He shook his head. "Blue," he whispered.

Carla raised an eyebrow, but turned back to the panel and extracted a few more options. She added them to the array on the counter.

Lansing squinted but nothing looked familiar. He could still feel the beat of his bag bouncing against his hip, though he stood still. Maybe it was his heart booming in his ears.

"What other colours are there?" he asked, his voice louder than he thought it would be.

"Oh come *on*," from the lineup behind him. He could feel its energy start to surge. But this was important.

"Just wait," he snarled over his shoulder. Then, gently, to Carla, "Do they come in green, or maybe brown?"

Carla glanced at the people behind him. "I can't bring them all out for you, hon," she said. "They're really all the same, ain't they?"

Lansing leaned forward, putting his whole weight against the counter. "Please, Caroline," he said. "Put an old man out of his misery, won't you?" He reached for her hand, gripped it. "For God's sake, Carrie, I know I've made mistakes, but don't be so hard, girl." He pressed her fingers between his own and squeezed. "You always were so quick to judge, Carrie, and so reluctant to forgive."

With his other hand, he pushed the stack of cigarette packages aside. "But your old man's come so far looking for you, Carrie, the least you could do is hear me out." Lansing was surprised to hear himself shouting, his throat suddenly feeling hoarse and damaged. He looked into the woman's eyes and saw fear reflected back, and then he felt the fear too. Confusion and loss, abandonment and longing. And regret, years of regret tumbling out. He reached for the woman's other hand and grasped it, squeezing both of hers in both of his as hard as he could. "Let it out, Carrie," he gasped, as tears pushed their way out of his eyes and down his cheeks. "Just let it out, lass." He tipped his own head back and wailed, long and loud, a siren, a warning.

The sound he made seemed to go on long after his mouth had snapped shut and his cheek had met the floor. He struggled to get out from beneath the crushing weight that pinned him. What fresh hell was this, he wondered. A heart attack, a stroke, and me so close to being finished, just my luck. Lansing Meadows just can't catch a break, he thought, not even at the very last minute.

I won't give in to this, he thought. I haven't fought all my goddamn life to go quietly now. And so he twisted and flailed and did his best to command his arms and legs to do the work they'd done so faithfully for years. He managed to turn himself over, but whatever had him in its grip was strong and relentless, and he couldn't rise.

"Stop struggling," it said. "Settle down, old timer, and I'll get off ya."

"Are you crazy? He's on meth or something. You can't let him up till the cops get here."

"You can't sit on his chest like that," a third voice came, "you'll kill him."

At that Lansing struggled anew and was forced even harder to stay down. "Give it up," the first voice came again, the one Lansing had thought was inside his head. He could feel hot tears and humiliation pooling. He wanted a cigarette. He wanted so much still and yet he wanted nothing at all.

Things came into focus. The thin, wiry man who held him down.

"A Miramichi tuxedo," Lansing said.

"The fuck are you talking about, grampa?" the wiry man said.

"Your outfit," Lansing said. "Jeans and a jean jacket."

The wiry man gave Lansing's chest an extra shove. "Fuck you."

"I'm Lansing Meadows," Lansing said. He worked again to bring authority to the sounds his voice was offering.

"I'm the goddamn Easter Bunny," the man said, "so shut the fuck up."

Lansing lay on the floor looking up at the man. He took a deep ragged breath in and let it out. As if it hadn't been bad enough to be marooned in Wawa, now there was all this to deal with.

He imagined describing the scene to the journalist who awaited him in Winnipeg or the adoring crowd that waited to hang off his every word. Lifetime achievement. What a fucking joke.

65

Evan leaned as far forward as the shield would allow, as if leaning could make the car go faster. Dacey apologized and he said first: "For what?" and then: "it doesn't matter," and he was surprised to acknowledge that it didn't. It was Lansing who mattered now. Getting to him, getting a look at him, figuring out what the fuck was wrong with him.

"I'm sorry too," he said, and meant it wholeheartedly.

"He'll be okay," she said. Her face was open and sweet, those two rivers of hair running serene and smooth alongside. She looked into his eyes and he ducked his head away. "He will," she said.

"I don't know how you can say that," Evan said.

"I just have a feeling," she said.

The BlackBerry in his hand rang and he put it up to his ear instantly. "Hello?" he said. "I'm in a police car, on the way to him. Think it's him, anyway. What? Oh. No. It's a long story. I don't know. We're here, I'll call you back."

The squad car had pulled into a truck-stop parking lot, lights flashing and siren whooping. Parsons and Grisdale leaped out. Evan grabbed for the door handle, but there was none. He pounded on the window. "Let me out!" he shouted, but either they couldn't hear him or they didn't care. The officers strode toward the little store. Evan fell back against the seat and groaned.

"Don't worry so much," Dacey said. "We're here now, the cops will help him, it'll be alright."

"It's a disaster," Evan said hopelessly. "I've done this whole thing wrong, made nothing but mistakes for days. It's all fucked up."

"Hardly," Dacey snorted. "Look, whatever's going on with Lansing has nothing to do with you. It's going to be fine, you'll see."

Evan squeezed his eyes shut, feeling the tears gathering again. He tried to think of what had gone wrong first, to work it back to the moment of his first misstep, but it jumbled together. Sometimes, Evan knew, Lansing was being a jerk on purpose. But the fear and confusion Evan had seen lately was real. Why hadn't he done anything about it?

He thought of Lansing on stage, the way he came vigorously alive in front of a crowd, the relentless way he held them from the moment he stepped into the warm bath of the spotlight till the final chord rang. The authority, the power, the deep knowledge and understanding that ran through the songs and the performances alike. Evan couldn't imagine how you got to be that kind of person, so sure, so steady. Lansing was so much himself, and Evan was trapped in the back of a police car weeping while God knew what was happening inside. He balled his hands into fists and used them first to push the tears off his face, and then to hammer once more at the windows.

Dacey put a hand on his shoulder, but he shook it off. "Lansing!" he yelled. "LANSING!" He tipped his face back like a stray dog howling for its pack.

"Oh, for Pete's sake," said Dacey Brown. She shrugged down in her hoodie in disgust. "Oh my God," she said, as an ambulance pulled into the parking lot. She joined Evan in pounding on the windows.

At last Parsons returned. "Quit it," she yelled, from outside the car. "Settle down or I'll arrest you both."

Evan sat back and pulled Dacey's arm down.

Parsons opened the door. "You Evan Cornfield?"

He nodded.

"He's asking for you. You can go in."

Evan scrambled out of the back seat and Dacey began to follow. "Not you," Parsons said. "We're not finished."

Evan looked back, trying to catch Dacey's eye.

"It's okay, Evan. You can't save everyone at once."

Parsons leaned into the door frame. "Just tell me the truth. You steal that car?"

"No ma'am," Dacey said. She put one hand on her heart and held the other up. "I borrowed it. And I tried to get Shara to come with me. I got the call from Evan and I knew I had to come right away."

Parsons had a hand on her forehead again and was shaking her head. "But you knew the car was stolen."

"What car? Evan's?" Dacey was shocked.

"Oh, for heaven's sake," Parsons said. "The car you were driving when we pulled you over."

"The se*dan*?" Dacey squeaked.

"Yes, bingo, the sedan. Stolen two days ago in Windsor, Ontario?"

"Cool customer," Dacey said. "She didn't let on at all. Glad I stole it back, in that case."

Parsons gave her a hard look.

"Sorry," Dacey said. "Borrowed it back." She gestured

toward the ambulance. "Is Lansing okay?"

Parsons stepped out of the way. "Go see for yourself," she said.

Dacey approached the little store slowly. She could see through the window a crowd gathered inside, and Lansing was sitting on a chair in the middle of the store, being seen to by paramedics. Evan stood close by, with his hand on Lansing's shoulder. Lansing looked tired, she thought. And something else, too. Sobered, maybe. She looked away.

Grisdale came out of the store and nodded at Parsons.

"Got all your stuff, Miss Brown?" Parsons asked.

Dacey turned. "Actually, my knapsack is in the sedan."

"We'll take you back to it," Grisdale said.

"I'd better wait for my friends," Dacey said. She looked back to the store and there was Lansing, shaking off Evan's arm, and pushing open the glass door.

"I'm fine," Dacey heard him say as he exited the store. "I keep telling you all, I'm fine."

"Sir, we really think you should come to the hospital," one of the paramedics was saying.

Lansing strode away from them, out to the parking lot, Evan and the paramedics following behind. "Yes," he said, "you've been more than clear about that. And thank you, gentlemen, honestly. Look. I'll put you on the list for my show tonight in Thunder Bay. Just tell them you're paramedics, they'll let you in." He turned to Evan who was hovering behind him. "Where'd you park, son? I swear I've got a mind like a sieve these days. Too worked up about that damn award." He looked around the parking lot for the Corolla and his gaze settled on Dacey.

"Well," he said. "The girl's come back to us." He elbowed Evan. "Maybe you didn't cock it up after all. Let's get going."

He looked around. "Seriously, son, where did you park, back in Wawa?"

Evan nudged Lansing toward the cruiser. "We're parked about a kilometre up the road," he said.

"Good plan," Lansing said. "Important to get a little exercise on tour." He eyed Parsons standing by Dacey's side. "Are you in trouble, lovey?"

"No more than usual," Dacey said. She swept an arm toward the cruiser's back door. "After you," she said, and Lansing slid in, Dacey fast behind him. Evan had doubled back and was conferring with the paramedics.

"Time's ticking, boy!" Lansing leaned past Dacey to yell. She stifled a grin. "These windows go down at all?"

"I don't think so, no," she said. Lansing was indomitable, she thought.

"Can you lay on the horn?" he asked Grisdale, "or run the siren or whatever will put the fear in him? We're on a schedule." He leaned back. "Jesus, listen to me. What have I become? Clock-watching is his job."

Finally Evan finished with the paramedics and jogged back to the cruiser to squeeze in beside Dacey. She smiled at him and he smiled weakly back. She put her hand on his knee and squeezed. The cruiser pulled back out into traffic.

Dacey drove in silence and her passengers were silent too. Lansing, chastened, had handed over the keys without a word when the cops dropped them off, and Evan had taken them half-heartedly.

"Want me to drive?" Dacey had said, and Evan nodded. Now he sat in the back seat looking broody and Lansing was up front, his face shuttered.

Dacey pressed the pedal down and watched the kilometres fly by. She was lost in motion when the jangle of the

BlackBerry startled them all. Evan pulled it out of his pocket.

"Hello? Oh no. It's all fine. Never mind. No, don't do that. No, it's fine. Yes, okay." He clicked the phone off and slid it back in his pocket. Lansing turned in his seat and scowled.

"Who was that, son?"

Evan arranged his features in innocence. "Who was what? Oh, on the phone? No one, wrong number."

"Now, boy—" Lansing said, and the phone jangled again.

"I should take this," Evan said. "Hello?"

"Did you know about this, young lady?" Lansing said to Dacey. She shook her head.

"No," she said, "but I'm not surprised. Lots of people care what happens to you. Including me."

"Bunch of foolishness."

"What?" she said, "people caring what happens to you? Or what you pulled back there at the gas station?"

"I didn't pull anything," Lansing said.

"Oh, that's great," Evan was saying from the back seat. "No, I'm sure he'll be pleased. Yes, thank you." He clicked off the phone and leaned forward so his face was between the two front seats.

"Now what?" said Lansing.

"Great news," said Evan. "In addition to giving you the lifetime achievement thingy, there's going to be a musical tribute to you with a bunch of other musicians singing your songs and a little short film as well."

"That's wonderful," Dacey said. She beeped the car's horn in celebration.

"Terrific," Lansing said. "I really can't think of anything I'd enjoy less. Can't they just give me the Order of Canada with a nice ceremony at Rideau Hall and let me pack it in?"

Dacey laughed, but Evan didn't. He leaned further in and

put his hand on Lansing's shoulder. "You don't mean that."

"Don't I?" Lansing said. "I feel like I mean it. Surely even you can see now that there's nowhere to go from here but down? Everyone who's ever gonna know my name or give a rat's ass about me already does. All that's left is for me to alienate and disappoint the fans I already have."

"Your fans will never be disappointed by you, Lansing."

"All due respect, boy, and you are still a boy, make no mistake. All due respect, you don't know what the fuck you're talking about. You're a beautiful dreamer, kid, and I love you for it. These fans, they are like jackals. And the other songwriters, the critics, the journalists. Everyone's waiting, watching to see if you stumble, if you fall. You need to know this if you're gonna keep strumming that guitar and writing those songs. There's no one who wishes you well but you."

Evan had slowly retreated till he slumped on the back seat. "I just don't think that's true, Lansing."

"And again, son, I say to you, you don't know what you're talking about."

"What about me?" Evan asked quietly.

"What *about* you?" said Lansing.

"I wish you well, I'm not waiting to see if you stumble. I'm not a jackal."

Lansing grinned. "Give it time, boy, give it time." He felt his pockets. "Goddamn it," he said, "I never did get any cigarettes."

Evan leaned back and closed his eyes. His feelings had all gathered to form a knot in his throat. He had promised the paramedics Lansing would be seen by a doctor in Thunder Bay. He both anticipated and dreaded what his sister would say in assessing Lansing.

He remembered those teenaged years spent listening to

Lansing's songs, the way he'd played and replayed those albums till he'd nearly worn them out. The way he'd almost hyperventilated, concentrating so hard on the lyrics. The way he'd sometimes have to stop between listens and try to calm down. "It was only a human who wrote this," he'd remind himself. "A human just like you."

He had a long way to go, he thought, before he was a human just like Lansing Meadows. For better and for worse.

66

"I can't find the tour bible," Evan said, panic in his voice as they pulled in to park in front of the venue, a folk club in downtown Thunder Bay. "Where the hell did it go?"

Lansing had one hand to his mouth, pinching his lips between his fingers. "Tour bible," he said, through his hand. "Threw that away."

Evan was startled. "You did what now?"

Lansing wiped his hands over his face. "Threw it away," he said. "Pretty sure I did. On the 17."

"Well, that's just dandy," Evan said. "How the hell am I supposed to—"

"Don't worry about that, boy," Lansing said. "Tour's all but over anyhow."

"It's barely half done," Evan said. "There's all of the prairies yet to do, and out to BC."

"It's all but over," Lansing said, and he got out of the car.

Dacey looked at Evan in the rear-view mirror. He shook his head and pushed open the door to get out.

The venue manager was eager and obsequious. "Lansing Meadows," he said. "What an honour, I'm such a fan." He reached for Lansing's guitar, but Lansing jerked it away.

"I got it," he said, gripping the handle tightly.

"Oh," said the manager, "of course." His face dropped a little, then he rallied. "This must be your *entourage*." He gave it the full French pronunciation, with a rolled *r* and everything.

"Dacey Brown," Lansing pointed her out. "You deal with her about the money." Evan appeared, lugging his own guitar and a suitcase full of Lansing's merchandise. "And this is Evan Cornfield. Young fella plays on stage with me." Evan tried to look confident.

"Excellent, excellent," the manager said heartily. He slapped Evan on the back, almost knocking the suitcase out of his hand. "Just through here, gentlemen."

The green room was dingy and several degrees colder than the club's main room. It was furnished with lumpy mismatched furniture. There was a veggie tray on a card table, some dip, and a bag of chips.

"Thought you might be hungry," the manager said.

Lansing swung his guitar case onto the lumpy striped couch. "Yep," he said. "Okay, thanks." A note of finality the manager couldn't miss. The man retreated and pulled the door shut behind him.

"Alright son, look," Lansing said. He had his hands on his hips and his hat still on his head. "I don't know how much longer I've got."

Evan shivered. He put down what he was carrying and brought his hands together in front of him. "Lansing, I wish you wouldn't—"

"No son, it's got to be said. You know by now I'm all fucked up. I keep losing time, and the other half the time, I don't know what the hell is going on. I would fight it, but the truth is I am tired. What happened today, I can't go through that again. I've been keeping you outside the circle and it's time to stop doing that." He sank onto the couch and rested against his guitar case.

"Maybe a doctor," Evan said, but Lansing interrupted him.

"Come on now, boy, you know the doctors don't know what to do with someone like me." He leaned forward. "I need your help, son. This is it. My last chance. I can't trust myself to get it right."

Evan twisted his hands and felt the familiar tightness in his throat. "Lansing, you're crazy, you don't need me. You've already made your mark. You are Lansing Meadows."

"That and two-fifty'll get me a cup of undrinkable coffee. Why won't you listen to me, boy? I cannot do what I used to do. I cannot remember my own songs anymore. I am this close," he said, holding up two fingers side by side, "this close to losing everything. The tiny amount I have." He exhaled hard, took off his hat. "On stage tonight, you call the chords if I look at you." Evan started to speak, but Lansing was louder. "You call them quietly, but you call them. And be ready to take a verse if I need you to. And Evan," Evan looked away as his tears began to run. "Don't do that, son. Evan, don't give me any guff. And don't let me down." He put his hat back on and stood up. "Better finish loading in. Don't want the crowd to see the man behind the curtain, after all."

Alone in the green room, Evan sank into a rickety kitchen chair and put his head in his hands. He was at sea and he knew it, but that was all he knew. The jig, he felt, would soon be up. How could he keep such a force as Lansing Meadows on the rails? It was an impossible task. He thought of himself three weeks earlier, how naïve he'd been.

He missed that Evan.

The door swung open then. Dacey Brown.

"Anything you need from me?" she asked.

My God, thought Evan, if you only knew. Here too he was far out to sea. He smiled at her. I'm terrified, he thought, of everything.

"I'm fine," he said.

She smiled back and he thought about his capacity for joy and how it could expand, just like that.

"Do me a favour, Dace," he said. He couldn't imagine what had possessed him to send her away. His only comfort was that he could get smarter from here.

"Anything," she said.

Love me, he thought. He pulled the BlackBerry from his pocket. "Take care of this thing. A bunch of his old friends are coming to Winnipeg and they're calling and I just can't. I think he's starting to suspect and it's making him squirrely." He chucked her the phone. Truth was, it was making Evan squirrely, like having a loaded gun. She caught it with ease and pocketed it. "I'll put it with mine," she said. "Oh, I almost forgot. Your sister's here."

Evan swallowed hard. "That'll make the show easier to do, Dacey. In no way, at all."

She smiled at him once more. "You'll be fine. You'll be great."

Evan nodded tightly. "I'll be puking."

"And eventually it'll be over," she said. "I'll leave you in peace now. Looks like it's gonna be a full house," she said over her shoulder.

"Not helpful," he called after her.

The door swung shut. Jesus Christ, his nerves. What a disaster.

Out front the room was filling in. Dacey had laid out Lansing's CDs for sale and the stickers and the buttons. She'd made a mailing list sign-up sheet.

"Hell is that for?" Lansing asked when he saw it.

"So you know how to get in touch with people who want to keep up with what you're doing," she said brightly.

He shook his head. "Busy night," he said.

"Yeah," she nodded. "Evan's really nervous."

"He should be," Lansing said. "It's a big deal."

Backstage, Lansing tossed his bag of patch cords and pedals down beside his guitar case on the lumpy couch. The case was open and Evan had the guitar out.

"I put on new strings," he said. He held the guitar out by its neck.

"Good job, son." Lansing took the guitar. He put it on his knee and strummed it. "Yeah." He stood it up in the case and then flopped down in the armchair. He took off his hat. "My hair hurts," he said, "right to the tips." He ran his hands over his head and the hair stood up, waving with static. "My God, I'm tired," he said. "I want you to cancel the rest of the shows."

Evan stared at him, blinking slowly. Lansing waited for it to sink in. Finally, the boy spoke. "Lansing, no," he said. "There's time off after Winnipeg. A couple days in one place, we'll get a nice hotel. We can do laundry tonight at my sister's place—"

"Oh, Evan," Lansing said. "This is bigger than a bag of dirty socks, son. Sometime you're going to have to accept that. I'm bone-tired, son. Fresh laundry won't fix that."

Evan's heart hammered. "But you said you wanted to go all the way across, Lansing, you were going to put your boots in the Pacific one more time. You fired the last guy because he didn't think you could do it, Lansing, but I know you can. What about all your fans? What about showing the naysayers, all the critics who say you've had your day?"

Lansing laughed low in his throat. "Oh boy," he said. "The naysayers were right. Never been more right. Jake was right. I can't do it."

"You're just tired, Lansing."

"That's what I'm trying to tell you, boy. I am tired, I'm done. Cancel 'em and don't try to change my mind. That's not what you're here for."

Evan bowed his head.

"Alright now, son, no need to cry over it. My God, when is life gonna toughen you up? End of the road, that's all. It was bound to happen. And we're not quite there yet, son. There's tonight."

Evan nodded, eyes still cast down.

"Okay then. What are we gonna play?"

Evan held out a square of paper, a list inked in black. Lansing looked it over. "No 'Ocean Curl'?"

"I don't think I can play that one," Evan said, his voice heavy and thick. "It's complicated. I don't really remember it."

"Oh, come now," Lansing said. He hefted the guitar again. "It's in G," he said. He started playing. "Come on," he said.

Evan blinked hard, then reached for his own guitar. Tuned it and fell in with Lansing. He played quietly, tentatively, but Lansing nodded encouragement and he leaned into it a little.

Lansing's face was like the sky after a bad storm. He started to sing and Evan rode the wave, the words that wouldn't stop coming. The song spoke of heartbreak and of carrying on, the timelessness of tides, the heart's failing beat. Endurance, love. It all came back to him and he brought his young voice up to meet Lansing's old one and when they met and wove and crashed together Lansing's eyes were bright, so bright Evan had to close his own. And still the words were there for him, and the chords too, a net thrown out on the tide of the tune, both working together to pull Evan into shore. And when the words were done and the final notes spilled down the trough of the wave they'd been riding, Evan opened his eyes again and Lansing was there, nodding at him.

"You see, son," he said, "you see that."

Evan nodded.

"Alright," Lansing said. "Why don't you warm them up with a couple tunes of your own. And I'll be out before too long." He drew a pack of cigarettes from his pocket. "Go on now, son. Give me a couple minutes alone."

Evan had thought the night would pass in a blur, but it was just the opposite. Most moments were slow and he could stretch them like taffy, stay in them and revel. Even standing in that bright spotlight, playing a few of his own songs. He hadn't been on a stage since that night at the Boite. But he felt none of the childish nerves he'd felt that night. He knew right away which songs he should sing. He had four that were strong and a fifth that was almost there. It wasn't much, but it was enough for this night. And he'd get more. He knew now that he'd get more.

Lansing's crowd was kind to Evan, but he could feel he had a long way to go before he could hold them on his own. And that was okay with him, too. He had come a long way, and now he knew a bit about that. He was on the path; he'd stay on the path.

He thought of Lansing Meadows, and the way he took a stage, all charm and stories and flirting. That wasn't Evan

Cornfield's way and it probably never would be. He had the beginning of a thought that maybe that was okay. That maybe it would be okay to just be Evan Cornfield and to get where he was going on his own time.

And when Lansing came out on stage, the crowd adored him, and Evan Cornfield stood on stage and felt the force of that adulation. Lansing gestured to Evan with his head and said, "How about my boy, Evan Cornfield?" And the crowd responded with stamping and whistles. It was hot already under the spotlight, Evan reddened a little more and hoped no one could tell.

The generosity that overtook Lansing on stage was doubled for Evan Cornfield. He bathed in its warmth and thought that it had all been worth it.

And in the end, Lansing hadn't needed him much, not really. The man on the stage with a guitar in his hands, he was real. Evan called the occasional chord, but mostly to justify his own existence. And the audience had been as hungry as ever. And Lansing—Lansing had stood on that stage in that warm bath and accepted it all. With a face-cracking smile that made Evan shiver, bobbing on a sea of emotions he couldn't yet name.

67

After the show, a pack of fans hung around, waiting for a piece of the man. Lansing changed his shirt backstage and smoked two cigarettes out the fire door, propping it open with his body while his face poked out into the night. That work done, he nodded at Evan, who was coiling up cord, and he went out front to where Dacey had set up the merch table.

Lansing both loved and hated this part. His natural curmudgeonliness sometimes melted away among strangers. He found he could be joyful in brief interactions he knew would have no lasting consequences. And of course, without these people who loved him without knowing him, there'd be no work. So thank God they didn't really know him, he thought.

There was a little crowd around Dacey Brown and Lansing could see she had them busy signing his mailing list. He felt a stab then, sorrow at what was inevitable, but he pushed it away and kept walking. If he thought he had another album in him—but no. He'd not deliver endless encores. He knew when it was time to take a final bow.

But that was business for another day. For now, he was still Lansing Meadows and no one was the wiser.

Dacey smiled broadly when she saw him and gestured to the little knot of fans around her. "Here he comes," she said, "let him through."

He set his face and mustered his breath to boom hellos. The little crowd turned away from Dacey and toward him as one. Like a school of fish in a documentary he'd watched late one night in some motel room, their finely choreographed, synchronized movements beautiful and little understood.

Easy as shooting them in a barrel to win their love, he thought. Until it isn't anymore. They could easily turn their attention elsewhere, turn away and never turn back.

The stage helped, though. It did something to a man. Put him up above the others—literally, of course, in most cases, but something else too. It conferred on him an automatic difference, an apartness that wasn't inherent to him, or to anyone. He was, as the saying went, someone who put his pants on one leg at a time, but that's not what these people saw when they looked at him. He was special because they believed he was. The difference between them was decided by the people looking, not by the one being looked at. In their eyes he had both more and less humanity than they did.

"Well, hello," he said again, pushing all the air inside him out into the world. He was jovial, he was self-deprecating, he was Lansing Meadows. A smattering of returned hellos, and lots of hands holding CDs for him to sign. He patted his pockets.

"That's silly of me," he said. "No pen." He looked at Dacey, who was ready with a Sharpie.

"Behind every half-decent man there's an outstanding woman who's already thought of everything," he said.

"Alright," he said to a middle-aged woman with wavy hair and long earrings. "Now, who's this for?" He leaned in close to her and she giggled.

"It's for me," she said, her hand still on it even as she offered it to him.

"Aha," Lansing said. "Okay, a woman who knows what she wants. What's your name, darlin'?"

The woman blushed to her roots. "Jenny," she said, with more giggling from her and her friends.

"Ah, Jenny kissed me," Lansing said. Jenny inhaled deeply at this, and her friends batted her with their handbags.

"You're a scoundrel, Lansing Meadows," the emboldened Jenny said.

"You finally noticed," he flirted, and handed back her CD, now bearing his expansive autograph.

She handed her purse to her nearest friend and squealed, "Take our picture." She grabbed Lansing around the waist and swung him around. As the flash died away, she gave Lansing's left buttock a squeeze and fled, amid peals of girlish laughter.

Eyes still dancing from the camera flash and invigorated by the sudden goosing, Lansing turned to the next fan in line.

"Not sure how you'll top that," he said rowdily, but the energy of the man who faced him was completely different. He clutched a grubby cloth grocery bag.

"I have all the records you ever made," the man said.

"Ah," said Lansing. "A true fan."

"I didn't like it when you went country."

"Okay," Lansing said, "well, that's in the past now."

"I still listen to that record, but I don't like it."

"I'm not sure what to say about that," Lansing said, the post-show vibe starting to ebb. "I'm sorry you didn't like it. You're under no obligation to keep listening."

"Your latest record has some good songs," the man continued. "But none as good as 'On My Honour.'"

Lansing steeled himself. "I'm glad you found something to like. I really should get back to signing CDs." He gestured toward the line.

"Aren't you going to sign mine?" the man asked. He hefted the cloth bag and Lansing realized the man wasn't being abstract when he'd claimed to have all Lansing's records.

"I'll tell you what," Lansing said. "I'll sign three of them, including the country one and maybe you can sell it to someone and get a good price for it."

"I want you to sign them all," the man said. His voice rose. "I came all this way."

Lansing tried to soothe him. "I came a long way too, and I'm happy to sign some of your collection right now, but I have lots of people to see here tonight."

"What they say about you is true," the man sputtered, backing away. "I've defended you in chat rooms, but they were all right."

Lansing reached out for the cloth bag. "Come on now, man, surely we can find a compromise—"

"He's an asshole," the man shouted, wrenching the bag away. "Lansing Meadows is a total dick."

"Stop the presses," Lansing murmured. Those closest in the lineup laughed, a nervous tide of brittle tittering.

"Fuck this," the man yelled, and then he was out the door.

"The secret's out," Lansing said, turning back to the line. "Anyone else want a total dick's autograph?"

The commotion brought Evan out front. "He okay?" he murmured to Dacey.

She nodded. "Better than okay. Some frustrated fan just blew up, but Lansing's doing great."

Indeed, the famous head was bent once more in conversation with an admiring stranger. Evan watched a moment longer, then turned at a tap on the shoulder.

"Little brother!" It was Elaine. She pulled him in for an embrace. "Ooh," she said, pushing him away again, "you reek."

"Rock and roll is a dirty business," Dacey said, sticking out her hand. "I'm Dacey Brown."

Elaine looked from Evan to Dacey and back again. "You two are together?" she asked. Evan felt his face go hot.

"We're both travelling with Lansing," Dacey said. "We're colleagues." She smiled at Evan whose ears heard only rushing blood.

"Uh-huh," Elaine said, speaking to Dacey but looking only at Evan. He shrugged at her and said at last, "It's nice to see you."

"You too," Elaine said emphatically. She grabbed his hands. "The show was great, you were great! Are you staying with us?" She looked at Dacey. "We have tons of room, you'd all be welcome."

She turned back to Evan. "You can do laundry. How long are you here for? Have you called Mom lately? Are you eating?"

Evan held his hands up. "Elaine, Elaine. I'm fine. We're only here overnight. I'll call Mom tomorrow. I am eating. Mostly french fries."

Elaine laughed. "I'm just so glad to see you."

"Me too," Evan said. "Write down your address, we'll be another twenty minutes here."

As the lineup of fans dwindled, Dacey repacked the merch suitcase and Evan loaded it and the guitars into the car.

When Evan returned, Lansing and Dacey had moved to

the bar at the back of the room. They were deep in conversation, their heads inclining toward each other. Evan felt a stab of jealousy, then remembered the feeling of being soaked in the brine of that pre-show moment with Lansing backstage, and he stepped back into the shadows before either of them saw him. He went back outside to the car and uncased his guitar. His hands still ached just to hold it, just to hold the guitar a little longer this night. And that would be enough.

68

"You know, the one I'm most worried about in all this is Evan," Lansing said. "Isn't that ridiculous? I barely know the kid." He was drinking whiskey, pulling it from the glass between his teeth and letting it slowly meet his tongue. "I just—I see the way he looks at me and I think, son, no good can come of that."

"I know," Dacey said. She folded a stack of ten- and twenty-dollar bills. "You did well on CDs tonight, by the way. I know, he looks at me the same way."

At this, Lansing hooted. "Oh, my dear," he said, "not quite the same way, no." He tapped her hand where it lay on the bar. "Aren't you gorgeous, darlin'. The look he has for you is a little different." Dacey began to protest. "No less hungry," he said, "I'll give you that. But not quite the same, no."

He took a long pull of the whiskey, rattled the cubes in the glass. "It's funny, isn't it, what a life comes to? If I had any sense, I'd be worried about Carrie. And I am, I am. I am worried. Worried she won't see me before it's too late and she and I will both lose." He sucked a shard of ice. "Mostly me, though," he said. "It's mostly me who'll lose in that one."

Dacey put her hand to her pocket where the BlackBerry

sat. It felt full to bursting and she along with it. One of her queries had borne fruit. How meaningful it would turn out to be, she couldn't yet say. She held back.

"Don't you ever get old, Dacey Brown. It's a terrible, terrible thing to get old."

"You're not old, Lansing, you're really not."

"Might as well be, lovey. I might as well be old. What's the point of having years left if you really won't be able to spend them? No, my dear, it's almost done. Old Lansing Meadows is nearly done." He drained the whiskey glass and patted her hand again. "Let's not keep the young man waiting any longer," he said. "I'm turning over a new leaf in my old age. Gonna try not to be such a total dick to those who love me."

He slid off the bar stool, rocked back on his heels. "Oopsy-daisy," he said. "Oopsy-Dacey." He laughed. "Fallsy-down-sies." He steadied himself and held out a hand for Dacey.

"Go ahead, Lansing," she said. "I'll just make sure we've got everything."

He wobbled to the exit and Dacey settled their tab with the bartender, then went backstage to make sure the green room was clear. She shut the door behind her, then pulled out the BlackBerry and typed a hasty email. She took a deep breath and pressed send.

69

Evan felt high, the adrenaline of the night still making him jangle, as he drove them all to Elaine's place. Lansing had been amazing, on fire, at the top of his game. How could they think of cancelling the rest of the tour? He'd find Jake's number in the BlackBerry, get him to send the tour bible by email. Lansing would rally, Evan believed, after the ceremony in Winnipeg. They would do the western leg. He would take better care of Lansing. Starting with having Elaine give him a checkup.

All the lights were on when they arrived. "Sorry it's so late," Evan said. "It always takes longer than you think it's going to."

"Not at all, not at all," Elaine said. "Come right in." She stepped back, her arms wide, welcoming them. "Chip," she called. "Wake up, they're here."

The house was in a nice neighbourhood, where well-kept houses sat on well-kept lawns and gardens. Even in the dark it was easy to see that Chip and Elaine had made a series of good decisions.

And now Evan, Lansing, and Dacey stood awkwardly in their front hall with well-kept Elaine, and Evan became aware of just what a motley crew they were. Lansing's face was haggard and there was whiskey on his breath. Dacey's once-smooth hair looked a little road-ratty. Evan thought back on all the times he'd wiped his french-fry-greasy hands on his jeans.

They smelled and it was late and Lansing had been drinking and they had all grown unused to nice surroundings. Evan felt a bolus of worry form in his throat. But Elaine was gracious and didn't breathe them in. She took their coats and hung them in her front-hall closet. "Let me show you the place," she said.

They filed up the stairs behind her. "Lansing, Dacey, you're in here." They left a trail of belongings first in one spare room then the other. "And little brother, you're in the basement. I'll show you the way. There's a bathroom here with lots of fresh towels. You just help yourself to whatever you need."

Dacey looked longingly at the stack of plush towels. "I think," she said, "if it wouldn't be bothering anyone ..."

"Not at all," Elaine said, sounding a note of triumph. "You go right ahead." She led the other two back downstairs. She steered Lansing toward the living room.

"Chip," she called. "We have guests. Wake up and get this poor man a beverage." She turned to Evan. "You come along."

He followed her, docile as he'd always been with his sisters. She clicked on the light at the top of the basement stairs. "You'll be down here," she said. "You're not still afraid of basements, are you?"

Evan shook his head. "Hardly at all anymore," he said.

"Now, Evan," Elaine said as they slowly descended, "there's no bathroom down here, though there is a laundry room with a big sink—but don't let me find out you peed in the sink in the middle of the night like when you were a kid." She laughed. "Oh my God, I'll never forget that. You were—what? Twelve? Fourteen?"

"Eight," Evan said, "and sleepwalking."

"Here's your room," she said. "It's a little rustic."

"It suits me fine," Evan said. The room had floor-to-ceiling wood paneling, a tightly woven orange carpet and a single bed with a flowery quilt Evan remembered from their childhood. "It's at least two steps up from every motel we've stayed at so far. Despite the lack of a bathroom." He smiled at his sister. "Can I ask you something?" He dropped his knapsack on the floor and tenderly leaned the guitar against the wall.

"Of course," she said. She sat down on the bed and patted the spot next to her. "Is this about Colleen?"

"Colleen?" Evan said, grasping for a moment to assign meaning to the name. "Oh, gosh, no. No, it's about Lansing."

"He's great," Elaine said. "What a good concert that was."

"He is good," Evan agreed, "but he's kind of going through something right now. He has these episodes. He calls me or Dacey by a different name sometimes. He completely freaked out at a gas station on the way here." He left out that Lansing had almost killed them both. "You're a doctor," he said. "Could you look at him?"

Elaine put her hand on Evan's knee. "Evan," she said, "what you're describing sounds serious."

"I know," Evan said. "That's why I want you to take a look at him."

"Evan, honey, I'm a pediatrician."

Evan thought about this for a moment. "Well, he often acts like a child," he said at last.

"I don't know what I'd be able to tell you. I can test his

reflexes and listen to his heart and give him a lollipop at the end of the appointment if he behaves himself, but other than that—Evan, if it's worrying you, he needs to see someone who knows."

Evan shook his head. "Not before Winnipeg. Nothing can come between him and that award."

"When does that happen?" Elaine asked.

"Day after tomorrow," Evan said.

Elaine shrugged. "I have no experience with this at all."

"Will you just look at him?" Evan asked. "You know, without him noticing."

"Oh, Evan," Elaine said. "Even when you were a kid, you had such a good heart."

In the morning, Elaine was up making coffee. She toasted bagels and set out a container of cream cheese and a plate of smoked salmon. When Evan came up from the basement, she said, "There's the sleepyhead," and Dacey and Lansing looked up from their coffee cups to smile at him.

"I've packed a bit of a lunch for you," she said. There was a thick paper bag on the counter.

"You didn't have to do that," Evan said.

"It was no trouble," she said. "Now go have a shower, don't keep your friends waiting."

He rubbed sage-scented shampoo into his scalp. He'd slept restlessly most of the night, reliving the moment with Lansing backstage and the string of amazing moments on stage with him. He turned over from every angle the question of whether Lansing could truly go the distance on this tour, whether Evan's role should be to encourage that or to facilitate a graceful winding-down of things. He was as much at sea as he had ever been. He would take it day by day—minute by minute if necessary—until the path ahead became more clear. He stood beneath the shower spray and let it all wash over him.

Getting back into his clothes he was struck by the need to get back on the road. He dressed quickly, his T-shirt sticking where he hadn't quite finished toweling off, his hair dripping thick beads of water.

Downstairs, Elaine was showing them old photographs.

"Oh now," Evan said, "is that really necessary?" There was a photo of him in his highchair, asleep in a plate of spaghetti. "Adorable," he said. "Really, Elaine."

She brushed the wet hair out of his eyes. "I couldn't resist," she said.

"And we're so glad you couldn't," Lansing said. He gazed at a photo of Evan as a toddler, bare-bottomed, wearing a paper pirate hat and holding a spatula. "I can't quite figure out just what's happening in this one ..."

"Time to go," Evan said. He looked at Dacey. "Unless you also wanted to make a smart remark?" She lifted her coffee cup to him in salute.

"A picture is worth a thousand words," she said. She pointed to a photo of Evan in Batman pyjamas, his fists raised at an inflatable life-sized clown, his face a map of determination.

"Seriously, you guys ready? Big day today. Technical rehearsal, interviews, not to mention an eight-hour drive."

Lansing laced his fingers together and stretched his arms out in front of him. "It always seems like such a good idea to have a taskmaster as your tour manager, until he starts to spoil all your fun."

"This is why you pay me the big bucks," Evan said. He

winked at his sister.

Before long the Corolla was loaded once more with their bags and gear.

Evan stood in the driveway with Elaine. "Well?" he said.

"I think he's lucky to have someone like you along for the ride," she said.

Evan ducked his head. "You have to say that, you're my sister."

"It's the only diagnosis I'm qualified to make. Take care, little brother. Travel well. Call your mother."

70

Evan drove fast in the empty early morning, with the radio on low. The road was bare and dry and the sun came up and began to pour in the windows. Music came to him as it always did now, the words bubbling up out of recent experiences, fermenting the visit with his sister into something new, streaming along on ribbons of melody.

The car was crusted with salt and dirt and the sun's glare magnified every speck on the windshield. He blasted it with fluid and watched the wipers do their thing and he thought about the way the car had grown around all three of them. It was a shell that carried their tender selves along, the motion of the wheels a kind of current they were caught in. The current propelled them. Evan felt himself reaching for what was next, his arms open to it all, even as he shrank from it sometimes when it appeared.

Dacey remained in many ways mysterious to him. They'd had moments of electric connection, but always she had kept herself apart. He thought about her face, that final day in Wawa. She'd been glad to see him, but not the way he'd been to see her. She hadn't been relieved, or eager, or bursting, or any of that. She'd seemed *alright* with seeing him. And then she'd gone and done her own thing anyway. She didn't need him.

He turned that over, tasted it. He didn't understand that kind of independence. What would it be like to be an island the way Dacey was? Lonesome, Evan thought. Then: safe. And Lansing. Lansing did need him. Because he had a car and he could drive. Because he could work the BlackBerry. Because he would put up with whatever.

But also, Evan thought, though it felt daring to, because of his intrinsic Evan-ness.

He let that sit for a moment. Considered it.

"You shouldn't let him talk to you like that," Dacey Brown had said that day in Toronto he'd fallen at her feet. Evan had made excuses for Lansing then, but he could see now that Lansing had been behaving very poorly. It didn't bother him. Lansing wasn't trying to take him down, he was trying to keep his own self afloat. Experience and mistakes clung to Lansing like contrails, marking his progress—and now marking Evan's too. He'd come to see that Lansing teased him out of affection.

And then there was "Ocean Curl." Evan tingled at the memory, longing for the sounds his voice could make when pressed against that of his hero. It was a kind of love. Platonic, romantic, somewhere in between. Evan didn't understand how that kind of love worked, but it didn't take a genius to understand he was in it.

He checked the rear-view. Dacey was looking back at him, all big brown eyes and smoothly rippling hair. "You good?" she asked.

"Yeah," he said, "I am."

"Did you really pee in the sink?" she asked.

"She *told* you that?" He rolled his eyes. "I was *sleep*walking."

He caught her eyes in the mirror and tried to look stern. But he knew he was young and ridiculous. "Dacey, are you and I—"

"Probably not," Dacey said. "I'm kind of—into flying solo." She smiled kindly. "I'd be no good for you."

"I'd like a chance to prove you wrong," he said.

"Not how it works," Dacey said. "You're young, Evan, and I'm—I'm on the move. You're going to find what you're looking for, I know you will."

"What about you?" he asked.

"Oh, me," she said. "You shouldn't worry about me. I'll find what I'm looking for too." She smiled at him, and her face was kind, but clearly said *case closed*. "Let's stop soon for coffee."

He nodded and they drove on.

When they stopped an hour later, the sun felt blazing.

"I guess that's it for spring," Lansing said. His face was ruddy beneath the hat.

"Feels like full-on summer," Dacey said.

"Radio says it's supposed to go up to thirty," Evan said. "Yesterday it was eight."

They'd made a little heap of their excess layers in the back seat and Evan was filling the tank while the other two stretched their legs.

"Want me to take a shift?" Dacey asked, but Evan shook his head. The day was made for him, and he wanted every part of it.

Lansing leaned against the Corolla. "What will you do next, Evan Cornfield?"

"Pay for the gas," Evan said. "Maybe get some beef jerky."

"You know what I mean, son. What will you do after Winnipeg?"

"I'm sticking with you, Lansing. You know that."

"Winnipeg's the end of the line, boy, and *you* know *that*."

"What's this?" Dacey said. She was inside the car rooting around in her pack for her camera.

"I'm hanging it up," Lansing said. "You don't keep going after a lifetime achievement. You're supposed to crawl off and die."

"Don't talk like that, Lansing," Evan muttered.

"Okay, fine," Lansing said. "You're supposed to exit gracefully, stage left. I'll be sixty soon, son. I'm losing my marbles. Time to get out of the way. Isn't that what you young people are always complaining about? Goddamn baby boomers won't get out of the workforce? Here I'm prepared to leave a corner-office position open, boy doesn't want me to." He slurped his coffee. "Kids today."

Seeing the stricken look on Evan's face, he said, "Evan doesn't like this talk, but it's not Evan's tour to cancel. What did you tell them, boy, when you cancelled those shows?"

"Didn't tell them anything," Evan said.

"Because you haven't cancelled them yet?" Lansing said. "Get on it, boy. I'm not kidding, and I'm not changing my mind." He got in the car.

Evan got in after him. "But aren't you feeling better? Because you seem better. Don't you want to do what you set out to do? One last shot? Give everyone something to remember you by?"

Lansing laughed. "I've given them plenty over the years, son. I'm not sure there's much more they want from me. They want 'On My Honour' and 'Cantina Heart' and they can hear them in any shitty neighbourhood pub in every small town across this great land. They don't need Lansing Meadows for that."

341

Evan remembered the first time he'd heard Lansing
Meadows. He remembered how young and confused he'd
been and how certain Lansing made him feel. "I need Lansing Meadows," he said.

"I should think you've had enough to last you a lifetime,"
the old man said.

"You'd think," Evan said, "but I guess that's the thing. Every
day that passes, every feeling, every experience, I'll wonder
what would Lansing Meadows say about this, how would he
mill this fucked-up situation into something beautiful?"

Lansing clapped a worn hand on Evan's shoulder. "You
definitely don't need me for that, son. It's all there in the
songs, every bit of it. There's nothing new under the sun for
me, boy. Now it's up to you. I hereby pass the mantle." He
lifted the hat off his head and settled it on Evan's.

"Stop it," Evan said. "This thing stinks." He pushed it
back on his head. "Seriously, I still want your songs."

"Seriously, no one's ever gonna take the ones you already
have away from you. Now leave an old man alone. I'm
going to fall asleep, perchance to dream of my glory days."
He took the hat back and drew it low.

Evan shook his head, but he couldn't help but smile. He
put the car in drive and nosed back out onto the Trans-
Canada.

There was blue sky above, but a bank of dark clouds in
the distance, and the radio warned of thunder showers.
Dacey had fallen asleep too, her hair a silky blanket, her
camera clutched loosely in her hand. The ribbon of road
and the companionability of the car and its occupants put
music back in Evan's mind and as he drove he composed
and memorized with a rising sense of joy. And when the
rain finally came, fast and hard, Evan Cornfield was so

ready for it, big fat drops that clattered on the windshield, a symphony of instruments tuning up, the chaos before the audience settles into what's coming.

This time he didn't worry about trying to see through individual rain drops. He just drove. The road was straight, the prairie flat as they left Ontario behind. He could look out the side window for long seconds, taking it all in, and still drive in a straight line without fear. What was a little rain to him, or even a lot of rain. It beat its hands on the roof of the car, insistent and raucous, washing all three of them clean, pummeling them soft and new, the old streaming off behind them, dirty streaks disappearing down a water-dark highway.

They sailed along like that, three souls in a steel and fibreglass body, windshield wipers keeping the beat of their hearts, clearing a view instantly filled in again, and Evan Cornfield felt safe and right. Safe with these near-strangers and their unparsed motives. Safe in this sealed world hurtling through prairie rain, their mingled breaths a sweet miasma he might otherwise have found stifling. Here in this new home, here with windows gently fogged with their breath, here he felt the feeling he'd longed for and never felt, the feeling he'd sought, shirt off, hugged up against the speakers of his boyhood stereo, the feeling he'd reached for every time he'd reached for a girl in the dying hours of any of a hundred adolescent Petite Riviere nights. It had eluded him then, but now he was in the thick of it.

His heart felt giant, beating blood out to every quivering outpost of nerve and sinew, the message coming back in seven-eight time: *this then, forever now this.*

He wanted to pull the car to the side and revel in it, leap out and let the rain wash him for real, but he couldn't change the rhythm of their progress, couldn't disturb the magic that held them all together for maybe the final time. He wanted to drive and he wanted to run and he wanted to lie in the lush expanse of grass that flowed alongside as he piloted the three of them to whatever would be next. He could feel something was ending, but something was beginning too, he had to believe.

His face was wet and he wondered if the rain was coming in, but he darted his tongue out to catch a rivulet and tasted salt, and for once he was not ashamed.

71

Lansing Meadows was ready. They'd had a day off in Winnipeg and Dacey had cleaned his hat, and Evan had made a cheat sheet for the song Lansing would perform during the ceremony. He'd thought about all the things he wanted to say and he'd noted them down. But beyond that, he was just ready. He'd been carrying his house on his back a long while and he was ready to set it down.

Backstage his guitar sat gleaming, propped up in its case. It had been some time since anyone had fussed over him in this way and he was determined, if not to enjoy it, at least to endure it with a smile. People—journalists, mostly, but not entirely—had been asking him all day about his legacy. A terrible question to ask of someone who was still alive, but he tried to give them what they wanted. There were a lot of people backstage, bustling about in various official capacities. Someone tried to make up his face, but he fought her off. For Chrissakes. It was too late for any of that.

Evan said that Matthew was coming, and that maybe Michelle was too. Lansing gave him a stern look, but he couldn't make it stick. It was good and proper for his friends who'd been there in the beginning to be there to see him out at the end. He had a feeling he'd been awful to Michelle. Well, he'd try hard to make it up to her. He asked about Marie, but Evan shook his head, and it was just as well. He was no good to Marie now, and the less said about it, the better.

Dacey appeared at his elbow at one point and whispered to him, and he turned to her, surprised and not.

"You won't stay then," he said, "to see me join the club, become legit?"

"I know who you are, Lansing," she said, and she gave him the widest smile he'd seen, and kissed his cheek. "Can I finally get my photo?"

So he smiled for her and then he said, "Travel well, Dacey Brown. You travel well, girl."

"You too, Lansing Meadows," she said.

"That's all behind me now, lovey," he said. She blew a kiss and melted away.

Evan was working the room like a proud papa at a wedding. The boy would be alright, Lansing thought. It might take a while, but he was strong; he just didn't know it yet.

Here was Evan now with some young woman on his arm. Nice to see. He was rallying already. And she was a lovely one. Old for Evan perhaps, but lovely, a short cap of russet curls and green-gold eyes. Like her mother, he thought.

"Oh, Carrie," he said, and he put his hand out to her. "Oh, Carrie you found me."

"Dad," she said. He could see the word was foreign in her mouth. A piece of glass. Smooth but unchewable.

"I wasn't going to come," she said, "but they told me you weren't well. Mama said I should come."

"Did she?" he said in wonder. "Fine, I'm *fine*, Carrie," he said, his voice trembling.

"Still a liar, I see," she said lightly.

"Maybe I should—" Evan said, making as if to leave.

"No, no, I should," said Carrie.

"You just got here, girl," Lansing said.

"I think I shouldn't have come at all."

"Of course you should have, Carrie. My God, it's so good to see you at last."

"You could have seen me any time, Lansing," she said.

"I couldn't find you, darlin'," he said. "I looked. Finally had some help from a young woman reminded me a lot of you."

"I mean before," Carrie said. "You knew where to find me before. When I was little." Here a hitch in her voice. Evan made once more to leave, but Carrie put her hand on his arm. "Don't."

"I did it for you, Carrie," Lansing said. "The things I did, they were for you."

"No," Carrie said. "No, Dad, they were for you."

She pressed a card into Evan's hand. The envelope said *Congratulations* in tight, tidy handwriting.

"I'm sorry," she said, "I thought it would be okay, but it isn't."

"At least let me kiss you," Lansing said, unable to believe it was over.

Carrie kissed her own fingertips and pressed them to his cheek. She turned, she ran.

"I'll clear the room," Evan said. He cleared his throat. But Lansing put a hand on his arm.

"No, don't. No need, boy. She's right. And I'm old."

Suddenly, it was time.

ACKNOWLEDGMENTS

Thank you Dave Gunning for telling me, some years ago, a story about Stompin' Tom Connors that gave me this book's title. Thank you Ron Hynes, Steven Bowers, Stephen Fearing, Erin Costelo, Matt Epp, Christina Martin, Rose Cousins, Jenn Grant, Jill Barber, Don Ross, Brooke Miller, and countless other artists with whom I've talked about life on the road, songwriting, fame, and fans. Thank you Corin Raymond, whose song "There Will Always Be a Small Time" was like a bug in my brain while I wrote. And thank you for giving me permission to quote the lyrics (from the excellent album *There Will Always Be a Small Time*).

Thank you The Common, my most excellent group of writing peers. Jaime Forsythe, Carsten Knox, Sarah Mian, Ryan Turner, you kick my ass and make me laugh. Each of you has made me a better writer. Here's to many more years of that. Thanks also ex-pat members Sue Carter Flinn, Sean Flinn, Camille Fouillard, Wanda Nolan.

Thank you Julie Gunning, John Parker, Ella and Ruby Gunning Parker. Meaghan Smith and Jason Mingo. Shayla Howell. Jen Laughlin and Aidan Brunn. Tara Thorne. Andrea Dorfman, Tara Doyle, Jackie Torrens. Andrew Kaufman. Catherine Bagnell Styles. Patti Hetherington.

Thank you Petite Riviere and Grand Falls. Neither actual place bears much resemblance to my imagined towns—and both are far finer places than either Evan Cornfield or Dacey Brown realizes.

Thank you Katy Parsons and Mackenzie Grisdale, who listened to lots of panicked talk about word count and plot. Thank you Kathy Large and Andrew Cochran, for affording me the time to write. Thank you Bill Roach and Alex Mason, who held down the fort while I was off doing that.

Thank you Penelope Jackson, who believed in this book early and often, and courted me hard. Our time will come, Penelope. Count on it.

Thank you Sue Goyette, who always knows what I need well before I do, and provides it with grace and style. Thank you amazing band of writers who took up the challenge and fed me while I wrote, including Roy Ellis, Alan MacLeod and Shandi Mitchell, Pete Munro, Elizabeth Peirce, Maggie Rahr, and Shannon Webb Campbell—who also gave me deadlines and a place to write one night. Thank you Chris de Waal for the celebratory steak.
Thank you Province of Nova Scotia, for supporting this book in its early days with a grant that gave me time.

Thank you Robbie MacGregor and Invisible Publishing for being so awesome, and Bethany Gibson, who didn't let me off the hook once. Her wisdom, insight, tact, and editing acumen were instrumental here, though where this book falls down is due to my own shortcomings.

Thank you Carmie Domet, Jeff Domet, Donna Domet, and my extended family and friends. You have each played a part in who I am.

And finally, thank you Kev Corbett, without whom, nothing.